Let Them Eat Cake

French Twist Series, Book One

Sandra Byrd

www.sandrabyrd.com

In Memory of Jane Orcutt
À bientôt!

To eat an egg, you must break the shell.
French proverb

One

Chaque personne sait où sa chaussure pince.
Each woman knows where her shoe pinches.

Catbert avoided catching my eye—never a good sign. He prowled the aisles all day but didn't stop to say hello or ask about my plans for the weekend.

My cubicle had recently been expanded by three inches to accommodate my new cellmate, Celine, who silently typed nonstop. The woman was a machine. I tried not to compare the stack of nutrition labels she had robotically processed since eight that morning with my own paltry offering.

I pulled up another document and studied it. *Hmm, I wonder why they used an emulsifier in this recipe?* I closed my eyes and thought about it. *And was this soft wheat?*

I heard a cough behind me and quickly opened my eyes.

"Should I help you?" Celine asked in French, eyeing the stack I still had to translate.

"Oh...ah...*non, merci*," I answered. "I was

thinking about the flour."

"*Bon,*" she said. She had a smile like sour milk. I'd asked her to lunch when she first joined us. She'd informed me that she didn't take lunches, and would I please stop burning lavender candles at the desk. *Les allergies.*

I glanced at the clock. It was nearly five. In order to get my quota done today, I'd have to stay at least another hour. Again.

Celine tidied up her station, turned off her Moroccan music, and bid me a stiff good night. Everyone else began to pour from the room like mice from a hole. I typed faster.

I felt, more than saw, him standing behind me.

"Miss Stuart?" Catbert said.

I turned around and looked up. "Yes?"

"Can you come with me?" He nodded toward his glassed-in office overlooking the cubicles.

"Should I finish these labels first?" I asked, cotton-mouthed.

He shook his head. "That won't be necessary."

Uh-oh.

I followed him into his office, and we sat across the table from each other.

"Your French is really very good," he said. "You simply don't translate enough documents in a day to make it worth your time...or ours."

"I'm just so fascinated by the business," I said quickly. "I enjoy seeing what's going into each product."

He nodded curtly. "But you are not here to

8

evaluate contents, Miss Stuart. You are here to translate."

"I see," I said, feeling desperate and hating myself for begging for a job that I loathed. "I can certainly work more quickly."

He shook his head. "That's what the thirty-day trial period was for. I wish you the best." He handed me my final paycheck and a cardboard box for the few items I had at my cubicle. "I'm sorry."

I nodded and took the paycheck and the box, not trusting myself to speak for fear of releasing the tears. What was I going to do?

I packed up my half-burned lavender candles, got into my car, and drove slowly in order to collect myself before pulling up in front of my parents' West Seattle house. I'd moved back in a little over a month ago to find a job and save some money for a rental deposit on my own place.

I left my box of cubicle gear in the trunk, stashed like a dead body. I pasted on a smile and walked into the house. My mother was just hanging up the phone and looked exultant.

"Guess what?" she said.

"What?"

"All the permits are in place, and we're ready to go."

"How long until your new place is ready to move into?" I asked, trying to dredge up enthusiasm from somewhere deep within.

"Six months," Mom answered. "No longer." She glanced at me out of the corner of her eye.

I'd lived for twenty-four years in a family rife with unspoken conversations and unstated expectations. I knew what she meant.

"Get a life, Alexandra Stuart. You have until July." I went into "my" room—recently the storage room, before that Nate's room—and closed the door behind me. Dad had stacked my mail, forwarded from my old apartment, on the dresser. I shuffled through the magazine subscription advertisements and a manipulative plea for alumni donations from the college I'd attended just an hour and a half to the north in Bellingham.

No wedding invitations so far this week. *God is good.* I opened the last envelope.

Washington Bank and Trust

Alexandra Stuart
102 Rhododendron Drive, Apt 2B
Bellingham, WA 98229

Check #206 has been returned unpaid. There were insufficient funds to cover this draft. The payee, GMAC Auto Finance, has been notified.

Thank you for doing business with Washington Bank and Trust.

Not again. I'd been overspending on clothes for a job I hated. Had Dad guessed what this was when he'd stacked the mail?

I sat on the bed, lifted the box that held my vase, and rested it on my lap. With the money from my last paycheck I had bought this tiny Chihuly bud vase from a friend who was moving to Spain. I'd always wanted a Chihuly piece, and it was a bargain. If I'd known it was going to be my second-to-final paycheck, of course, I'd have applied it to the final five car payments on my coughing VW.

I set the vase, still carefully swaddled, on the shelf in the corner of the closet. Chihuly would debut in my real apartment. Or maybe in my room at the downtown YWCA shelter.

I walked into the hall, shut the bedroom door behind me, and went into the kitchen. My mom stood in front of the stove, wide-checkered apron hugging her postmenopausal curves.

"What time will they be here?" I lifted the lid on the homemade spaghetti sauce my Italian family calls "red gravy." A thick tomato steam, flecked with dried summer twins, basil and rosemary, rose into the air. Mom chopped fresh mozzarella and dressed it with balsamic vinegar. I could taste the tang on my lips even now.

"About seven. You can use my curling iron if yours isn't unpacked yet."

Subtle, Mom.

They say trouble always visits in threes. My hypochondriac lawyer brother, his *très* successful lawyer fiancée, Leah—who graduated from high school a year after I did—and my outspoken Nonna were coming to dinner. At least Nonna posed no problem to the job conversation.

No, absolutely not true. Nonna was always stirring up trouble.

"Can I help with anything? Make some shortbread for dessert?" I asked. "I perfected a new recipe with vanilla beans before Christmas—the cookies I gave away in tins. Everyone said they were great."

"No thanks, honey. I have it all under control," Mom said. "What's a mother for except to cook for her family?"

"All right. I'm going to run to the mall for a minute," I said.

Mom nodded absently, tasting the sauce.

When I'd escaped to my car, I sat for a moment and sighed before turning over the motor. I loved my mother, of course, but I missed living on my own.

I headed toward the discount Supermall. My phone rang, and the caller ID flashed the name of my best friend, Tanya.

"What are you doing?" she asked.

"Going to the mall."

"What's in your wallet?"

I dug it out at a red light. "One hundred and fifty-six dollars, a Tully's Coffee card, and a creased photo of Greg with a nose ring penciled in." Greg and I broke up almost a year ago. Everyone said I should be over it.

"No way." Tanya laughed. "Don't spend too much."

"I'm not going to buy a lot," I said, wincing at how pathetic I sounded. "I just need time to think. *And* I can use the clothes for job hunting."

"Job hunting? You have a job."

"Uh-oh, light's green. I'll call you later. Bye!" I hung up.

I parked in front of the Rack. Even if I couldn't afford Nordstrom, I could afford their remainders discounted at Nordstrom Rack. I tried on a pair of slim black pants that hid the extra pound or two hitchhiking on my hips, and some black pumps with a skinny-yet-sturdy heel. I headed to the register, and the clerk took out a marker.

"Wait," I said.

The shoes hung in midair. The ten people in line behind me let out a collective, irritated sigh and shifted their feet.

"Yes?"

"Do you have to write that number on the bottom of the shoes?"

"Yes. It's loss control. Company policy."

"Can you make it small?" I asked. The clerk wrinkled her nose but wrote it small. Okay. As long as my feet stayed flat on the floor, no one would know my shoes were discount. I paid, left, and drove home.

Now that the retail therapy was over, I felt sad again and blinked back tears. But I managed to put on a happy face and get out of the car, wondering what I'd say at dinner if they brought up my job. I couldn't let on.

Nate, Leah, and Nonna arrived precisely at seven. At the store I'd felt so chic in black pants and a white shirt, but now I felt like a hostess at Bakers Square. Even though I was unhappy living with my parents, it still felt good to be back home and near my crazy friends and family again.

"How *are* you?" Leah said, hugging me. I hugged her back, warmly. It wasn't *her* fault that she was pretty and successful, or that she had graduated a year behind me and was already clerking at a law firm in town, or that, to top it off, she was a Pied Piper to children and small pets everywhere.

"Really good to see you, Leah," I said, meaning it. Hey, if I never found another job, maybe I could nanny their kids!

"Hey, sis," Nate ruffled my hair, the same rich dark brown as his. But I scored the blue eyes and dimples, for which I offer a hearty thanks to all recessive genes everywhere.

Nate and Leah kicked off their shoes, and Nonna slipped off her loafers after brushing a feathery kiss on my cheek. As soon as everyone had gone into the dining room, I turned Leah's shoes over, hoping to see a scribbled number on their soles. Nothing. Just soft leather. Real leather.

I am so pathetic.

I followed them into the dining room, where we all sat in the same seats we had used our whole lives, with Leah as an addition, of course.

"So." Nate looked at me, twirling ribbons of linguine around his fork. "How's the new job?"

Everyone looked at me, smiling. There had been vast relief when I'd finally scored a job. I knew there'd be major disappointment when they found out I'd lost this one. I'm all about postponing pain.

"The company is interesting," I said evenly. "They translate nutrition labels from English into French so they can be used in Canada too. It's a Canadian requirement that all labels are published in both languages."

Nate grinned and ate another bite. Leah, more sensitive to the vibes, looked up in alarm. She knew I'd neatly dodged the question. Catbert-like, I avoided eye contact.

"I guess studying Madeline and Tintin was a great career decision after all, eh?" Nate forked another mouthful of linguine, and Leah elbowed him slightly. I couldn't decide whether to be glad that someone finally disciplined my older brother or jealous of his and Leah's intimacy. They were getting married in June.

"I studied French *culture*," I said, "and *literature*. Contrary to popular opinion, the literature goes way beyond the Madeline books."

"They sure never read up on how to fight a war," Dad snickered. "They haven't won anything since Napoleon."

Nonna gave him a hard look.

"Excuse me," he said, pushing his chair back. "I'd

better refill the water pitchers for Margaret." Dad always called my mother Margaret, even though everyone else called her Peggy.

"Would you like to have lunch this week?" Leah asked me. "I only get forty-five minutes, but we can go somewhere close or eat in the atrium of my office complex."

"Thanks," I said. "I'd really like that. What day works best for you?"

She thought for a minute. "Wednesday? Do you have enough time to get away for lunch?"

"I have a lot of time at lunch," I said. *More than you know*. "I'll bring something good for both of us."

"You sure?" she asked. "I invited you, after all."

"I'm sure," I said firmly, not wanting to be the designated charity case.

I hoped I could buy something both classy and cheap. I didn't want to show up with homemade sandwiches like Red Riding Hood and her picnic basket.

After dinner we talked for a while, mostly about Nate and Leah's wedding.

"You'll help me shop for dresses, won't you?" Leah asked.

I nodded. "Of course! It'll be fun. I'm glad to be back in town for that reason, if nothing else. I'd like to give you a shower, too, if no one has spoken up for it."

"I'd love that," she said.

"I have three possibilities to escort me to the wedding," Nonna chimed in. "One has a walker, so dancing might be tough. I may have to choose between the other two."

"Maybe you can give one to Lexi," Nate teased.

I threw a balled-up napkin at him. "How do you know I don't *have* a date for your wedding?"

He raised his eyebrows, but Mom walked in with a tray of cookies right then, which thankfully stopped the conversation.

"Do you?" Nonna whispered.

I shook my head and winked. "But I will. Promise."

"That's my girl."

After coffee, Nate got ready to drive Leah and Nonna home. I gave Nonna a peck on the cheek. Her skin was soft and floury with face powder, like freshly kneaded dough.

"*Bonsoir*," Nonna said, kissing me back. She was the only one who tried to speak French with me.

"*Bonne nuit*," I answered.

As soon as they left, I called Tanya. "Come over," I said. "I need some get-a-life support."

She laughed. "I'll be there in a few minutes."

I hung up the phone and began to unpack a few books. I opened a bookstore bag and took out the three I'd bought earlier that week. When I was a freshman, I'd decided to buy books at the local bookstore, save the receipt, read them, and return them for credit. I did it twice before I'd realized it wasn't right.

Things were so tight now. Was it really that bad? I looked at the books on the bed--*Where Is God When It Hurts?*; *Baking Illustrated: A Best Recipe Classic*; *Quarterlife Crisis: The Unique Challenges of Life In Your Twenties*—unwilling to return any of them.

I shredded the receipt and sprinkled the confetti into my garbage can, then started hanging up my new clothes.

A knock sounded on my bedroom door, accompanied by a soft "Hey."

"Help!" I called from inside the closet. "I've been swallowed by a shrine to Nate's childhood!" When I'd moved out, my mom had changed my smaller room into her sewing and craft room. When I moved back in, only Nate's old room was available.

Tanya came in and helped me lug Nate's old dartboard out of the closet.

"I barely have enough room for *my* stuff," I said. "I'll put it in the garage. Or he can take it to his apartment with the rest of his stuff."

"He might want to wait until he and Leah have their own place," Tanya said.

"Yeah, or she may want me to deep-six it." I grinned.

"How'd it go tonight?" she asked.

"Dinner was a little rough." I sighed and plopped down on the bed.

"Nate and Leah doing well?"

"Yeah. It's not their fault they're both great. It's

just that I seem so...so...*unproductive* next to them."

"You're not unproductive." Tanya sat on my floor. She nodded at the open box of books. "Want me to hand these books to you while you put them on the shelf? We can talk while you do. You'll feel better when they're up. It'll feel like your own space."

I frowned. "I don't want it to be my space at all. That's why I hadn't unpacked yet. And anyway, it can't be my space for long. In six months, my parents are moving to a fifty-five-and-older community nearly two hours away."

"You'll have your own place then, which will *really* be your own space."

"My room at the Y?" I joked. I sat down next to her. "Tanya, I lost my job today."

"Oh, Lex, I'm sorry. I thought maybe you had when you said you needed to go job hunting. What happened?"

"I wasn't translating enough labels quickly enough."

"Are you sad?"

"Sad? A little. I feel like a loser, but I hated that job. I counted every minute I was there. I made no friends and did no meaningful work. Scared? Yes." I rubbed my fingers over a worn guide to Montreal. Then I handed it to Tanya. "I should have stayed there. I had my own place. I liked it there."

"So why did you come back?" Tanya asked.

"I was broke, as always. Once it wasn't part of a room-and-board agreement with the college, I had no choice."

"You'd wanted to go to France instead, anyway," she reminded me.

I nodded. Montreal had been my second choice.

"So what *are* you going to do?"

"I don't know. My parents are moving to the retirement house right after the wedding. They're listing this house for sale soon. I guess I'll try to find a job and then a place to live."

"How about teaching?" she asked. "You could so totally get a job at the French American School." Tanya taught fourth grade and lived with another teacher in a two-bedroom apartment. She had started with a local school district and planned to transfer to a private Christian school nearby, but she'd signed a two-year teaching contract and a two-year lease with her roommate. She was stuck for now.

"You want to know the truth?" I asked.

"Lay it on me." She handed me a copy of Baudelaire.

"I don't like kids." There. I'd said it. The pillars of the house didn't fall in and crush me. I hadn't been struck with boils.

"Really? I never knew that."

"I just never felt brave enough to admit I don't like them. It's watered-down blasphemy to a lot of Christians."

She opened the can of Diet Coke she'd brought. "Well, are you ever going to have kids of your own?"

"First of all, that assumes I'm married at some

point."

"Lots of time," she said. Tanya wasn't interested in dating, and I knew why. I'd tried to talk with her about it again a couple of months ago, but she'd shut me down.

"And second, they'll be interesting to me because they'll be *my* kids. I'm just not into kids in general."

"I get it," Tanya said. "Teaching is out." She handed me last year's stack *of Paris Match* magazines. "What *did* you want to do with a French degree?"

I shook my head. "I don't know. I just like the language and the culture and all. Diplomacy or something." *I thought I'd be married.* "I worked for that French import firm for a few months after college," I reminded her. "I had high hopes when I started."

"Until they made it clear only family moved beyond receptionist."

"Uh-huh. Then I tried freelance translation, but there was never enough work to make ends meet. Part of my credit card debt is from then. I ate ramen noodles and eggs like everyone else."

"What about the account manager job?"

"Phone sales," I said. "Totally bait and switch. A grunt in a sweaty cubicle begging people to buy extended warranties on their home appliances before midnight."

"Didn't your uncle help you find that last job in Bellingham? Marketing executive?"

"Yeah, but, you know...I lost that job too."

"I know," Tanya said. "I'm sorry I brought it up. Does your uncle know you were 'not a good fit'?"

I shook my head.

"Something good will come up soon. Either a job or a place to live."

"Or a guy," I said.

She rolled her eyes at me, and we stood up. I knew she thought it was totally impractical to be thinking about men at a time like this, and maybe it was. But when we were in junior high, there was a questionnaire our friends passed around—I love questionnaires—that asked, if you had to pick getting married *or* having kids, which would you pick? Tanya wanted the kids. I wanted a soul mate. If I could have both, great. If not...

I hung Nate's old dartboard on the robe hook on the back of my door. I tore out a piece of notebook paper and ripped it into twenty pieces. I wrote "Guy" on four of them, "Job" on six of them, "Place to Live" on six of them, and "Guy" on four more (hey, a girl needs an advantage!). Then I arranged them on the dartboard, sticking them in the twelve, pizza-slice-shaped sections.

"What are you doing?" Tanya asked.

"It's biblical."

"What?"

"It's the twenty-first-century equivalent of casting lots," I said.

"Mmm-hmm."

I threw a dart. I aimed hard for *guy* but got *job* instead.

"Two out of three," I said.

I threw two more darts, aiming for all I was worth toward *guy,* and got two more *jobs.* Well, maybe that wasn't too bad. I mean, I needed a job before I could get a place to live, right?

I closed my eyes and threw a fourth dart.

"Hey," Tanya said. "I thought you said three."

Even blind, the last dart came up *job. Oh, all right. I'll be responsible.* I felt with certainty that if Nate had thrown three darts, he would have hit *job, place to live,* and *wife* once each. Winner takes all.

"Give me those darts," Tanya said. "Maybe something miraculous will come along and release me from my teaching contract."

She threw one dart, then two. They both hit *guy.*

"I quit," she said, disgusted.

"Stupid board." I took it off the hook and stuffed it back into the closet.

Tanya checked her watch. "I'd better go. Are you coming to church this weekend?"

I shook my head. "Nah. Maybe next week."

Even girlfriends have unspoken conversations and unsaid expectations. I didn't push her; she didn't push me. For a while, anyway.

Sandra Byrd

Two

L'eau trouble est le gain du pêcheur.
There's good fishing in troubled waters.

Everyone went to work the next morning. Dad went to the recruiting station where he worked his jaws with other military cranks about the good old days, and Mom drove to Curves to work out before heading to the church's preschool where she taught. I slipped into my brown suit and shoes, pretending to be going to my old job, but instead I got my leather résumé case out and drove downtown to try to elbow my way into the work force.

But first, a *café crème.*

I hadn't noticed L'Esperance last time I was downtown, but it caught my eye now. I parked, got out, and walked to the restaurant. The front doors were French, of course, and opened up into a lovely café with about twelve tables. The counter at the front was long and brass and perfectly clean.

There's a certain smell to a bakery when it's really, truly French. It's yeasty and soft and crusty all at the same time, like a real baguette should be, perfuming the street for blocks around. It has a hint of bitter chocolate dust around the edges. The coffee smells like a fine-burning pipe tobacco with an edge of chicory. L'Esperance smelled right. It was a good sign.

I stood at the counter for almost five minutes before a lazy fake blonde hung up her phone and came to stare at me. Good thing I didn't have a job to get to.

"I'd like a café crème." I said it in English, of course, but pronounced "café crème" properly.

"Coffee with cream?" she asked. Her nail polish was chipping. She helped it along as we talked.

"Uh, yeah, café crème," I said. The bakery's name meant "hope" in French. I hoped nothing dropped off her nails and into my coffee.

Just then a man appeared from the back.

He had the buff build of a baker—they're physically working all day—and long blond hair pulled back into a queue, like Russell Crowe in *Master and Commander*. But younger than Russell—twenty-seven, maybe twenty-eight years old.

"Please help them load, yes?" He motioned the chipping-nail blonde toward the back and rolled his eyes. "*Café crème, tout vite!*" he said to me.

Not only would he make it, he'd make it quickly! I smiled at him.

A small rush of people came into the café, tinkling the door chimes over and over. By the time he was done making my coffee, there was a line five deep.

"Voilà," he said, handing it to me with a flourish. "Mademoiselle, a beautiful cup of coffee for a beautiful lady."

Frenchmen are such flirts. I love it.

I paid him and sipped my *café crème*. It was delicious. I hadn't tasted anything this French since Montreal my junior year. It was just the right thing to start the day.

Bracing myself, I walked back out to the street. January is a blustery month in Seattle, drooping from post-holiday depression and rising barometers. In spite of urban legend to the contrary, most Seattleites use umbrellas. Unless you like that wet-dog look and smell, it's a necessity.

After polishing off my coffee, I rode the elevator up to the twelfth floor of the first building on my list. The day before, I'd carefully mapped out a plan based on the Sunday ads, a lead Nate's golfing buddy had given him more than a month ago, and a list of names from the yellow pages. I faced off with Receptionist Number One at 10:00 a.m.

"Hello, I'd like to leave a résumé," I said.

Without saying a word, she wearily waved to the stack of résumés spontaneously generating in the in box. My résumé floated down, settling on top of what I hoped were résumés of completely incompetent and unqualified individuals.

I got into my car and drove four blocks south. At least the car was my own—until it was repossessed. I parked at a coin meter and went into the next building.

"Hello, I'd like to talk with someone about your marketing jobs," I said to Receptionist Number Two.

I loathe marketing.

"Do you have marketing experience?" she asked.

"Yes." *Unfortunately.*

"Do you enjoy phone work?" She smiled, revealing a fleck of lipstick on her tooth. I restrained myself from telling her. My mother had a compulsion to tuck in exposed shirt tags on people in front of her in church or the grocery line. Horrified, I realized this personal appearance correction habit might be genetic.

"Kind of," I answered. I could see where this was going.

"Leave your résumé," she said.

She didn't look at it before I left.

I spent another two hours trying to look both perky and positive as well as professional and grown-up. I'd waited for fifty minutes at my last call—prearranged via computer over the weekend— for a woman who never showed up. Her assistant kept apologizing. I left a résumé, smiled, and left. I decided to go home, look at Monster.com, and plan for tomorrow.

On the way home I drove by the huge tower housing Leah's law firm. I wondered which floor was hers. I envied her the job but not the cubicle.

The next day I wore my navy skirt and a subtle string of pearls. I'd had no résumé responses from Monster.com and was politely turned down by three recruiters.

Tanya called me on her lunch break. "I'm taking a sanity break from my students. I have two girls catfighting and a boy who eats erasers when he's nervous. I imagine that makes him constipated. Where are you?"

"Don't ask."

"I'm asking."

"I'm parked outside the French American School."

Tanya groaned. "Do you think French girls have catfights? Do French erasers constipate?"

I laughed. "Maybe it's a good job option," I said. "I could sub."

"You could," Tanya said, "but would you enjoy the work? And it'd have to be full time eventually to make enough to live on. Subs make about a hundred dollars a day, maybe four to five times a month."

"Oh." I knew in my heart that I wouldn't enjoy teaching all day. It wouldn't be fair to the kids—or to me. I just wasn't meant to be a teacher. "You've been a great help to me," I said wryly. "See you later."

As soon as we hung up, I started my asthmatic VW. It seemed to be choking—just like my career.

When I woke up the next morning, I put my workout clothes in a gym bag. I needed to locate some endorphins.

My mom was finishing up breakfast, decked out in matching Sag Harbor sweats. Who thought of naming a line of clothing for women Sag Harbor?

"Mom, take the headband off. You look like a Jane Fonda wannabe."

"Jane Fonda became a Christian, you know." She began wrapping up the breakfast rolls.

"I know, I know. Do you see her at Curves?"

I caught the soft roll she threw at me, and we both smiled.

"Don't forget you're meeting Leah today," she said.

"I know."

My dad brought his cereal bowl to the sink, washed it with hot water and soap, and dried it. Then he put it in the dishwasher.

"Dad, it's clean," I said.

"Needs to be sanitized." He pulled on his cap, then took it off, kissed my mother, kissed my cheek tenderly, and put it back on. "I thought I'd come to your office and meet you for lunch," he said, "since you've got these long lunch hours now. You're past the thirty-day trial period, and I want to make sure it's not some two-bit, low-paying job going nowhere professionally. It's got benefits and a future, right?"

"Sorry, Dad, I'm meeting Leah today. Maybe next week, huh? Pretty busy this week."

That was true. I hoped he wouldn't just drop in.

Once they'd both left, I headed to the gym. Surrounded by strangers as I worked out, I felt lonely. I had Tanya, of course, but Tanya had a life, and I needed one of my own.

I showered and dressed for my lunch with Leah in my favorite jeans, a cute red sweater, and a pair of flats. Leah always looked pulled together. I still needed to pick up something for us to eat. I could hear Tanya's voice. "*What's in your wallet?*"

I looked. Eighty-three dollars, a Tully's Coffee card, and Greg's picture. With a nose ring *and* an earring this time. He looked like Johnny Depp in *Pirates of the Caribbean*. I laughed and snapped my wallet closed. Where to pick up lunch?

Of course! L'Esperance! I could buy myself a *café crème*, get us both a sandwich and an Orangina, and perhaps a chic little *salade niçoise*.

I drove to L'Esperance, which was only two blocks from Leah's office. When I went in, the blond girl was nowhere to be seen, and the line stretched almost to the door. Without her, they were seriously short of counter help. A girl with multiple piercings helped each customer as quickly as she could.

The café windows were draped in burgundy linen, pulled back with gold cord. Fleurs-de-lis speckled the walls. I could hear soft music and laughter in the back room from whence the yeasty-earthy-divine scent emanated. Baking smells.

When I reached the counter, the Frenchman who'd served my coffee two days before had emerged from the kitchen to help.

"You're back!" he said, eyes twinkling. Everyone seemed to move more quickly when he was around.

"*Café crème*," I said in French. "And two *salade niçoise* luncheons to go."

"A Frenchwoman knows quality coffee." He winked at me. He thought I was a *française*!

When my order was finished, he packed it into a chic little to-go bag. He didn't rush me even though there was a line. His eyes crinkled. I looked at them a little too long, and he held my gaze.

Reluctantly, I left the shop and walked to Leah's building. She was waiting for me in the atrium, and we claimed a table. I unpacked our lunch.

"So how's it going?" Leah tore off a piece of her roll and buttered it.

I opened our plastic containers of salade niçoise and set one in front of her. "I'm not working at the translating place anymore."

She nodded slowly but didn't look surprised. "I suspected as much. Things didn't work out?"

As much as I wanted to, I just couldn't tell perfect Leah that I'd been canned again. "It was really boring," I said truthfully, opting to look irresponsible rather than stupid.

"I'm sorry," she said. "There are times when I think I don't like law either. I think I might have liked to go to massage school."

"Really? So what are you going to do?" I asked,

setting out the rest of the lunch. *Where are our cookies? I bought the package lunch with cookies.*

"I'm going to be a lawyer," she answered. "I'm deep in the groove now. I have to make it work. And I will."

I nodded. We chatted about clothes and her wedding and a new massage therapist she'd found who had become a friend. "I'll pray for your job," she said as she headed back to the elevator.

"Thanks," I said. "Oh, and Leah?"

She stopped and looked at me.

"Don't tell anyone yet, okay? I'm going to try to find another job before I mention it to my family."

She hugged me. "Mum's the word."

Sometimes I envied her drive. Right now, though, I felt sorry for her and her high-paying career that she had to make work. On the other hand, at least she had a job to make work.

What was so wrong with me that I couldn't hold a job, find a guy, or live on my own?

I headed back to L'Esperance to get my promised cookie. I needed it. I needed to eat Leah's cookie, too, on a day like today.

I stepped into the shop and found the counter untended. I heard some voices in the background, raised, so I decided not to stick around. Maybe God was saving me from over-indulgence, anyway.

Just as I turned to leave, I spotted some papers on the counter. As I glanced at the content, my face flushed. I reached toward one, but my hand hesitated in midair. Finally, I tentatively took one.

L'Esperance Job Application

Want to work where you love to eat? L'Esperance is looking for fun and friendly counter help. Six-month commitment required. Interested? Please fill in your personal and professional information below and return to L'Esperance.

I slipped it into my résumé case and turned to leave.

Three

Elle qui aide d'autres est aidée.
She who helps others is helped herself.

A couple of days later I called Tanya while I got dressed. "I think I'm having a heart attack." I held the phone between my cheek and shoulder, sat on the edge of my bed, and pulled my pants over my knees.

"You're only twenty-four."

"Nate has lots of strange ailments, and he's my blood relative."

"That's Nate. He's a whole different story," Tanya answered matter-of-factly.

I tugged the khakis on and stood up, smoothing the creases out of the stiff sailcloth fabric. *That'll do.* "I have constant pressure in my rib cage, and my arms really ache."

"How often have you been on the elliptical?"

"Every day this week." I stepped into the bathroom, avoiding the scale lurking under the sink. "Burning up nervous energy."

"Your shocked muscles are rebelling. And you're anxious." On the other end of the phone I could hear Tanya's kids tumble into her classroom. "It's going to be okay."

"Thanks."

"Meet you at The Ballroom for pool tonight," she said before hanging up.

I pulled a black sweater over my head, slipped in some seed pearl earrings, and turned off the curling iron. On a whim, I gathered my hair into a neat French twist and decided I liked it. Maybe I'd make it my signature style.

I walked into the kitchen through a cloud of fading breakfast fumes.

"Here, I'll scramble an egg for you before you go," my mother said, reaching for a pan.

"No thanks, Mom."

"It's not good to leave for work without eating breakfast."

Good thing I'm not leaving for work then.

"Protein will keep you going all day."

"I know, Mom; I'll eat later."

She sighed her reply. She meant well.

Once in the car, I chucked three unopened water bottles, an old Organic To Go bag, a pack of new iPod skins, and a Western Washington University hooded sweatshirt into the backseat.

I should get rid of Greg's sweatshirt. It whispered his spicy-smooth aftershave in my direction as it flew through the air, and my heart wavered at the memories the scent dredged up. I

36

could still recall his unshaved cheek against mine. Maybe a ritual burning was in order. Of the sweatshirt, not Greg. I clarified this to avoid the temptation to think vengeful thoughts.

The one thing left in the front seat was a black spiral notebook. Did it still hold my neatly filled-out application? It did. I'd purposely kept the application in my car and not in my room where others helpfully "dusted."

I know we've been having a...um...lack of communication, God, but I'd really appreciate it if you'd let me know if this is the right direction.

No giant professional compass appeared in my mind. *On my own again.*

I grew up in a home where my mom washed and dried us and took us to church every Sunday. She found God and her peace there, but I hadn't, really. It felt stifling to me. Not God, the church itself. I was glad when I went to college and left it behind, but it left a void. God was still there, but I couldn't find him.

Last week, while driving down the highway, I saw a billboard that said, "Need directions? Follow me. God."

I did need direction. My mom's church may have been stifling, but no church at all was—well, lonely. Empty.

I'm trying to follow. But I have to see where you're leading in order to do that.

I drove across the West Seattle Bridge and into the city. Quarters jingled a muffled tune in the closed cave of my ashtray, stocked for on-street parking. I hoped I'd find a spot.

I passed Pike and Pine, turned the corner, and drove past Saint Rita's, Nonna's church. Nonna once told me that Saint Rita was the patron saint of desperate, seemingly impossible situations. Maybe I'd ask her to give me a hand.

A long line of Spanish-speaking men loitered on the corner outside, hoping for a car or van to pull up and whisk them off to a day's worth of work. Idling at a red light, I watched a construction truck slow down and several men leap into the back. The ones who missed out stared dejectedly at the spidery cracks in the sidewalk or scouted down the road, hoping for another chance. Most day laborers were hired before nine, but I'd seen some picked up into the afternoon.

We all need a job. Value. Worth. A way out of desperate, seemingly impossible situations.

Help them, Lord, I prayed reflexively into the Great Void. *And me.*

I rounded the corner, drove past Leah's building, and parked as soon as I could, pulling into an open parallel spot.

My hand shook a little as I grabbed the black notebook and locked my car. I fed the coins into the meter.

Go get 'em, killer.

I walked into L'Esperance, heels clicking against the polished wood floor.

The French baker was in. I could see him

through the door into the bakery area, biceps flexing as he rolled dough. He chatted boyishly with one of the other bakers one minute, then commanded another the next. I reached up to make sure my French twist was neat.

The café tables were filled with perfectly coiffed morning gossips, rumpled newspaper readers, and sleepy coffee drinkers. I waited my turn. Pastries sparkled in the lit display case stretching across the storefront area beneath the brass counter. Tiny blueberry pearls glistened inside pastry seashells. Sassy *Tartes Tatin* blushed cinnamon red.

No blonde behind the counter; I assumed she'd been guillotined, and that's why I was here. The stack of applications was thinner, but still there. A woman about my age with a short brown bob and a baker's dozen earrings clinging to her left ear caught my eye.

"Can I help you?"

The moment had arrived. "I'd like a half-dozen croissants," I said. Before she could turn away to bag them while I bagged my original intent, I blurted, "I'd like to leave an application too."

She looked me up and down, paying particular attention to my high heels and black sweater. I looked her over, too: rubber-soled shoes and powdered sugar dusted across her apron.

"I'll give it to Luc," she said coolly.

Luc. Aha. He of the perfect café crème draw and gorgeous crinkly eyes.

I paid $9.59 for the croissants and put them in

my trunk for safekeeping. Next to the cardboard box of entrails from my gutted cubicle.

I stopped by Washington Bank and Trust and paid one car payment; then, as a vote of confidence in myself, I went into a shoe store and bought a pair of Dansko Ingrid clogs. Soft-soled, good for someone on her feet all day. I left them in the box with the receipt nestled in the toe.

Out of the store and back on the street, I glanced at the electric trolley pole next to me. It was washed in raw, dried tar and stapled with fliers for concerts, raves, sample sales, and, at the bottom, a condo for rent.

Condo For Rent

If you want to live in style in a perfect location, this is the rental for you. This condominium is walking distance to Key Arena, the Seattle Center, and the Space Needle, as well as many restaurants in Belltown. Both the living room and bedroom have a beautiful view of Elliot Bay and the Bainbridge Island Ferry. One bedroom, one bath, deposit required. Please call for more information.

I tore one of the phone number tabs off the condo flier and stuck it in my wallet, next to doodled-on Greg, who was paper clipped to the emergency twenty-dollar bill my dad insisted I always carry.

After dinner, I met Tanya at The Ballroom. The buzz was low, punctuated with laughter and chatter. Glasses clinked against one another, forks clinked against plates, and billiard balls clanked against the soft-sided tables. Most of the people were between twenty-one and thirty, hanging out after work. *Oh, that I had work to hang out after.*

Tanya was already there, noshing on chicken wings.

"Put our name in?" I asked. The pool tables were all full.

She swallowed. "Yeah. Should just be a couple minutes."

Tanya and I had been pool sharks since junior high, when we took on the guys after youth group every Wednesday and usually won. If we were gambling girls, we could have won a lot of money from men who didn't think women could shoot pool. *Just call me Minnesota Fats.*

On second thought, no, please don't.

Tanya held up her glass of Diet Coke, a lemon slice darting among the ice chips. "Did you already eat?"

I slid into the booth and ordered a glass of wine and a glass of water. "Yeah, with my dad."

"Tell him where you went today?"

I shook my head. "Might as well wait and see if

anything happens first."

"I told my mom you were applying to work at a French *boulangerie* and she thought I said you were going to be selling French lingerie."

"Oh great!" I said. "Let's hope *that* doesn't get back to my dad."

We laughed together, and she checked her watch. "I have to be out of here by eight. I have a meeting with someone about being on an adult coed volleyball team. Maybe."

Tanya coached volleyball at the school where she taught. "Great," I said. "With school?"

She shook her head but didn't say anything else.

"You're holding out on me," I said. "You love volleyball. What's up?"

Tanya took a deep breath. "Remember when I subbed at that Christian school last year, before I got this contract?"

I nodded.

"One of my students had an older brother who came in during family day, and we talked volleyball. I thought nothing of it. You know, family chatter."

"Okay..."

"Well, he somehow got my number from the school and called to ask if I'd be interested."

"In him or in the league?" I joked.

She drained her Diet Coke and set the glass down on the cardboard coaster. We were tiptoeing toward troubled waters.

"Ah," I said. "Maybe he meant both?"

Tanya smiled, looking unsure. "I do like to play

volleyball, and it seems like a good way to meet more people. I'm so not into the singles group at church. The Impact Group. It sounds like an asteroid."

"Meat market," I said. Neither of us had gone. Nonna called them "ripe fruit," but as far as she was concerned, anyone over twenty-one who was unmarried and not contemplating childbirth was quickly ripening and about ready to fall off the tree. The group consisted of holdovers from the college group who hadn't managed to get themselves married in the last decade. The whole thing had a whiff of desperation about it, and I had enough of that clinging to me as it was.

"Maybe he meant both," Tanya admitted. "I don't know. I'm just interested in the volleyball. What if he gets the wrong idea?"

"Did you get a good vibe?"

She considered this. "I guess so."

I touched the back of her hand lightly. "I think you should go," I said softly. "It seems like he might be a nice guy. Who knows? Maybe he's only interested in volleyball too." I doubted it, though, and I knew she could read me.

"I don't know. I'm not ready, Lexi."

I knew she didn't know if she was ready, but I thought it was time. I wasn't going to push her though. Not yet. I'd wait and see what she said the next time she brought it up.

They called our number across the speaker to let us know our pool table was ready. I grabbed a cue stick from the rack and chalked up the end, while Tanya racked the balls. She ran her hands across the soft green felt. Tanya always wanted everything to be perfect and in control.

"How was *your* day?" she asked.

I told her about putting in the application. "The counter girl said that Luc would call me."

"*Luc!*" Tanya teased as she sent the cue ball slamming into the other balls, scattering them across the table. "*Ooh la la.*"

"Yeah," I admitted. "Ooh la la. He's definitely a bonus. Nice to look at and talk with *now*—who knows as I get to know him better? But I'd like the job no matter what."

"Would you get to bake?"

"No." I shook my head and neatly planted one ball into the side pocket and one into the corner.

"How much does it pay?"

"Ten dollars an hour," I said sheepishly.

She drew in her breath. "Lex..."

"I know," I said. "I know. If I don't hear by the end of the week, I'll start looking again."

"Are you okay with ten dollars an hour?"

I stood next to her, leaning on my cue stick. "No. I'm not, really. I feel angry and sad. I mean, I did everything right, you know? I studied hard. I didn't party all night. I went to college and worked my butt off. I walked all the way up the mountain that my parents and every school counselor said I had to climb, and when I got to the top, there was no great job, no guy waiting, nothing meaningful. I fell off into this ditch by the side of the road."

Tanya clucked sympathetically.

"I'm whining, I know." I pocketed a ball and dropped my voice. "I've disappointed everyone, including myself. It's embarrassing." I looked at my watch. "You'd better go if you're going to meet that guy."

"Steve," she filled in. "I think I'll call and cancel. We haven't even finished our game."

"No, you need to go. You *want to* go."

Suddenly the cool, in-control persona dropped from her face. "You think...?"

One by one, I rolled each ball into a pocket. "Game over," I said softly.

We paid and walked out the door.

On the way home, I stopped at the grocery store and bought a card to mail the next day.

A truly brave person
carries on in spite of fear.
She moves forward when the path is dark.

Am looking forward to cheering at a volleyball game and vetting Steve to see if he's worthy.

I'm proud of you. Go, Tanya!

XO,

Lex

When I got home, my parents were in bed watching TV. I kissed them good night, rubbed our old black Lab's ears, and then closed their door behind me.

I went into my room to change. My dirty clothes had been taken out of the hamper, washed, dried, and folded into precise little piles. She'd done my laundry! At least she hadn't put my clothes away or, worse yet, cleaned the drawers.

I looked at the vase box in the corner of the closet. *I have got to get my own place.*

I pulled out the tab I'd torn off the post earlier, closed my bedroom door, and dialed the number on the tab.

"Hello, we're sorry we're unable to take your call, but please leave a message, and we'll get back to you. If you're calling about the condo, it's still available. Thanks."

I cleared my throat. "Yes, I...ah...I'm interested in renting the condo but wanted a few more details. Please call me back when you get a chance. Thanks." I left my name and number and hung up.

Downtown. Perfect. Part of me knew how much it must cost. Part of me didn't want to think about it.

After throwing on some sweats, I went into the kitchen and dug out the croissant box from deep in the pantry where I'd hidden it behind a huge bag of pinto beans, the only place to keep them safe from Dad. I pulled out pistachio paste to spread on each half of the sliced croissants and the ingredients required to make the syrup to brush on top. I rough-chopped some roasted, salted pistachios to sprinkle on as a finishing touch.

Half an hour later, I'd prepped the pastry to make six croissants. I could pop them into the oven first thing in the morning so they'd be crispy and fresh. Six was enough for Mom and Dad to each have one tomorrow morning, and I'd take one each for Leah and Nate when I met Leah for coffee. That left two, one of which was tagged for Tanya.

They sure looked good. They smelled good too. My mouth watered.

Eating mine tonight couldn't hurt. Wouldn't want to serve anything I hadn't tried myself, after all.

I revved the oven up to four hundred degrees and popped one in. Five minutes later I slid it out of the oven.

Flaky. Refined brown butter taste. Smooth, silky nut texture—*better than almond,* I thought. Browned pistachio chips clung to the top, easily flicked off with my tongue, straight into my mouth.

Délicieux!

I watched TV for a while before turning in for the night. I took my phone with me, just in case the condo people called back.

Sandra Byrd

Four

Elle qui a un choix a l'ennui.
She who has a choice has trouble.

A couple of decades—I mean days—went by. By the end of the next week, there'd been no call from the bakery or the condo.

"Are you coming to church with me tomorrow?" Mom asked.

"I don't think so. Hey, Mom, can I help you with dinner?" I'd had a great idea—chicken puttanesca.

She clucked at me. "No thanks. You know I love to make dinner for my family. It's part of being a woman."

"Mom, I *am* a woman," I reminded her.

She looked at me, and I realized she still thought of me as a girl.

"I'm going for a drive," I said.

I drove down the hill to Alki Beach. I pulled a blanket out of my trunk and sat down on the sand, not caring that the wind whipped my hair and roughed up my skin.

"I'm not a girl anymore, God," I said. "I'm a woman who needs a home and a job and respect and *hope*. I have no hope. I hear nothing from you. What's the point of going to church? I don't feel you here, there, or anywhere."

What was the alternative? Not believing? That wasn't an option, because I really did believe. When I was growing up, my mom and the youth leaders provided me with a spiritual map. *"Be here at this time. We're studying this book."* I went along with it. But I hadn't made a map—or a home—for myself now that I was an adult. I needed a place to live in more ways than one.

I had gotten back into the car and started home when my phone rang. I pulled over on a side road and glanced at the number. I didn't recognize it.

"Hello?"

"Hi, I'm returning your call about the condo," a man said.

"Oh yes," I said, fumbling for a pen and paper. My pen had fallen into the passenger seat crack. I grabbed the car registration from the glove box to take notes on. "Can you tell me a little more about it?"

"It's beautiful. Has a peek view of the Sound, new appliances, Bosch oven."

Bosch oven!

"Secure building."

Good, Dad would go for that.

"There's a one-thousand-dollar deposit," he continued.

I thought I might be able to swing that. Maybe. What could I sell?

"And the rent is twelve hundred dollars per month."

I sucked in a breath and held it. Twelve hundred per month was three hundred per week. Too much even if I did get the job. Which seemed unlikely, since I hadn't heard back.

"I'm sorry," I said. "It's just too much for me."

"Do you have a roommate you could split it with?"

"No."

The guy seemed genuinely kind. "I'm sorry. I think you're going to have a hard time finding anything downtown in a good neighborhood for less than that. Maybe you could try some studios."

"Thanks for your time," I said. As disappointed as I was, I knew I needed the job first. Not the house, not the guy. *Maybe I should apply at the Starbucks up the road.*

When I got home, I saw a note propped on my dresser. I opened it.

"I'm sorry if I made you feel like you weren't a woman. Would you like to take over cooking dinner on Monday nights? Sometimes even moms say dumb things. Love you."

I sat on my bed. I didn't really want to take over on Monday nights. I wanted to cook in a cool new Belltown condo with a secure building, a Bosch stove, and a peek view of the Sound.

I walked into the kitchen. I hugged my mom,

relishing her comfortable arms, her thinning hair, and her thickening waist.

"I'll come to church with you tomorrow," I said.

Mom went to the early service, but it was just as well. No one I knew was likely to be there at eight in the morning. The Impacts met later, and my high school friends who already had babies wouldn't be up that early. A lot of them had moved on. I was sure to get the inevitable, "And where are you working now? Have you moved back home for good?"

My mom went all by herself, week after week, since Dad didn't do church, and I know she was glad for my company. She had lots of friends who rallied around her, but most of them had someone to hold their hands in church. Mom didn't.

I closed my eyes and tried to listen to the sermon, but all I could focus on was the occasional squawk of a child who had not been placed in the nursery. "Weeeek!" Then five minutes later, from another corner of the room, "Waaaak!" They sounded like pterodactyls.

I folded my bulletin so many times that my mom leaned over and whispered, "Origami?"

I smiled at her, put the paper down, and held her hand for a minute. I wasn't my dad, but I had to believe it helped.

On the way out of church, we stopped for a coffee at the self-serve bar.

"Is it hard for you to do that alone every week?" I asked.

Mom looked at me affectionately. "It can be lonely, but I'm not alone. And I'm not there for myself. I'm there to worship."

I drained my latte and said nothing in response.

As we got out of the car at home, I watched as my mom set her Bible down on the counter and prepared to make lunch for my dad, without a word of reproach to him for sitting at home. He patted her hand and kissed her cheek. Maybe she *is* the woman around here.

I spent the afternoon highlighting want ads and searching Craigslist for jobs and condos, town homes, or apartments for rent.

"Professional piercer, clean tattoo shop. Bring portfolio." *I could practice on a potato first and say I had experience. Nope.*

"Work with the French." *Now here was a possibility!* "Be an usher with Cirque du Soleil when they're in town." *Temporary work. Nope.*

"Learn how to make a six-figure income." I clicked on it. "Sales/Marketing/PR." *Nope.*

I printed out a few possibilities. Executive assistant. Personal assistant able to work her way up in a busy salon.

I'd told my parents once, as a girl, that I wanted to be either a teacher or a hairdresser. After a few moments of dead silence, my dad firmly explained that if I were a teacher, I could have a fun time doing hair with my friends. My mother had looked on, smiling too brightly.

Even at that age, I got the hint.

I lined up three or four places to call in the morning, then began doodling a possible Monday menu. Dad liked meat, potatoes, and Italian food. If something was green, it had better be a salad or beans. It didn't leave me a lot to work with.

I logged into Allrecipes.com and scouted for ideas. I wanted something American enough for my family, yet clean and fresh and new enough for me. Continental *and* American.

I heard my phone ring, and I ran into my room to answer it. Another strange number!

"Hello?"

"Bonjour, may I speak to Alexandra?" A man's voice. *A French accent!*

"Yes, this is she."

"Hello, Alexandra, I am so sorry to call on a Sunday night, but it has been a busy week. My name is Luc, with L'Esperance. I have your application. Would you be available for an interview tomorrow at the bakery?"

An interview!

"Ten dollars an hour," the schoolmaster on the left shoulder whispered. "Say no."

"In a bakery! With French people!" the cheerleader on my right shoulder shouted. "Say yes!"

"Yes, I can make it," I said. "What time?"

"Six o'clock," he said.

"In the morning?"

"Is that a problem? This is a bakery, you know, so we keep early hours. It's not for everyone."

"Oh no," I quickly recovered. "It's fine. I was just clarifying." Usually I was in deep REM at six in the morning.

"Good, I'll see you then. Good evening!"

"*Bonsoir,*" I answered in French.

Silence on the line. He hadn't hung up. "*Vous parlez français?*" he asked.

"*Oui*, I do speak French." *I can't believe I forgot to put that on my application!*

"*Bon*. I will see you tomorrow then."

I hung up and dialed Tanya. She had a long weekend with Martin Luther King Jr. Day and had gone with her mom to their cabin in the mountains. I left a message.

"I have an interview at L'Esperance tomorrow. Call me after school is out, and we'll plan to meet this week. And I want to hear all the details about the volleyball guy! Bye!"

What should I wear in the morning? I dug through my closet. Khakis were okay, I knew, standard restaurant wear. I had a button-down white shirt I could wear. Mom would iron it.

No, I would iron it. With starch.

I held the box with the Danskos in it. If I wore them and I didn't get the job, I'd be tossing out all that money, because I'd need to return them for clothes money for the job I did take.

I wanted to look both pretty and ready for work, though. I set the box on my bed and went to set up the ironing board.

Late that night I paged through a couple *of Paris*

55

Match magazines to brush up on my language skills. I opened my Bible and took out the much-creased bulletin from the morning and looked it over, avoiding reading the real book. I slipped it back into my Bible and set the Bible on the side of my bed.

Let me know what you think, God, okay?

Silence.

I woke up well before my alarm, which was set for five. I hoped to be out of the house before anyone asked exactly where I was going at that time of day.

At least that early I wouldn't have any trouble finding a parking space. I parked right in front of the café and walked up to the bakery section of L'Esperance. Through the large windows that faced the street I could see Luc, sleeves rolled up, feeding dough into the massive industrial kneader.

I knocked on the window. He flashed that wide, boyish smile and invited me right in. When he opened the bakery door, warmth flooded into the cool morning air.

"*Bonjour.* You must be Alexandra." It rolled off his tongue. I love that even "Which way is the restroom, please?" has an earthy oomph in French. *Veuillez m'indiquer les toilettes, s'il vous plaît?*

For some reason, I didn't ask him to call me Lexi. Alexandra just seemed to fit better, and it sounded sophisticated coming from him.

"Yes, I am. *Bonjour,*" I answered.

He wiped the flour off his hand and offered it to me. I took it, and he shook my hand gently, holding on a bit longer than was necessary. If we knew each other better, a Frenchman may have kissed me once or twice on each cheek in greeting. Maybe that was a custom we could adopt in the good old U.S.A. Let the change begin with me!

"Coffee?" he asked as he led me into the café, still silent and dim at this early hour.

"Yes, please. *Café crème.*"

"Ah, *oui,* the *café crème* girl," he said. "I remember you now." He grew warmer, and so did I.

Before beginning the interview, Luc gave me a quick tour of L'Esperance, which was divided into several sections. It was much bigger than I thought and very, very French. Large floor-to-ceiling windows allowed passersby to watch the bakers prepare what Luc said were the nearly fifteen hundred croissants and several hundred loaves of various kinds of bread made each day.

Oh, how I wanted to sink my hands into that dough. Three men with their hair pulled back in nets cut the dough into squares with what looked like pizza cutters.

"*Bonjour.*" One of the three men nodded, his handlebar mustache dipping up and down.

"*Bonjour!*" I answered to their wide grins. I could see myself working here.

Six-foot racks of glistening baking trays were already lined with flaking almond croissants and *pains au chocolat,* little nubs of dark chocolate winking from between folds of buttery dough. My mouth watered in spite of my self-discipline. Maybe one or two wouldn't bloat me into *l'homme Michelin;* you know, the fat tire guy.

The tour complete, Luc showed me to a table in the café section, made two coffees behind the counter, and brought them to our table.

"Mademoiselle, à *vous,*" he pronounced with that Gallic grin. I took the coffee with both hands, in the French manner.

"I see on your résumé that you have a college degree and have already worked at a few jobs, corporate jobs," he started. "Can you tell me about that?"

I read between the lines and felt infused with confidence. "Yes, I can," I said. "I have a degree in French studies and tried to find a job that would match my interests and experience after college. I was unable to do so right away. After giving it some thought, I realized that I don't want to be in an office all day. I enjoy cooking and baking and an environment where that's happening."

Luc looked at me with a bit more appreciation. "You understand this is a counter job. You'd be serving customers, boxing their purchases, helping to box or deliver special orders. Clearing the dishes in the café and bringing them to the kitchen. That kind of thing. No baking. No cooking."

"Yes, I understand." I did, and that was sad. But it was a place where people spoke French, where they appreciated food, where bakers were baking and people were eating and enjoying life. I could hear laughter in the background. There were photos of the *Arc de Triomphe* on the wall. There were no cubicles. And who knew what the future held here?

Also, I was desperate.

"The pay is ten dollars an hour," Luc continued. "Reviewed after three months, but even then, there won't be a big raise. I'm asking for a six-month commitment. We're growing, as is our sister store, La Couronne, and I'd like there to be some stability in the shop."

"I understand."

A phone rang in the small office off the café. "*Je m'excuse,*" he said, excusing himself to answer it.

I leaned forward. Well, who wouldn't eavesdrop if she could? I mean, just a little. And he seemed to have forgotten I spoke French, or else he didn't care if I overheard.

"Yes," he said to the person on the other end of the phone. "I am getting the staffing set here. Everything needs to be running well when Margot and the others come over. Patricia, of course, will return to France. I'll return for the summer too, or at least part of it. We'll figure it out. We'll have to find someone to manage L'Esperance while I'm gone. It's time to hire an assistant manager, anyway. I can perhaps promote someone from within. That will free me to bake and supervise the growth of the shops."

I sat back in my chair. *Mais oui!*

Maybe I wasn't really overqualified. I could be an

assistant manager! The potential was there, at least. I'd learn all I could as fast as I could. The accounting class in college wouldn't be wasted. I'd take human resource seminars online. I knew I could do it! Given a little time, I'd prove to Luc that I was up to the task.

He hung up the phone and returned to the table. I drained my *café crème* to cover my excitement.

Before we could resume our conversation, though, the woman with all the earrings who had accepted my application came through the bakery door and into the café.

"*Bonjour,* Sophie," Luc said.

"Good morning, Luc," Sophie answered.

"Sophie works the front of the shop," Luc told me, "but we need two people."

I smiled and held out my hand to Sophie. "Hello, I'm Lexi," I said.

She managed a slight smile but didn't offer her hand in return. Instead, she gathered our empty cups from the table.

Deciding not to be put off by her behavior, I turned to Luc and asked, "Do you sell all your baked goods here or deliver them to other places?"

Luc laughed and covered my hand with his own. I felt a zing race through my hand, which was totally stupid because I'd only had three boyfriends in my life and I didn't even know the guy. But he was cute. And French.

He looked a few years older than me, maybe Nate's age. And the hand he used to cover mine was his *left* hand, and he wore no ring.

"That's a good question, Alexandra. I like that." He stood. "Follow me."

He led me back to the pastry room. To some people it might have been nothing but a room lined with stainless steel—racks, carts, a huge walk-in cooler. Long, smooth, chilled countertops to keep pastry dough cool while it was worked. But to me: nirvana.

I could definitely see myself working *here*!

"My cousin Patricia is our pastry chef," Luc explained. "Our family in France owns several *boulangerie/patisserie* shops, making both bread and pastries. We've opened two here in the U.S. now, L'Esperance and La Couronne, which is over in the U District. La Couronne is smaller and mostly sells pastries and bread that we send over."

I absorbed everything.

"I bake bread in the early morning, and Patricia does pastry a bit later in the day." He looked at his watch. "We'd better get out of her pastry room, or there will be trouble. She's very territorial. *Quels problèmes* if she finds us in here!"

Luc led me back into the bakery and tied his apron on again. His eyes were jade green but warm, and he had just the tiniest bit of a shadow growing on his chin. It made him look roguish.

Okay. Now I sounded like a Harlequin ad.

"I'll call in the next few days," he said.

I tried to sound professional. "Thank you for the interview. You have a terrific place."

Maybe it was because he knew I spoke French and was comfortable with French culture. Or maybe it was something else. But as I held out my hand, he kissed my cheek in the French manner instead. *If only all my wishes were granted so quickly.*

I turned to go, but he called out after me. "Alexandra."

I faced him again. "Yes?"

"I normally don't make such quick decisions, but I feel you'd be a good match with L'Esperance. You ask good questions, you're enthusiastic, you speak French, and that will come in handy from time to time. If you really don't mind working in the café at the counter, and you promise to stay for six months, then the job is yours."

Something behind Luc caught my eye. I looked over his shoulder and glimpsed Sophie listening in, scowling, before she popped back into the café.

I could hardly fault her for eavesdropping since I'd just done the same thing. She didn't seem to have any warm fuzzies for me, but honestly, I didn't for her either.

"Think about it for a day or two and get back with me," Luc said. "I'll need to know by Wednesday so I can interview some of the others if you decide it's not for you."

Now this is progress! "I'll get back to you. Thank you so much."

I slipped out of the bakery door, the three men rolling croissants bowing and calling out, "*Au revoir,*" as I left.

At ten dollars an hour, what could I afford in rent? Eight hundred, tops? Where was I going to find that downtown?

Maybe my parents' house on Whidbey Island would be done late. Wasn't construction always late? With a few months of grace, I could save up quite a lot. If I could get promoted to assistant manager, a job which surely made more money, I'd be fine. I had the education for it. And the desire!

I'd live cheap. Everyone had to start at the bottom, even my venerable father agreed with that. It would work!

I pulled up to the red light by Nonna's church, next to the men hoping for day labor. They probably worked for less than ten dollars an hour, and most had families to support. I just had me and didn't even know how I could make that work.

One thin man in particular stood shivering in the drizzle. My heart moved.

Suddenly, I knew what I could do. I reached into the backseat and grabbed Greg's WWU sweatshirt. I rolled down my window and motioned to him.

He approached the car hesitantly, "*¿Si?*"

"Here, you look cold," I said as I handed him the sweatshirt. On impulse, I opened my wallet and took out my emergency twenty-dollar bill. This was an emergency, wasn't it? The light changed and people started honking, so I had no time to unclip the bill from the photo of Greg on which I'd doodled an earring and a nose ring.

"*¡Gracias!*" the man called after me as I drove

63

away, and I burst out laughing at his puzzled expression as he tucked both the bill and Greg into his pocket.

"Well done," I heard Someone say quietly. It was a voice I hadn't heard for a long time. Two words, nothing more, spoken deep within me.

I smiled. "Hey," I said aloud. "I remember that voice. It's been a long time."

I didn't want to go home too early, so I returned some books to the library, wandered around downtown, hoping to stumble across a gorgeous and affordable apartment, and then called Leah to see if she wanted to meet during her lunch break. She agreed we'd meet at her atrium. "For a walk," she said.

A few hours later she met me at the table we'd had lunch at a few days ago. We hugged, and she slipped off her leather pumps and put on a pair of walking shoes. I saw her push her iPod back into the bag.

"What's on your playlist?" I nodded toward her iPod.

"Law cases being argued."

"Oh yeah," I said. "That's on my playlist too. Sheesh. Don't you guys ever get tired of law?"

"Nah," she said and grinned. "Gotta make it work. So what's on your job agenda?"

I hesitated. Should I tell her?

"Well, I've been offered a job," I said.

"Great! Are your parents excited?"

"They don't know yet. Actually, I haven't accepted the job."

As we headed outside for a brisk walk around a couple city blocks, I watched young professional people my age rush in and through the atrium, on their way to real jobs. Jobs that required a suit or pantyhose and a briefcase. People who hadn't let their parents down or squandered the vast amounts of cash poured into their college educations.

"Where is it?" Leah asked.

"L'Esperance."

"The bakery! You're going to be baking!" Leah beamed. "*So* cool."

"Well, not exactly. It's a counter help job. For ten dollars an hour."

Leah's stride hesitated for a second, and I saw her struggle to maintain her smile. She did. She'd have a good lawyer poker-face. "Ten-dollar-an-hour counter help? Oh. Are you excited?"

I nodded. "I think I am. I'll get to learn all about the bakery, and I think they're going to have an assistant manager's job available in a few months."

Leah's face relaxed. "Well, then, that's different. I'm so glad for you. But you know you won't find someplace to live alone on that in Seattle, right?"

"Right," I said. She *was* right.

Since I didn't want to hog the entire lunch hour with my news, we talked about her wedding.

"Nate and I were supposed to register for the gift

65

list last night," she said, "but he had a migraine. Maybe tonight."

Nate *always* had a migraine. Or a pulled muscle. Or a strange ailment of some other undiagnosable sort. It drove me crazy growing up, because my mother always coddled him. I didn't think I could take it if Leah was going to do that too.

I said, "Hopefully you guys will be able to do that soon. When are we going to look at dresses?"

"My mom had a great idea."

I couldn't tell by the tone of her voice if she thought it was a great idea or not.

"She thought all the women in the family—yours and mine—could go together. As a bonding experience."

And so her mom could approve what everyone else wore.

"Is that okay with you?" Leah asked.

"It's your day. It's your wedding. I'm here to do what you want me to do."

"I did make sure the wedding was small, even though she wanted it large," she said, sounding defensive.

"You did," I reassured her.

"Detail-oriented" was a kind way to describe Leah's mother. She made sure everyone around her agreed with, or at least abided by, her details. Thin and rich, she made certain everyone knew her daughter was going to be a lawyer and was marrying a lawyer as well.

"Mom wants me to drop a few more pounds

66

before the wedding," Leah said, her voice more casual than I knew she felt.

I'd like to drop a few pounds too. Right on her head. "You're going to be the most beautiful bride ever," I said. "No doubt. My brother already thinks so."

We giggled and chatted and eventually made it back to my car. I turned the engine over, happy, and decided to get the car washed in celebration of the sweatshirt-free backseat.

I pulled up to the gas pump first, hoping my credit card had enough wiggle room to cover it without an over-the-limit fee, then started clearing out the car.

Out with the Organic To Go bag, the water bottles, and the crusted boots that didn't fit anymore anyway. Out with the papers. Out with the coffee cups squished between driver's seat and center armrest. I found something in the glove box and stared at it.

AMERICAN RED CROSS BLOOD DONOR

Alexandra Stuart
Type B Positive

I *liked* that. Alexandra Stuart would "B Positive!" I stuck it into the flip side of my visor as a daily reminder. Cheesy, yes, but everyone needed a little cheer once in a while.

When the car was finally clean, I drove home. My

parents were still at work, so I busied myself planning dinner. I nibbled on blue cheese-stuffed olives and logged on to Epicurious.com. Great for me, but too fancy for my parents. They just weren't going to do fava bean bruschetta or braised chicken with morels.

I, on the other hand, didn't want frog eye salad or hamburger green bean casserole.

Was there no middle ground?

I browsed Allrecipes.com, which offered a few possibilities, but in the end, I decided to make up my own recipe. I'd tinkered with one before leaving Bellingham, when I'd had roommates to cook for. Something good and hearty and tasty for a cold winter night. My old roommate had called it boyfriend bait. Tender, toothsome meat that didn't need a knife, silky cream sauce sliding over perfectly cooked noodles or tender grains of rice.

Maybe I could soften Dad up before I dropped the employment bomb. Maybe Frenchmen like beef stroganoff, too. *Les possibilities…*

Boyfriend Bait Beef Stroganoff

Ingredients:

1 1/2 pounds beef tenderloin, well-trimmed, cut into bite-sized pieces (about 1" square)
4 Tbs (3/4 stick) butter
1/2 cup finely chopped shallots

2 1/2 cups sliced mushrooms
2 cups canned beef broth
3 tsp corn starch
1 cup sour cream
2 tsp Dijon mustard

Directions:

Over medium-high heat, gently sauté beef tenderloin in 2 tablespoons of butter for about 2 minutes, till just seared on all sides. Red will still be visible. Remove from pan and set aside in a rimmed dish.

Over medium-high heat, sauté shallots and mushrooms in remaining butter until soft and wilted, about 5 minutes. Mix corn starch into cold beef broth, whisk to blend. Pour into pan, and stir together with shallots and mushrooms till thickened, 2 or 3 minutes.

Add sour cream and mustard, stir to blend. Add beef and juices from dish; stir over medium just till warmed through. Serve immediately over noodles or white rice, salt to taste.

Sandra Byrd

Five

A force de choisir, on tombe à terre.
He who hesitates loses.

Nate couldn't take any time off from the law firm that Friday, so he said he'd drive up and meet Mom and Dad and me at Whidbey Island later in the evening. I told my parents I had the day off. It was true, in a way, but I was tired of dancing around honesty. I'd have to tell them. Tonight.

We didn't really do family vacations any more, but I thought that one was important to my parents. After Nate and Leah got married in June, we wouldn't do anything with just the four of us anymore. I didn't mind—I loved Leah—but it brought closure to our family of four.

Also, my dad was excited to show us the new house. My parents had never had a house they could call their own. We lived in base housing when Nate and I were little, and then we rented in a neighborhood near the naval air station on Whidbey. When we moved to West Seattle, it was only because my grandmother died and left the house to my dad.

This new house was my parents' dream home, and it was all their own. I was caught between excitement for them and the hope that construction would be delayed by six months.

Would I find my own place too? A place to call home in the literal, figurative, and spiritual sense?

The trees were taller in Whidbey, and there were more of them. I felt the saltwater tighten my face and sizzle on my tongue. The clocks ran slower, and people waved more. It would be a good place to retire.

"Well, here we are, out in the boondocks," Dad said with a smile. He eased the Jeep down a long gravel drive, which would eventually be paved, and onto their property. He parked exactly square with a log he'd set out.

"Wow, Dad, the land is all cleared!" I said. Last time I'd been there, it had been a rain forest from the Jurassic period.

Not good, not good. Land was ready to be built on, builders eager to finish their work and get paid. Was a labor strike possible?

"And the foundation's almost poured," he said. "Now that we have the financing all lined up, we can get building. It's supposed to be done in four months—barring no problems, of course."

Please let there be a few problems. Nothing terrible, nothing to derail things. Just enough to give me some time to save up. Minor flooding.

Sump pump problems. Wood rot.

"The thing I'm looking forward to most," Dad continued, "is having someone else landscape this place. It's a mess. I'm done with mowing and planting and hauling. A local company is going to come in and do just what your mother orders while I sit on my porch, drinking iced tea."

"The financing worked out so great," Mom said. "Because the property in West Seattle has appreciated so much, we won't have a mortgage at all for this, once that house is sold. We can just pay off the bridge loan. Dad has his military pension, of course, and we'll have Social Security, but not much else. So it's a great relief to us."

In other words, as much as we love you, we have no money to support you in any way, shape, or form.

"If we're careful with what we spend," Dad said, "it will be just enough. I want to make sure we're secure, no matter what. And it's nice that everyone in this community is our age. We'll have some friends to play golf or cards with or reminisce."

"And no teenagers!" my mom teased, looking brightly at me again.

Or twentysomethings.

"You guys have done so much for others. It's good to have something to look forward to for yourselves," I said.

"We were glad to put you and Nate through school," Mom said, beaming in on my thoughts. How did she do that? "We didn't want you to have student loans as you launched your professional lives."

I flinched at the words "professional lives," but my mother didn't notice.

We checked into the small bed-and-breakfast where we usually stayed. It had a military discount, and Nate and I could have small single rooms to ourselves. Nate arrived a few hours later, and we went to dinner at my dad's favorite steakhouse.

Before entering the restaurant, Nate removed his earbuds.

"Let me guess, law cases being argued." I gestured at the iPod.

He looked at me, amazed. "How did you know?"

"I'm smarter than I look." I wasn't about to give out my secrets. "Can anything be more boring than that?"

"I have a friend in medical school who listens to hour after hour of heartbeats so he can learn to recognize a murmur," he answered.

"Question withdrawn."

Nate laughed.

I wanted to spend my life with someone who shared my interests, like Nate and Leah did. We could talk about the same things, learn about the same things, and be interested in adding to each other's body of knowledge. Best friends *and* husband and wife. I yearned for that. Even looking at my parents, preparing to rediscover one another in their new house without kids, I longed for that togetherness.

An empty spot gaped inside me. I felt like a puzzle with pieces missing, and I felt those holes like bruises. Would I find someone to fill them?

We were seated quickly, and everyone began examining the menu.

"I'll just have the salad bar and a baked potato," Nate told the waitress.

"No meat?" my mother asked.

"My stomach has been acting up again," he said. "I'm trying to go easy—soft foods, nothing too spicy—and they spice all the steak here."

I refrained from rolling my eyes.

We chatted until the food arrived. I'd figured I'd let them all get something into their stomachs so they were good and mellow before I dropped my news. I'd chosen the restaurant as a safe place to tell everyone because my parents, especially my mother, never wanted to make a scene. My mother hated drawing attention. If she weren't Italian, she would have been Japanese. I'd read that a favorite Japanese proverb was, "The nail that sticks up gets hammered down." I was surprised it wasn't hanging, a framed needlepoint, on our living room wall.

"This is good, but not as good as the beef stroganoff Lexi made the other night," my dad said, polishing off the last bite of his steak. He folded his napkin into a neat square and placed it just under his plate.

I beamed at him.

"Sure, she *has* time to cook," Nate teased. "She doesn't work the hours I do."

75

Must everything be competitive with him? At least he gave me the opening I needed.

"Actually," I said, sitting back in my chair. "I've been offered a new job, and I've accepted it."

"Oh," Mom said. "I thought you were happy with the job you have now."

Dad leaned toward me, but not too close. He didn't want to tip a chair or drop a napkin or in any way impose on someone else's personal space.

"What is this new job?" he asked. I could tell he wished he'd met me for lunch after all.

I decided to try a ploy I had used as a teenager. Maybe it'd still work.

"I am going to be a massage therapist," I said, thinking of Leah.

Dead silence. Dad put both hands flat on the table.

"No, no, really," I said, "I decided I'd like to be a beautician after all. Remember? I always wanted to do that as a girl."

"Oh," Nate said.

Dad, on the other hand, said nothing. His bald patch turned pink.

I held up my hands in mock defense. "I'm kidding, you guys. I've accepted a job I'll really like at L'Esperance downtown. It's a French bakery. Great culture, wonderful food, and the people are fun. They speak French! I'm going to learn a lot and fit right in."

"What will you be doing?" my mother asked. A little too politely, but at least she was no longer holding her breath.

"I'll be counter help," I answered, holding *my* breath, instead, as I watched my dad's face deflate.

I knew they'd react this way, but knowing something in your head doesn't always prepare you for the hit to the heart when you see that you've disappointed your parents yet again.

Later that night, I heard a light rap on my door at the bed-and-breakfast.

"I know you might be too old for this kind of thing," my dad said when I opened the door, "but I was thinking about walking down by the docks for a while. Would you like to come?"

"Sure, Dad," I said. "Let me get my coat and gloves."

"I'll wait for you outside." He walked down the hallway in precise steps.

When I was a girl, my dad and I walked the docks by the naval base, looking at the ships coming in and going out. He would relax a little, comfortable in that world, and even hold my hand from time to time. Those walks meant a lot to me, so I was glad he remembered them too.

We walked down to the dock, watching the lights twinkling on a carrier getting ready to ship out.

"Did you really hate that other job?" he asked.

"Yes," I said, thankful I could finally be honest. "I was slow. I felt dumb. And bored. I'm interested in

77

things other people aren't always interested in, like baking and art."

"There's more to life than what you're interested in," Dad said. "When I was a kid, I wanted to go to law school. But I had no father, and Grandma had no money, and the navy seemed like a good way to go. It wasn't always fun, but I adjusted. Then your mother and I got married, and Nate was on the way soon thereafter. I had health insurance. I had stability. I had security and a place to live."

He brushed a fleck of dust off his coat sleeve.

"I appreciate all that, Dad, and everything you've done for us. But you wanted security. I want meaning."

He stared straight ahead, military bearing in place. "Sometimes if you take one, the other comes later."

"I'm hoping it will be that way for me too," I said. "Just the other way around."

He nodded, and we talked some more, but only about little, inconsequential things. I couldn't tell if he approved or disapproved of my choice. Maybe I needed to get over wondering.

Whether or not my parents liked the idea, the job was still mine, and I wanted to make the best of it. But no matter what time I arrived at work, Sophie was there before me.

"You're here early," Sophie said as I walked in

the door my second week on the job. "You can't clock in early."

"I know." I tied my apron around my waist. I was wearing khakis and a light denim shirt, thankful for my Dansko clogs. Lifesavers. If I weren't saving like a maniac, I'd have already gotten a foot massage at the spa down the street. "I just thought I'd come in early to help you," I said. "I know there's a lot going on."

"I'm good," Sophie said.

Fine. Two could play The Chill.

We worked straight through the mornings, slipping warm loaves of bread into sacks and setting them in neat, soldierly rows on the bread rack. I took over the pastry case, something Sophie seemed to have no interest in, while she kept up with the sandwich station. There was enough work for both of us during the morning and lunch rushes, but in between it was quiet. Only enough work for one, and that was usually the experienced one—Sophie. She was an efficient organizer and, when she remembered to smile, good with the customers. I noticed she was particularly soft toward the kids who came in.

Each morning I artfully arranged the pastries Patricia had prepared and stored in the cooler the afternoon before. Most days there were tall, round opera cakes, frilly Chantilly cakes, and tarts. Sometimes I brought in fresh flowers and arranged them in the pastry case while whistling "La Marseillaise," the French national anthem. Sophie pursed her lips and said nothing.

I couldn't figure out why the tarts had slices of fresh lemon on them instead of candied lemons. Candied lemon slices were *de rigueur*—tart with the potential for sweet all at once.

"Do you know why these slices aren't candied?" I asked Sophie one day.

"Ask Patricia," she said, ending the conversation.

No way. Patricia was the *dame formidable* in the kitchen. Everyone kept out of her way—Sophie and I, the croissant rollers—even Luc gave her a wide berth.

At every break, I read *Paris Match*. I peppered my conversation with French, even with the non-French-speaking customers. *Pourquoi pas?* Why not?

"*Tres belle*!" Luc said, looking at the flowers in the case one day. "This is very pretty. Who arranged this?"

I smiled but said nothing.

He smiled back. "I need a break. How about a *café crème* and some conversation? I haven't spoken French all morning."

My heart skipped a beat. I untied my apron, and we sat together at a cozy café table.

"So tell me how things are going," Luc said. "Do you enjoy the shop?"

I did! I told him how I enjoyed arranging the cases and serving the customers. I liked the hustle and bustle and hurry of things. I didn't mention that taking this job was causing serious stress at home or that Sophie seemed to wish she could cast a spell and make me disappear. What good would it do?

He surprised me by opening up about his village near the famed Palace of Versailles, just outside of Paris. Fairy-tale land.

"I miss it," he confided. "Not as much right now, but soon, when spring is here, I will miss it. But I go back this summer, for personal and family business. Have you ever been to France?"

I shook my head. "I've always wanted to go," I admitted, "but my family didn't have the money."

"*Alors,* you've not lived life," he said. "It's truly *charmant.*"

"I've studied all of France," I said longingly. "The rich history, the art, the literature. The palaces. Versailles."

"Ah, you must visit, Alexandra," Luc said. "*Je regrette.*"

"I went to college, but college was my parents' dream for me. I guess I followed their dream instead of mine."

"I wanted to go to college," he said, "but that wasn't for me. My family wanted to open bakeries in the U.S., and *voilà,* here I am. So neither of us got our dream. We each got someone else's, eh, Alexandra?" He smiled and leaned closer as he picked up his coffee. "But now, perhaps, we have to make our own dreams."

"There's always time to do new things...," I said, blushing. Blushing was a bad habit that I couldn't always control, but no guy had made me blush since

81

Greg.

"That's what I like about you, Alexandra," Luc said, holding my gaze. "You fit in well at a restaurant named for hope. We'll have to drink coffee together more often."

"Thank you." I stood up. "I'd better help Sophie."

Was he being polite? Trying to help me fit in? Was it just that the sense of personal space was smaller for a Frenchman than an American? Or was he starting to feel a little personal about me? Did I like him? Or was it a crush on a Frenchman, and any Frenchman would do?

I just didn't know.

Later that night, I went to watch Tanya coach volleyball. I walked into the gym and saw a swarm of girls encircling her, sweaty and pink with excitement, their ponytails bobbing. Tanya waved.

During the game I clapped and cheered and scanned the bleachers for an attractive man who just *might* be the mysterious Steve. *Non.*

"Go, girls! Dive for it, Amber!" Tanya called. One of her players did just that and came up right under the ball as planned. "Well done!" Tanya yelled as the girls applauded loudly.

After the game, I helped put the balls away and listened to Tanya coach.

"You girls did a fine job," Tanya said. "You overcame adversity and didn't listen to the rankings—Snohomish was supposed to whoop you tonight, and you won!"

A cheer rose from the girls.

"Go home, celebrate, get some rest, and I'll see you at practice tomorrow," Tanya said, looking as happy as I'd seen her in ages. Volleyball was a place she felt safe letting her guard down.

As the girls filed out, I sidled up next to her and said, "I remember when you were one of those girls."

"And you were in the stands cheering me on," she answered, pulling her car keys from her purse and grinning.

"I baked cookies for the team," I reminded her.

"Indeed you did. And that brought a lot of cute guys around too. *Muchas gracias.* Or should I say, *merci bien.*" She'd taken Spanish in school while I'd taken French. It was the only place my grades outdid hers: language.

We drove to the International House of Pancakes.

"So here we are, together again in a romantic restaurant on Valentine's Day," Tanya said. College students, retired folks, and young couples with babies peopled the room, which was thick with the smell of maple and coffee.

"Yeah, here we are," I replied. Greg and I had broken up last year just before Valentine's Day, and Tanya had come up to spend the weekend with me.

"Greg was way out of your league, anyway," a "friend" had once told me. I supposed she was right. It wasn't too long after the breakup before I saw him with a business major whose family was in real estate. Their fingers had been laced together intimately.

Was Luc out of my league too?

I snapped back to the present. "So, no Valentine's volleyball rendezvous?" I asked Tanya, expecting her to tease back. She'd been playing on that coed volleyball league for a few weeks now.

"Well, I had an option for that," she said. "Steve asked what I was doing after the game. I told him I was busy."

"Did you want to go?" I opened up three creamer containers and set them on the table, ready for my coffee.

Tanya looked at me. It meant everything to her to remain in control, but if you lingered long enough, you sensed her vulnerability. I think it was attractive to guys, though, as was her seeming lack of desire to be paired up. It made her mysterious and enticing. I feared I, on the other hand, was a needy open book.

"I think I *might* have wanted to go," she said.

"You can go on a date with someone and not have it be serious."

"I know."

I walked gingerly around the issue. "Do you like him?"

"I—I might," she answered. "I liked *him,* though, too."

She still never spoke Jason's name, more than two years later. It had happened on a date, after

84

dinner. They'd gone for a drive to a remote part of town—a high place, deserted—to see the city lights. There wasn't anywhere for Tanya to run, but he'd locked the car doors anyway.

I'd gone to counseling with her, but since then, she'd been uninterested in guys. She'd sort of dated one guy in a halfhearted effort to deflect questions from her family, whom she'd never told about Jason.

"You know Steve's sister," I said, bringing her out of the past and into the future. "And you know his family."

"Yes, and he goes to church. He's asked me to come with him to a church ski outing in a few weeks. Before the snow melts."

"See how it goes until then," I said. "You never know. He might just be what he seems to be. And you said he's cute!" I let my eyes twinkle.

She smiled. "He is."

Progress!

I dug into my pancakes.

"Things going okay at work?" Tanya asked, nibbling some hashbrowns.

"The good news: I like the environment. It's fun. I love matching customers up with food and doing the little touches." I told her about the flowers in the pastry case and how I'd noticed a few things missing on the pastries, but how busy Patricia was. "I especially love it when I get to interact with the food."

"Terrific!" Tanya said. "I'm so happy for you.

85

Anything else going on?"

"Luc had coffee with me today," I said, knowing what she meant. "And you know, he seemed a bit more interested. I haven't seen him have coffee with Sophie."

"Yeah, but Sophie's not new," she pointed out.

"And," I added triumphantly, "she can't speak French!" I knew I sounded pathetic, but it had to be worth something. Certainly that would be an important skill for the assistant manager.

"Is he a Christian?" Tanya asked, doubt in her voice.

"He wears a cross necklace."

She laughed. "Madonna wears a cross necklace. Marilyn Manson wears a cross necklace."

Well, you never know. I wasn't going to judge.

"The bad news," I said. I fished my paycheck stub out of my purse and handed it over. She hadn't even had to ask me what was in my wallet.

"Oh, Lex, you can't live on that," Tanya said. "I'm paying tonight."

"No way. I don't want to be everyone's charity case."

"What are you going to do?" she asked.

"Pray."

Suddenly, I remembered a verse from Jeremiah that I'd memorized long ago in order to earn points for a youth group ski trip.

"'For I know the plans I have for you,' declares the LORD, 'plans to prosper you and not to harm you, plans to give you hope and a future.'"

I wish I knew that plan. Actually, I'd like to direct and approve of that plan. I decided to look the verse up later. I wondered when I'd last looked anything up in the Bible without having a teacher, leader, or pastor suggest I do so. Never, maybe. I read it, but not on my own initiative or with fresh, adult eyes, driven by my own desire.

It was something to try. After all, I *had* asked for God's direction.

I checked my watch. "We'd probably better go. Work night." I grinned. "I want to do a good job."

She nodded. "Day starts early for both of us."

When we walked out to our cars, she bumped into me.

"A couple of cups of coffee and you're all jittery," I teased. "You're a Seattleite, girl!"

She winked at me, then got into her car and drove away.

I opened my purse to take out my keys, and as I did, I noticed a folded piece of paper with something scribbled on it. A twenty-dollar bill was folded inside the note, repaying my share of the meal twice over. She must have slipped it in when she bumped into me.

Why can't I cheer you as you reach for your dreams, too? I can't bake cookies but I can buy pancakes and watch from the stands as you prepare to become an Assistant Manager.

Tanya

87

Sandra Byrd

Six

Chacun croit aisément ce qu'il craint et ce qu'il désire.
We soon believe what we desire.

The next work week rolled by pretty much as the week before had. Sophie and I worked side by side during the rush, quietly uncomfortable during the down times. She was the organizer. I was the beautifier and food innovator.

One day I decided to powder the *gâteau basque,* Basque cake, with sugar. It'd been parked in the pastry case for a day or two, and soon it would be too old to sell. I dusted some sugar on the top and arranged early rosebuds on the side. I nodded, pleased at the effect.

A few minutes later, Patricia came into the café to hand off some tartes Tatin, apple tarts. She took one look at the powdered gâteau and barked, "What happened here?" to Sophie, not even looking at me.

Sophie shrugged. "Ask Lexi."

Patricia turned to me, and I felt my face flush.

"I wanted it to look nice and sell. You work so hard on the cakes, and I didn't want it to go to waste," I explained, barely taking a breath.

Patricia shrugged and hustled back to the pastry room. *Victory!* I'd evaded a royal scolding and claimed nothing said as tacit approval.

"I'm going for a break," I said to Sophie. I hadn't taken a break in the month I'd worked there.

"That's okay. I'll hold the fort. As always," Sophie said. Sneered, maybe? I didn't know or care. She couldn't hurt my job, but I needed to win her over if I was going to lobby for the manager's position.

After the lunch rush, Sophie restocked the paper goods. "Would you arrange the special orders?" she asked me. "They're really important to our business. I know Luc's trying to develop that line."

"Sure," I said, happy to learn more about the daily operations. At least she wasn't freezing me out of new information.

"Here's what you do," she said. "In the bakery, there's a big corkboard. The pastry special orders go on one side, general special orders on the other. We just write them down on one of these slips," she pointed to a pad by the phone, "when people call in. We pin them to the board in the back—filed by date under either pastry or general—when they come in. That way Luc and Patricia know what to prepare and when to have the order ready." She showed me the board in the back. "Got it? Really easy."

"*Even for you,*" I sensed unsaid in her voice.

"Got it," I said. I copied the orders that had been scribbled on various napkins and wrote them neatly on the order papers. I took them into the back and tacked them to the bulletin board under the proper dates and with the proper person.

"Hey, come here, Alexandra," Luc called, motioning to me. "I'm trying something new. Taste it." He handed me an almond croissant. "I'm glazing it and putting the almonds on before quick-toasting them in the oven, sealing the sides shut so the pastry filling stays fresh longer. Another day of shelf life."

I loved almond croissants. I'd eaten them often in Bellingham.

"Go on," he urged me. "Try it. I'm really interested in your thoughts." He watched and waited like he really cared.

I bit into it. It was crispier all the way around, not just on top. And the inside, just as Luc said, was still fresh. The nut filling was both smooth and coarse, with the texture of rough sugar.

"Delicious!" I said. "It might work even better if you put just a dab of glaze on the inside of the croissant before you bake it, to seal it from the inside too." I'd tried that with my pistachio ones last month.

"*Voilà!*" he exclaimed. "That will work even better. Go on," he urged. "If you like it, finish it. One little croissant isn't going to spoil a pretty figure. Croissants are good for the soul. Just ask my *maman.*" He winked, but he seemed genuinely pleased that I liked his new idea.

I wolfed down the croissant and went back to work, fighting a smile. Oh yeah, I'd heard right. My pretty figure!

That afternoon I went home to find Dad there, organizing the pantry.

"Hey, Dad," I said. I watched as he moved from the pantry to the laundry room cupboards. He was orderly, but this was above the norm.

"Hi, Lexi." He seemed agitated, but unless I wanted a fifty-minute lecture complete with overheads and laser pointer on whatever political "moron" had annoyed him, it was better not to ask.

It was Monday, my dinner night. "Just you and me tonight, right?" I asked. "Mom's at an early-planning meeting for the Easter celebration at church."

He grunted from inside the pantry.

"Anything special you want?" I asked, still trying to put a finger on the vibe.

"Whatever you make is good," he said.

Uh-huh.

I did some research on Allrecipes.com and finally found some inspiration. I kneaded some dough and set it aside to rise. Then I went to put some things away in my room.

Just for fun, I unwrapped the Chihuly vase and held it up to the window. Even the muddy mid-February twilight cast a lovely glow through the handblown vase. I would find a home for it—and for me. I had tucked away last week's paycheck in savings. I'd tuck away this one too. Soon I'd have enough for a deposit, if I could find someplace willing to work within my budget.

I sat on my bed and looked at my Bible, unopened since my foray to church with Mom about a month ago. I had to give her props. She asked if I was coming to church with her the next week, and when I'd said no, she hadn't pushed or even asked again.

Remembering the verse I'd thought of at IHOP, I flipped to the concordance in the back and looked up "plan." The reference sent me to Jeremiah 29:11-13.

"For I know the plans I have for you," declares the LORD, "plans to prosper you and not to harm you, plans to give you hope and a future. Then you will call upon me and come and pray to me, and I will listen to you. You will seek me and find me when you seek me with all your heart."

With all my heart. With all my heart, I'd chased a job. With all my heart, I'd chased a man. With all my heart, I was scoping Craigslist.org every day to find a new apartment or condo. But seeking God? Not so much.

I set the Bible aside and put one of Mom's bud vases on the table with a rose I'd brought home from L'Esperance, then checked on my dough.

I stretched the dough out nice and thin, Italian style, and let it rest and rise. I cranked the oven to "phoenix"—four hundred and fifty degrees—so the bricks I'd laid in the bottom of the oven would get nice and hot. I'd have to take them out and stack them in the garage when I was done. Mom didn't like bricks in her oven.

I cooked down tomatoes, sugar, salt, and a pinch of basil, then spread it over the rising dough. Now, for toppings: what did we have?

After rummaging through the fridge and cupboards, I diced artichoke hearts, pitted Kalamata olives, chopped feta cheese, and put thin shreds of Italian salami on my Athens-Meets-Rome Pizza.

"This is really good," my dad said when we sat down to eat. "Not as good as that beef stroganoff that you make, though. Where did you get the recipe for *that*?"

I beamed proudly. "I made it up myself."

"Wow!" he said. "I thought you got it off that recipe site you're always visiting."

"Nope. I didn't like what they had to offer, so I tweaked a couple of recipes till it became what I wanted it to be."

Dad chewed his pizza and took a sip of his beer before answering. "Why don't you put your recipes on there too? You make things that are good but still simple American food. Do they pay you for those recipes?"

I wish. "No, they don't pay."

But why didn't I post my recipes? Well, what if no one else liked them?

Silence extended well beyond the time needed to chew and swallow. In fact, it seemed to stretch into the time it would take to digest the food!

Dad finally spoke. "It doesn't sound like the

cooking and baking thing is going to pay, Lexi. Why not let your old dad help you? I have several contacts who might be able to find a decent job for you."

"I'm doing okay, Dad."

"You can't live on what you're making, Lexi."

"I could live on the assistant manager's salary. And it's a place to start."

"You had time to start, Lexi. It's long passed. And who knows if you'll get the manager's job?"

He should have been a lawyer after all.

"I *will* get that job, Dad. I'm a natural for it. I love food, I'm motivated, I understand both baking and French."

"I could ask Uncle Bennie to look."

I stood up. "No, Dad. Don't mention anything to Uncle Bennie." I started clearing the table. "I don't want any help. I want to do it on my own now. And I've made a commitment." *I don't want you to know I was fired, Dad. I want you to be proud of me.*

"Have they made a commitment to you?" Dad asked.

My silence was my answer and he knew it, but at least I hadn't given in.

He opened his wallet and pulled out a business card, then slid it across the table.

"Peterson's Food Distribution. Mack Allan, Manager, Information Services," I read aloud. "What is this?"

"A friend," Dad said. "They're hiring."

Food services. Hmm.

95

"What is he hiring for?" I could tell by the rigid way Dad held his head that I wasn't going to like it.

"Information input. But it's a big company, Lexi. They deliver to restaurants, gourmet stores, and bakeries all over Seattle. There might be something else down the road. They have benefits, you know."

A cubicle. My dad looked so earnest, though. I knew he was trying.

"All right, I'll apply," I said, knowing that even if I got the job, I couldn't take it. I'd promised Luc the six months.

Later that night I went to Allrecipes.com again. I did have some good recipes, and maybe others would enjoy them too. Or maybe they'd hate them, or no one would try them. And then I'd lose the only thing I felt good about in my life right now.

I'd register. *Why not?* It'd be fun.

Dad, unknowingly, had suggested the perfect user name. I logged on, entered the name, and set myself up.

I wouldn't check my feedback for at least a month. Okay, two weeks. Maybe one. Definitely not tomorrow because I was *not* going to base my worth on what people I never even met said about my food.

I had enough trouble with people I knew.

One day I took an early lunch and went to Peterson's. I knew all about them, because they delivered to L'Esperance: yeast, tinned peaches from

France, that kind of thing. I made sure I had no flour on my clothes and walked into the human resources office.

"May I have an application, please?" I hoped my clogs didn't look too out of place in the neutral-toned office.

"For which job?" the receptionist asked.

I showed her Mack's card. "Information inputting."

"Ah," she said. "That job was filled last week. But if you want to fill out an app and leave it here, I'll make sure it gets to Mack."

Okay, I tried. I'd followed through on my dad's good intentions and found the door—thankfully—closed. I left my application and drove back to L'Esperance, where I quickly tied on my apron. I glanced at the clock. Five minutes late.

"You're late," Sophie said, aiming her voice in Luc's direction.

"I'll come in early tomorrow," I answered as sweetly as I could.

After my shift, Mom came to pick me up so we could get Nonna and then go shopping for dresses with Leah and her mother. Mom wanted to see where I worked. I didn't mind. I was proud. Well, mostly.

I could see her waiting patiently at the back of the café. It was the first time she'd ever been to L'Esperance.

It was near 1:30, but I was leaving early to spend some time with my mom. The café had pretty much

97

cleared out. I watched my mom as she watched me bus tables. She had a look in her eyes, kind of forlorn. She didn't have to say it, but I knew what she was thinking.

"You didn't go to college to do this."

Yeah.

I took my apron off and beckoned her forward. "I'd like you to meet Sophie," I said.

Sophie acknowledged the introduction, but just barely.

Then Luc came forward, calling out to me in French about the pastry shelves. I answered in French, and then said in English, "Luc, I'd like you to meet my mother, Peggy."

"Ah, Peggy," he said, picking up my mother's hand and kissing it. "Now I know where Alexandra gets her extraordinary beauty."

My mother—my *mother*—blushed. "My real name is Margaret," she said charmingly.

"Margaret," he said soothingly. Mom smiled.

We chatted for a while, and Luc complimented me on the bud vases I'd dug out of an old storage cupboard and placed alongside some IKEA tea light candles on each table.

As we left, I saw Luc and Sophie sit down together at a café table. They looked friendly. Sophie smiled genuinely. I hadn't seen *any* sign of closeness between them before now.

Shake it off, I told myself. *It's nothing. Luc is merely being polite.*

Mom and I parked in front of Nonna's retirement center, right around the corner from her church.

"I noticed you let Luc hold your hand for a few extra seconds," I teased as we walked up to Nonna's apartment.

"It was nice to meet him. I've noticed the...ah...*warm* tone of voice you use when you talk about him." Mom gave me a knowing look. "Though I wouldn't know what you two were talking about in French, it sounded nice to hear you speak it," she admitted. "I always wanted to speak another language and have a glamorous job and an exciting time in my life. And then I wanted that for you."

"What else did you want, Mom?" She never opened up like this.

She stopped walking. "You know that Nonna worked my whole life, so when I came home from school, I cleaned, watched my siblings, and started dinner. I took care of everyone. It's been my role my whole life. From when I was a teenager until...now."

I'd never thought of it that way. Nonna seemed so forward-thinking when she was a working mother all those years ago, but had that somehow been at the expense of my mom?

"It would have been fun to travel. Have a good job that brought in my own money. Been independent before having kids. But, you know, I met your dad, and Nate came along, and I went from keeping house to keeping house."

"You're good at that, Mom," I said. It was lame, I knew, but I meant it. "And now you have all the time you want to do something else."

"Bosh, I'm too old for that now," she said. She started walking again, ending the conversation.

We rang Nonna's doorbell, and she arrived at the door, hair curled and makeup on. Just inside her door lay a stack of magazines.

"Nonna," I said. "I didn't know you subscribed to *Martha Stewart Living*. And *National Geographic*. And the *Atlantic Monthly*."

She smirked.

"Nonna," I reprimanded her. "*Nonna!*"

"Mother," my mom said, sighing. "Not again."

"I read them *very carefully*," Nonna protested, "not creasing a page, and then I return them to the right mailboxes. No one knows. Betty doesn't even remember to read her magazines. She only subscribes so she can get into the sweepstakes. Would she mind? No. And Mr. Jones will do anything for me. I've decided. He's going to be my date at the wedding."

She looked pointedly at me. "Got a date yet?"

"*J'ai des possibilités,*" I answered in French, implying a Frenchman.

"Ooh la la." My mother fanned herself with her hand, and we burst out laughing.

We met Leah and her mom at Bling, a dress shop. On the way I prayed, *God, let this be a good day for Leah. Let her stand up to the people who*

*treat her poorly. Let her mother see that this is
Leah's day and wedding. Thank you for my family.*

I felt his warm presence. I felt hugged.

In the end, Leah did choose the bridesmaid
dresses, a beautiful smoky rose. My mom got a dress
at the bridal shop that, while several sizes larger
than Leah's mom's dress, was beautiful. We told
Nonna she couldn't wear strapless or a plunging
back.

She winked. "We'll see."

On the way home, I decided to talk to my mom in
the family language, that is indirectly.

"Leah's mother means well," I said, "but she bugs
me. She's always picking on Leah. She expects her to
be just who she wants her to be, instead of accepting
Leah for who she is."

The windshield wipers whispered against the
glass. The interior of the car stayed quiet.

A block or two from home, Mom finally spoke.
"Leah's mom was pregnant when she got married, so
her parents wouldn't give her a wedding. Maybe she
just wants for her daughter what she couldn't have
for herself."

"Maybe that's not what her daughter wanted,
though. Wouldn't she rather have her be happy?"

"Young women don't always know what will
make them happy in the long run."

I sighed. We both wanted me to be happy. We
just had different ideas about what that looked like.

As we rounded the corner to the house, I saw
something in the yard. A big white pole with a sign

hanging on it. "What's that?" I asked.

"Oh goodness," Mom said. "I had no idea it'd be up so quickly. Dad must have given her the go-ahead while I was at school this week."

As we got closer, I read it aloud with increasing alarm.

Windermere Real Estate

FOR SALE

Listing Agent: Teresa Ranft
Phone: 206-555-4855

Seven

Si vous avez seulement un oeil, salut pour ne pas le perdre.
If you only have one eye, take care not to lose it.

Sign's up, eh?" Tanya and I sat parked in her old Mazda in front of my house. We both looked at the For Sale sign. "Looks like the fliers are gone," she said.

"Yeah," I said. "The real estate market is still hot." *Too hot.* "The house already has offers, but the agent wants to hold one more open house to make sure she's getting maximum dollars."

We sat in the car for a minute.

"What are you going to do?" Tanya asked.

"Nate's helping me look for a place. I have two small studios lined up to view, maybe tonight, and one grand, glorious apartment." I gathered up my purse and apron and looked at my hands. "I'm feeling kind of desperate."

"It's going to work out," Tanya said.

"I'll borrow your faith." I opened the car door.

Dad was neatly edging the lawn. He was so precise, you'd think he was trimming a hemophiliac's beard.

"Hi, girls," he said, the same thing he'd said to us for more than ten years.

"Hi, Mr. Stuart," Tanya said. "Lawn looks great."

Dad gave her a thumbs-up. He liked Tanya. Their personalities meshed well.

While Tanya walked toward the porch, Dad called me over. "Did you apply with Mack?" he asked.

I softly said, "I tried. Job's already filled, but thanks, Dad."

He looked so disappointed. In me, or in the lack of a job, I didn't know. I wanted him to be proud of me. I walked slowly to the mailbox, spring taken out of my step.

I pulled the mail from the box and met Tanya at the front door.

"Want to come with me to look at those places tonight?" I asked. "I'd love your opinion."

"I wish I could, but I have a date."

"A *date*!" I squealed, cheered again. "Really?"

"Yeah. With Steve. Dinner and a movie. It feels teenagerish, but, you know…"

Tanya had agreed to a date! A mix of emotions filled me: elation, anxiety…jealousy? Maybe a little. But mostly, I felt elated.

"I'm proud of you," I said. "When do I get to meet Steve?"

"Soon." She grinned.

I looked up the studios and apartment on MapQuest and left right after dinner to see them.

The first studio was within walking distance of work, which was a plus, but over a Greek restaurant, which was not.

"Come, come." A whiskered woman answered the door, and I followed as she lumbered up some side steps. I could hear a tambourine shimmying in the background and smell garlic, onions, and brine.

The studio was small, but it actually had a tiny bedroom. It overlooked a minimarket from the back windows, and a large ventilation system whirled noisily. As soon as the vent shut down for a moment, I could hear the tambourines downstairs. It was Friday night, I knew, but I didn't think I could live with the crash of plates and "Oopa!" every weekend.

Besides, there was no stove—only a toaster oven and hot plate.

"Thank you so much," I said, shaking her hand. "I'll call you if I want it."

The look on her face told me she'd heard that before.

I drove to the second studio, hopeful. It was in a better neighborhood and in a building of fifteen apartments. I was slightly taken back, therefore, to see the place wrapped in plastic like a giant, microwaved potato. Tentatively, I knocked on the manager's door.

"Yes?"

"I understand you have an apartment for rent?" I showed her my printout from Craigslist.org.

"Oh yes, yes. Well, right now," she swept her arm toward the building, "it's being fumigated. A little bug problem. We've tried to get rid of it before, but it never worked. I think it will this time." She winked at me. "Come back next week, okay?"

I agreed but didn't commit. *Bugs. Ugh.*

I drove by the great apartment and took a leasing flier from the lobby. All they had left were fourteen-hundred-a-month doubles. I crumpled it up and threw it into the trash.

I went home and watched TV with my parents before going to sleep in my brother's childhood room.

Things were not looking good.

I got to work before Sophie the next day without even trying. I hoped she didn't think I was trying to one-up her anymore. The *Trois Amis,* the three croissant-rolling friends (as I had dubbed them), let me in through the bakery door, grunting. They were under a lot of stress because our croissant orders had doubled this week for a special order from the university.

Luc was already in the café, and he hugged me and kissed my cheeks when I entered. "Ah, the spring flower of L'Esperance has blown in for the day."

We smiled broadly at each other. He held my arm just a bit longer than natural. I felt the imprint of his hand through my muscle, and the touch of it stayed there after he'd let go.

Did he feel it, too? I couldn't tell.

I opened the café.

It was nice to be there on my own in the morning. I felt ownership. I felt empowered. I could see myself managing this. *What would I do differently?*

Sophie came in after I had everything chugging along and gave me a rare smile when she saw the place set up. "I'll bag the bread," she said.

I noticed she had a stud in her nose. It looked like a small bug napping in the nose cleft. "New?" I asked.

She touched it gingerly. "Like it?"

It was the first time she'd ever asked my opinion. *Everything I need to know I learned in kindergarten: honesty is the best policy, but find something nice to say.*

"It looks really good on you," I answered.

Luc wheeled in a big rack of bread and croissants for us to bag, place, and showcase. He noticed Sophie's new piercing and tutted in her general direction. "Sophie, *la passoire.*"

Sophie narrowed her eyes and leaned toward me as Luc went back to the bakery.

"Sophie, the sieve," I translated for her, watching to see if she'd be offended. Luc clearly was not a fan of multiple piercings.

"I am what I am," she said. "Thanks for the translation." She turned away to wipe down the espresso machine. Her tone didn't sound very thankful.

The breakfast rush came and went, and Sophie and I washed the tables ten times each and tidied up already-tidy areas. I watched the clock, waiting for the lunch rush.

"I think I'll put some fresh flowers in the pastry case," I said. I headed to the florist three doors down and traded a few chocolate croissants for some daffodils and narcissus. I arranged them in the case, and even Sophie gave her approval.

Very managerial, Lex, I told myself.

During the lunch rush, Sophie handled the sandwiches while I ran the register.

"Do you sell this jam?" asked an older man, a regular customer. He held up his half-eaten croissant spread with wild strawberry *confiture.*

"No, I'm sorry," I said. "It's a special confiture that Luc, our owner, brings over from France. It's like strawberry heaven, isn't it?"

"I'd like to bring some home for my wife," he said. "She doesn't get out much these days."

I grabbed a foam cup from the shelf, scooped several large tablespoons into it, and snapped a lid on top. "Anytime." He held my hand in thanks.

I grabbed the phone while Sophie ran the coffee machine. "*Bonjour,* L'Esperance. May I help you?"

"Special order," said a male voice on the other

end. "Catering for Davis, Wilson, and Marks." I jotted it down: several loaves of bread, prepped, cheese tray, fresh fruit. Silver trays. Expensive look. "Nothing sweet," he insisted. "Not a pastry tray. Lunchtime stuff."

Sophie looked meaningfully at me over her shoulder. The line was out the door, and she needed help. *Oh well,* I thought to myself cheerfully, *job security, right?*

I ran the special-order note back to the bulletin board in the back. On the way, I noticed the pastry case out front was getting low.

"Can you bring forward some pastries?" I asked Luc as I breezed by. Where was Patricia anyway?

"Can you?" he answered, his voice edgy. "I'm a little busy here, in case you didn't notice." He glared, and I turned away.

Wow. I blinked back tears. *Sorry you're so busy, but you've offered to do that numerous other times.* I grabbed some pastries from the cooler and went back to the café to help Sophie.

"Who was on the phone?" Sophie asked once things had calmed down again.

"Davis, Wilson, someone," I answered. "Special order."

"Oh good!" she said. "I think they're an accounting firm. They used to do special orders every week for their business meetings, but we haven't heard from them for the past couple months. They always placed big orders, and they influence a lot of other companies in their building."

"Well, they're back!" I said. Maybe Luc would be happy with us all when he saw the order. Me in particular.

Sophie counted out the register, Luc put it in the safe, and she left an hour early, as we'd planned earlier in the week. Before Luc left to take care of business at La Couronne, he came to chat, calmer now.

I told him about the man who wanted to buy some jam. "I told him I'd give him a little cup of it anytime he asked, but it made me think—what if we had a small baker's rack of *produits de la France* up front? Some confiture, some truffles, some chocolate, French roast coffees." I joked, "Cans of escargot for the sturdy at heart." No one would buy snails. He knew I was kidding.

Luc ran his hand over his jaw and then smiled. "Eh *bien,* I like it, Alexandra. Good idea. It will bring in a little more revenue while providing something special for our customers."

He seemed pleased but also a little distant. Distracted? Mad at me?

He grabbed the deposit bag and his business case. "Look into it. There are some supplier lists in the back with Web addresses. Let me know what you find out."

He left, the door swinging jauntily behind him. He grew more attractive by the day, his temperamental nature enhancing rather than detracting from his allure. I wasn't immune to the bad-boy appeal.

I spent the evening browsing through lists of products offered by our distributors, jotting down a short list of contenders. Then I checked Allrecipes.com to see if I had any feedback.

Two Allrecipes.com comments for Simply American's Boyfriend Bait Beef Stroganoff

Four stars! What a great recipe! A snap to make and the result was elegant enough to make me feel like an accomplished chef. My meat-and-potatoes teenage boys loved this, as did my husband. I'll definitely make this one again. Thanks, Simply American!

Five stars! This is delicious, it's worth using the tenderloin, as the finished product is much classier than stroganoff made with ground beef. I was tempted to replace the shallots with onions, but I'm glad I didn't; shallots give this dish such a rich, distinct flavor. I felt confident serving this dish to guests.

The day of the last open house arrived, which meant I had to clear out of the house for the whole day and evening. With offers coming across the tram as though ours was the last house available in Seattle, I knew it wouldn't be long before it sold. My time was running out.

I drove to work in the morning not planning to go home until late that night. I had two more studios to look at, but not in Seattle. Out in the suburbs. Far from ideal, but I was short on options.

"Alexandra?" Luc sauntered into the café after the lunch rush. "I am going to Pike's Market to examine the competition: a line of new bakeries. They've opened their first shop. Would you like to come with me? Another set of taste buds..."

Sophie looked down.

"Regrettably, Sophie, since you won't eat the food, I can't have you come," he said.

I had noticed she ate very little at the shop. Weird. I wondered why.

"*Oui,* I would *love* to come," I said, glad he had an excuse to take me and not Sophie. I hoped there was more to it than the reason given.

We got into Luc's little Renault—I'd never ridden in one before—and zoomed down to the market.

"You're not in France, Luc," I joked, pretending to clutch the door handle as he raced the few city streets to the market.

"True," he answered, "but I can still drive like I am."

I teased him and wondered aloud if he had an international driver's license.

Once he'd parked, he motioned for me to stay in

the car while he walked around and opened my door for me.

Score one point.

We wandered down the produce rows first, pinching and smelling and even tasting the wares stacked in fetching displays. Vendors hawked the spring produce with calls and samples. We walked down the aisle of flower stands: so many beautiful combinations, set like nature's jewelry. I wished he'd buy a bouquet for me. Instead, he bought some fresh pears to make into tarts for Sunday and gave me one. We walked toward the bakery with pear juice all over us.

"Eh *bien*," he said, pointing across the way to the shop name. "Hot Cross Buns. Sounds English," he sniffed.

I smiled to myself. *Gallic pride.*

The girl behind the counter looked a lot like the nail chipper Luc had fired before hiring me, but upon closer look, it wasn't really her. Luc ordered a pain au chocolat, a plain croissant, and a bread pudding. We sat down at a café table, and he divided each one in two.

"Well?" he asked me after he'd tasted everything.

I took a bite of the croissant. "Tough."

He looked pleased. "Didn't proof long enough, and they overworked the dough."

"Poor quality chocolate," I said after tasting the pain au chocolat.

"*Exactement!*" he agreed. "And last?"

Suddenly, I had the feeling this was not just a fun

day out, but some kind of quiz. I've never been a brown-noser, so he was going to get the truth whether he wanted it or not.

"The pudding is really good," I said. "Better than any I've ever had."

Luc smiled. "I think so too, Alexandra," he said, leaning closer to me to pick up the leftovers and the napkins. I could feel his breath on my hair. As he pulled away, he looked me right in the eyes. "I'm glad you came with me. I value your opinion."

As for my breath, I couldn't seem to find it. "I'm glad you asked me."

As I helped Sophie close the café, Tanya stopped by. The weather was a little chilly, but we were going for a power walk on the boardwalk at Alki Beach.

"Where's Luc?" she asked under her breath.

I shook my head. "Already left for La Couronne." I wanted to know what she thought of him, but part of me was glad he hadn't met her. Like I said before, every guy who met Tanya seemed drawn to her mysterious vibe, and while normally that was okay, this time...

I introduced her to Sophie. Sophie smiled nicely at her—nicer than she ever was to me.

I took my apron off, and we drove to Alki, got out of the car, and strolled into a rare, sunny spring afternoon.

"My school project last night was great," Tanya

started off. "Another teacher and I applied for a Gates Grant for computers for low-income classrooms—and we got them! Each of my kids has a computer at his or her desk now." Tanya beamed, her face pinking up with pleasure and sunlight.

I held my face to the sun. I needed some of that warmth after months of hibernating in the northwest gloom.

"We installed them last night after the kids left," she continued, "so when they come back on Monday they'll find them on their desks. I don't know. I might not want to move schools after this contract. It's growing on me." She stopped talking. "Lexi, are you paying attention?"

"Oh...uh...yeah," I said. "So did you get the computers installed?"

"You are *not* paying attention," she said in her teacher's voice.

When we were kids, Tanya always played the teacher. Then she was the teacher's aide. Her mom regularly visited the school to celebrate her awards. My mother regularly visited the school to bring in my forgotten homework or lunch.

"What's up with you?" she asked.

I told her about the French products rack I was working on. "I hope Luc likes what I've picked out," I said.

"Somehow I don't think you're distracted about a product rack," she said. "Even if it is very managerial of you."

I giggled and told her about my "date" at Pike's

Market with Luc that afternoon.

"Was it a date?" she asked.

I shrugged. "I don't know. Probably not. But close."

"Do you think it'd be a problem to date him? I mean, since he's your boss?"

I bit my lip. "I don't think so. It's a small place, and we'd keep it professional. We're not at that level yet, anyway. Not by a long shot."

"And you don't know if he's a Christian, do you?" Tanya asked.

I shook my head. "I don't. Maybe soon we'll have a conversation about that."

"He doesn't talk about God, though?" She tightened her ponytail.

"No. But neither do I," I admitted. "I'm busy working hard. I want that promotion."

After our walk, I drove Tanya back to her school to pick up some papers she'd left. On the way, I noticed the Church on the Hill on Ballard. It looked small and inviting, and I'd heard someone mention it, though I couldn't remember who. Maybe I'd give it a try.

We stopped by the café to pick up Tanya's car. After parting ways, I still couldn't go home because the open house was in full swing, so I drove to Nonna's church. I checked my watch. She usually went to the Saturday afternoon Mass. I parked by the side of the road and decided to slip in.

I saw Nonna ten or twelve rows up. Most of the church was empty, and I sat in the back. I didn't usually participate at Nonna's church, but I could greet her after the service this way. And who knew? Maybe this was the church for me.

The sanctuary was dim, and the stained glass windows strained to reflect what little light still dribbled through the March skies. The smell of hot candles mixed with the musty scent of old stones and the ancient vapor of rosewood incense. It seemed old and continuous, like people had passed the baton of faith over and over again, and I liked that.

I sat on one of the hard oak pews and closed my eyes.

I felt awed; I felt holy and reverent. But as beautiful as it was, and as much as it was Nonna's spiritual home, I knew it wasn't mine.

After the service, people began to file past me, old and young. Nonna's face lit up when she saw me. "Lexi!"

"Hi, Nonna. I thought you might need a ride home." I held out my arm, and we linked elbows.

"No date tonight, eh?" Nonna teased and wagged her finger.

"Thanks, Nonna," I said. "You always go right for the jugular."

"I'd rather ride with my girl than the retirement center bus any day," Nonna said. "Come out this way. I want you to meet my friend Pete."

She led me down the cool corridor—as a girl, my mother took her first communion there—and into the kitchen in the back.

"There's my lady!" A man with a wide apron held his arms out to Nonna. She reached up and patted the crown of her hair to make sure her slowly expanding bald spot was covered.

"Pete, this is my Lexi," Nonna said. She turned to me. "Pete's in charge of the Saturday night dinners they hand out to the homeless. They line up on the sidewalk," she pointed out the door, "and get hot soup and bread."

"Bread if we're lucky," Pete said. "We have our food donated, prepared in a commercial kitchen. The grocery store down the way provides the soup, but our bread supplier is uneven."

"I work at L'Esperance just down the street," I said. "We often have leftover bread. I'll ask if I could bring some by on Saturdays."

"There, it's done," Nonna said, snapping her fingers. "Lexi will make sure the bread gets here. See? What a good girl."

"Well, but, wait..."

"Thank you!" Pete took my hand in both of his and shook it. "I knew the Lord would provide." He turned back to the soup and the other volunteers waiting to ladle it into large to-go cups to hand out at the door.

"Too bad he's not a little younger," Nonna said. "He'd be perfect for you."

"Nonna, he's like forty years too old, and not my type, and, *Nonna,* I don't know if I can bring the bread. I have to ask."

"It'll all work out, dear. You were here for some

reason, weren't you?"

I sighed. We walked to my car, and I took her back to her retirement community. During the drive, she told me all the activities her complex had planned: bingo, craft sessions, after-church potlucks.

If the studios I was going to see that night didn't work out, maybe I could don a wig and move in with Nonna.

Sandra Byrd

Eight

Un homme averti en vaut deux.
Forewarned is forearmed.

When I arrived at work two days later, I said,
"*Bonjour,*" to the *Trois Amis,* but no one even said
hi. "*Bonjour,*" I said to Guillaume, one of the bakers,
directly.

"You didn't close the walk-in door tightly enough
yesterday, and now the pastry cream is runny," he
said. "No pastries today. We had to take some from
La Couronne to fill a special order, which left both
display coolers empty."

Oh no. Patricia was going to kill me.

"Lucky for you the cheese delivery is tomorrow,"
Guillaume continued, "and therefore there is no
cheese to spoil, or you'd be out of a job already."

I knew they were crabby because of the week's
work load, but still...everyone makes mistakes. I'd
been helping clean up last night—off the clock—after
a special order prep, which Patricia ran back to La
Couronne. I'd just wanted to help, and instead I'd

ruined an entire day's worth of pastry.

I did my best to make up for it by working like a dog. I took one small break in the morning to call the cute, cheap studio I'd found on my drive last night only to find out they had a stack of applications already. They'd be in touch. *Right.*

Luc shouted into the phone at someone from La Couronne, stopping to point at a huge stack of supplies when I walked by. "Can you put those away quickly?" he asked me.

Sure I could! I dragged them behind the counter and got down on my hands and knees, placing things in exactly the right spot. I scooted over, pushing the box ahead of me, trying to pack in as many bundles of napkins as possible.

"Ouch!" Sophie cried. I had shoved the corner of the box into her leg.

"Oh, I'm sorry," I said.

"Watch what you're doing!"

I took a deep breath. *I am too old to cry.*

Then the lunch rush started.

At the sandwich station, I cranked out creamy tuna salad sandwiches, thick ham and cheese sandwiches, red roast beef, and pâté with tiny *cornichon* pickles, all on baguettes. I worked the knife so fast, I worried I would cut my thumb off. I could hear the hustle in the back too, as Luc and the *Trois Amis* rushed to fill orders for both L'Esperance and La Couronne.

I pushed my hair off my forehead with the back of my hand, the latex gloves rolling at the wrist and trapping moisture underneath.

"Hurry!" Sophie hissed under her breath.

I plated a sandwich, then a pastry, with silverware and a napkin. I assembled sandwiches and put half of them into to-go boxes. The line stretched out the door, and I could see people shuffling from foot to foot and checking their wrists, watching their lunch hour tick away.

A man came toward the pastry case. He tried to get my attention, but I avoided eye contact, irritated. *Why isn't he in line like everyone else?*

He waited impatiently for a few minutes, slipped his business card into the fishbowl for a free lunch, and then checked his watch again.

Finally, he waved Sophie down. She softened, seeming to recognize him. She smiled. I turned and watched them.

He was nice looking, what my mother would call earnest. What Leah would call clean cut. What Tanya would call sweet. He had on nicely cut pants, a crisp white shirt, and suspenders. Definitely not Sophie's type, which usually ran to Charming Bad Boy in Need of an Immediate Cash Infusion.

I liked the suspender look, but I wasn't ready to award any points since he'd bullied his way to the front of the line.

I overheard Sophie say, "Yes, definitely. I saw Lexi write it down."

Me?

She nodded at me to come over. "Could you take care of this man while I finish up the lunches? He's the one who called in the special order from Davis, Wilson, and Marks the other day." She turned her back to him. "Remember?" she whispered. "The corporate account we lost and now might get back?"

Ah yes. So he hadn't bullied his way forward. He was here for a pickup.

I tried to look pleasant. "I'll go see if it's ready."

He smiled at me, and I relaxed for the first time that day. Clean cut and earnest. Cute? Cute! It had been a long time since I had noticed a guy in that way...except Luc.

"Thanks," he answered. "The meeting starts in about fifteen minutes, so I need to get out of here. It should be a large platter of sliced breads, cheeses, and fruit."

I rolled off the gloves, pitched them into the trash, and headed back toward the cooler. The order should be ready. Luc always did the special orders first thing in the morning.

I pulled open the cooler door. Racks of *choux* pastry, neatly folded like tablecloths, waiting to debut, rested between sheets of plastic wrap on one wall. Huge tubs of choux cream, ready for *mille-feuilles* and other pastries stood patiently to the side. Fruit, meats, and cheeses for sandwiches were there but not the kind appropriate for a platter.

No special order.

Ah. Here was a box.

"University of Washington afternoon meeting." I looked inside. Meat and cheese, fruit, pastry. No pastry in the Davis, Marks guy's order, and he wasn't with the university.

I shut the door and went back to the bakery to find Luc. "Did you do a special order today for Davis, Wilson, and Marks this morning?"

His eyes lit up, the first time he'd looked happy all week. "Oh, *bon*! They are back, that is good. Very influential firm," he told me. Then his face went flat. "Today? *Non*. No order for them was prepared today."

"I put it on the board last week," I said. "Sophie and I even talked about it."

Luc walked over to the bulletin board, and I followed. He looked down the side of the board marked for the bread makers. Nothing was there. He reached out and untacked the lone order on the board. Yes, that was it. I recognized my handwriting. Relief flooded through me. At least I couldn't be blamed for this!

Luc pointed at something on the order. "*Mon Dieu,* Alexandra. You wrote down the wrong date! This order says it is for tomorrow!"

"*Ooh la la,* Alexandra," Luc said. The oven buzzer went off. "I have to get that. Then I'll come and take care of this *problème*."

"No, I can do it," I said.

He looked skeptical, but the buzzer sounded again, and he raced to pull the baguettes.

Dear God, please help me.

I returned to the front, where the man waited impatiently. I moved close so every customer in the place didn't hear.

"I'm sorry," I started, "but I wrote the wrong date on your order. It wasn't filled."

His eyes widened. "What? But our meeting is in just a few minutes. And this is a very important meeting!"

"I'm so sorry. Can I make up something else?"

"Like what? I can't just throw a box of doughnuts at this level of client. My boss is going to kill me." He ran his hands through his hair. "All right. A pastry tray will have to do."

"I'm sorry, but we're out of pastry trays right now," I said. *Because I left the door to the walk-in open last night,* I thought, crushed.

"This is so unprofessional." His voice rose, and he leaned toward me in his agitation. "What am I supposed to do?"

As he glared at me, my day, week, month, and life came crashing down.

I could please no one.

I couldn't please my parents—they wanted me to have a job that reflected their years of hard work and money and what they saw as my own abilities. A *career*.

I couldn't please Nonna because I had no man.

I disappointed myself. I had such high hopes for the kind of life I'd have: travel to France in college, cool and meaningful job afterward, good church and good friends. A "ring by spring." Had that happened? *Non.*

Luc was unhappy with me. Sophie was overrun with lunch orders and scowling in my direction.

God seemed to be in and out of my life.

And now this perfect stranger was upset with me too.

I pointed to the reach-in, my voice rising to match his own. "Let them eat cake!"

He stared at me, shocked, and I stared back.

Fine. I'll get fired from my ten-dollar-an-hour job and eat soup and bread on Saturday nights at Nonna's church.

After a few seconds he took a deep breath. "Well, then, could you box some cake up for me?"

Blood rushed to my face, my anger draining away. I really needed to think before I spoke.

I took several of the nicest cakes from the case and carried them back to Patricia.

"What is this?" she asked in broken English. She refused to speak French with me. She looked at me, mad, I knew, about the loss of the pastry cream.

"Rush order," I said.

"I am busy," she said. "You will have to do it." She turned back to the fruit tarts covering the counter.

I grabbed a silver catering tray and set a doily on it. I saw some fresh lemons in the cooler and plucked the shiny, waxy leaves off them. I arranged them on the silver tray with a dozen of our nicest, freshest *petit fours. Please God, help this look okay.*

From the bread room, I knew Luc watched me out of the corner of his eye, but he didn't come back. He was too busy getting the bread onto the cooling racks, and I think he assumed the situation was under control—which it was. Maybe he was testing me, to see how I handled it.

I also cut a gâteau basque into bite-sized pieces and artfully added both mini lemon tarts and fruit tarts. Some chocolate cakes with chocolate crème inside finished the tray. I took a few fresh flowers out of the pastry case and put them on the tray, then double-wrapped everything in plastic to make sure it didn't slide or slip. I set it in a large box and brought it forward to the café.

"*Voila!*" I said. "I hope this works out."

He had softened some, but still looked at his watch. "I do too. No time to check on it. I'll send someone back to the shop with the tray."

We locked eyes for a minute, and then I turned away.

He dashed out the door, and I put on my happy and confident mask and helped Sophie through the lunch rush.

After the busyness, we cleaned up in silence. I wiped off the tables, replaced candles that had burned down, and smoothed out the cover of the *Paris Match* on top of the stack of magazines.

"I'm going back to the cooler for a while," I said.

After checking with me to make sure I'd gotten the special order out and checking with Sophie to make sure lunch was taken care of, Luc had run to La Couronne for the afternoon. The bakery and pastry area was, therefore, blissfully quiet. Even the croissant rollers had left for the day. The café closed in fifteen minutes. Only Patricia was left fussing around in the back, freezing tomorrow's mille-feuille before she locked up for the day.

I went into the cooler, sat down on an upturned bucket, and faced the wall. I let the tears silently roll down my face.

How could I mess up that order? Worse yet, how could I raise my voice at a customer, no matter how angry he was first?

Sophie opened the door.

"Who's up front?" I asked.

"Patricia locked the door," she said. "It's three o'clock."

I tried to wipe the traces of tears from my cheeks.

She held out an almond croissant. "Hungry?"

I shook my head.

"You haven't eaten at all today," she insisted.

"What about you?" I asked. "I never see you eat anything here."

She gave me a friendly look. "I'm a vegan."

"A vegan!" I couldn't believe Sophie and I were talking.

"Yep. All I can eat here is bread, French onion soup, and the lettuce and tomatoes we line the sandwiches with." She held out a napkin for me to blow my nose. "I know you love to cook and bake," she said, avoiding the obvious topic of today's disaster.

I stood, brushing the wrinkles from my pants. "Well, I'm working on it. I have faith that it'll lead somewhere other than a soup kitchen."

Like an assistant manager's position in a French bakery in Seattle. I left it unsaid. I had no idea if Sophie knew Luc was looking for such a thing, since I wasn't supposed to know. We'd certainly never discussed it. We'd never discussed anything, really, before now.

"Faith, huh?" Sophie said. "What kind of faith? Or do you just do your own thing?"

"I'm a Christian," I admitted, feeling weird. I didn't want my temper tantrum with the customer to make Jesus look bad by association.

"Oh," she said. "I kind of do my own religion. You know, combine the best of everything. But I'm into checking stuff out." I heard the roar of a motorcycle outside. "My ride's here. Lexi, I'm sorry about today. You were in a tough spot, and we all make mistakes."

"Thanks, Sophie," I said. I smiled at her and she at me. For the first time, I felt that maybe we could be friends.

"Maybe I can visit your church sometime since I'm looking around."

"I'd like that." *First I'd better find a church myself.*

"Take it easy. You can deal with this when you come back tomorrow," she said. "I'm sure Luc will want to talk about it."

I put my head back in my hands. I wondered if I could line up another job in one night.

Maybe for minimum wage. If I broke down and called Uncle Bennie.

That weekend, Nate and I finally got some brother-sister time.

"Lane is ready for Simon and Garfunkel," a nasal tone called over the bowling alley intercom. "Again, lane ready for Simon and Garfunkel."

I chuckled at my cleverness, took Nate's arm, and dragged him to the desk to see which lane was ours.

"So am I Simon or Garfunkel?" he asked.

"You're prematurely balding, so you get to be Garfunkel," I said. "Just don't grow a giant Chia Pet 'fro to distract from the fact.

Nate patted the top of his head with increasing panic. "Do you really think my hair is thinning?"

"No," I said. "I'm just teasing."

"Because it *is* a possible side effect of one of the medications I'm taking for acid reflux," he said. "I've got to keep an eye on that."

Oh man. I hadn't meant to initiate a round of obsessive worry.

It had been a long time since I'd been bowling, and I was glad Nate chose it for our outing. I loved the waxy floor, the sixties lamps, the molded, orange plastic seats. I decided I looked good in bowling shoes. They were kind of retro and funky without being too out there.

God, this is a small prayer request, but if there's any way you can bring bowling shoes back in style, it would be nice. I'd have an edge for once.

I held the little nub of the pencil and the sheet with Simon and Garfiinkel printed on it and prepared to keep score.

"Remember when Mom and Dad used to bowl in a league?" I asked Nate. "And we'd sit in the game room and pump quarter after quarter into video games?"

"Yeah," he said. "That little machine that 'guaranteed' a win of a Tootsie Roll or something. I wish life was that easy now."

"Me too," I said. "Speaking of which, how's work? Is being a lawyer in a high-powered firm everything you hoped it would be?"

Nate nodded. "Yeah. It's hard, and I have to prove myself for the first few years. We newbies have to do the grunt work, but it's a fair firm, and I know I'll work my way up."

"But lawyers are always looking for how someone else is wrong, and you're always arguing," I said as he grabbed a black, fourteen-pound bowling ball. "Hey! I should get some kind of professional bonus for training you throughout our childhood. Like royalties."

Nate elbowed me in joking protest. "It can be fun. However, I got into an argument the other day with one of the other lawyers. I spouted off. I feel bad about it, because I know I'm supposed to live at peace with everyone as much as possible, Romans 12 and all that. But it's interesting work. Not like being an accountant or something, punching numbers day after day."

"Accountants," I groaned. "Spouting off." I stepped up to the ball return to get the neon green ball I'd chosen.

"What's wrong with accountants?" he asked.

"I got into a tangle with one last week." I explained the situation with the Davis, Wilson, and Marks order.

"Oh man, Lex," he said. "Not good. Was your boss mad?"

I slipped my thumb and two fingers into my ball and stood with it on my hip for a minute. "I don't know. He hasn't seemed mad, but he hasn't been as chipper either. He might be mad."

Nate looked thoughtful. "Or maybe he's got other things on his mind. Women always assume that if a guy is distracted, it's about them, and mostly it's not."

I cocked my head and smiled. "It's nice to have a big brother, Nate. I'm going to miss you when you're married."

He looked surprised. "I'm not going anywhere."

"I know," I said, "but you won't really be a big brother in the same sense anymore."

"It'll be okay," Nate said. "Just different. Speaking of getting married—I need to get Leah some flowers and drop them off on the way home." He threw his ball and scored a split.

"It's nice that you still pursue her," I said.

He updated the score sheet before he replied. "She still pursues me too. Guys don't like to be taken for granted either. We want to feel wanted just as much as girls do." He gestured toward the lane. "Get bowling, Simon."

I did the handy, foot-at-ninety-degree-angle-behind-the-left-leg trick and I made a strike.

After the game, we sat at the bar and had some appetizers.

"Do you think you'll keep the job?" Nate asked.

I shrugged. "I think so. I've made a commitment through mid-June. Luc hasn't indicated that things will change, though things are slow outside the breakfast and lunch rushes. And he hasn't mentioned my special product rack project again."

Nate seemed sympathetic. "What about asking Uncle Bennie to find something for you? I mean, he is a human resources guy, and he has a lot of connections."

I squeezed a lemon into my Hefeweizen and sipped it, then ate a fry. "Nate, do you remember the job Uncle Bennie set me up with in Bellingham? The last one I had before I moved back?"

"Yeah, the one that you got laid off from," he said. "Tough luck."

"I got let go."

He set his glass down. "Really?"

"Yeah. The job was totally boring, and some of the people were irritating. I was doing a lot and no one appreciated my effort, but I wanted to keep the job, just to make something work. I guess they could sense my boredom."

"You know, Lex," Nate said quietly, "you can't be

the vice president right out of the chute."

"I know," I said. But did I really? Wasn't I doing the same thing at L'Esperance, counting on an assistant manager job that had never even been mentioned to me?

No, I decided. That was completely different. I was earning that position, not expecting it to fall in my lap.

Right?

"I haven't had any luck finding a place for you to live," Nate said, changing the subject, for which I was grateful. "I haven't even had time to help Leah find something for *us* after the wedding."

"It's okay," I replied. "Soon I might not have a job to pay the rent with anyway."

"You should talk with your boss," Nate said, "just to make sure the air is cleared."

I agreed. I hadn't talked with Luc about the bread for Nonna's church either. Last Saturday I'd bought the loaves remaining in the store and delivered them to Pete, who called me Saint Alexandra. I looked her up online later and found out she'd been a closet Christian.

Somehow, that was unsettling.

"Can I help in some other way?" Nate asked. "Just name it."

I shook my head. "No. But thanks."

After another hour, we parted ways. As I pulled up in front of the house, I felt it—like a kidney punch—more than saw it.

SOLD!

Sandra Byrd

Nine

Le courage donne naissance à la surprise.
Courage gives birth to surprise.

I got up early the next Sunday, but it was like sleeping in compared to my usual hours at the bakery. It was a rare sunny morning in March. I'd asked Sophie if I could come in late on Sundays, and she'd agreed if I would open on Saturday mornings. She liked to come in late on Saturday because she was usually out late on Friday night.

"Ready?" my mom asked cheerfully, jingling the car keys in my direction.

"Yeah."

"Why did you decide to come with me today?" she asked once we were in the car. "Not that I mind. I'm really glad you're coming with me, but I just wondered."

I rubbed the seamed edge of my small Bible. "I'm tired of feeling separated from God. Someone told me that everyone wants to be pursued and that one person in the relationship shouldn't have to do all the heavy lifting. I guess I've been expecting God to do all the heavy lifting instead of seeking him out too."

I didn't tell her who said it. I didn't want the conversation to veer off toward Nate's finer qualities right now.

Mom nodded.

"And I have a friend at work who might want to go to church with me," I added.

"Luc?" She looked hopeful. I wondered if she understood that Luc was my boss. I wasn't sure I'd ever made that clear, but then, I knew why. My dad would give me a ten-point lecture about officers not fraternizing with the enlisted personnel. In other words, no dating your boss.

"Not Luc," I said. "Sophie."

"Sophie? She doesn't look like the church type."

With self-control worthy of a tightrope walker, I stopped myself from rolling my eyes or pursuing that discussion. I knew she meant the piercings.

Mom parked, and we walked into the building. I sat in the pew my mother had been sitting in since I was a child, and looked around, willing myself to tune out the squawking kids.

Ever since I was a kid, this one rich woman has always waited until almost the last moment every single week, then paraded down the runway—I mean the aisle—to the very front, ensuring that everyone saw whatever outfit she was debuting. She didn't seem very Christian.

I felt bad as soon as I'd thought it. I made as

many assumptions about people as my mom did. I closed my eyes and repeated, *Live at peace with everyone* ten times.

The worship songs began. As I sang, I felt the urge to stand and hold my hand toward God in freely expressed faith. I'd yearned for it, but had never given in. I'd overheard Nonna once, when I was a girl, pointing out people raising their hands on TV as being showy. So I'd never mentioned it or attempted it. The last thing I wanted to be was showy.

I lifted my hand a little and caught my mother's distressed look out of the corner of my eye. She didn't like attention called to her in public, and we were in her most sacred public. I hesitated, torn between honoring two kinds of parents.

I put my hand down and hoped God understood.

For the rest of the service, I didn't fold the bulletin into a Japanese crane or mentally circle how many letter *e*'s were on the front page of the bulletin, as I had as a teen. I didn't scan the congregation to see if any of my friends had married or compare myself negatively to anyone around me. I focused on the service, on the message, as though I'd be tested later.

It was okay, but like Nonna's church, it didn't feel like *me,* somehow.

We drove home, and Mom pulled up in front of the house. She leaned over and kissed my cheek. "I love having you in church with me."

I kissed her back. "I loved sitting with you too." I

hoped she didn't notice that I'd dodged responding exactly in kind.

I slipped into my Jetta, tossed the Bible on the passenger seat, and took off for L'Esperance. Maybe I'd read through Matthew, just to hear Jesus's voice more. That's what I said I wanted, wasn't it? Why not start at the beginning?

I'll seek you. Please find me.

The rest of the day went by quickly. Luc told us he was closing the store on Mondays, traditionally our slowest day. We would all still get our full forty hours, but he wouldn't have to keep the store open on the seventh day.

As we cleaned, preparing for the closed day, Sophie looked at me out of the corner of her eye. We both wondered if things were slowing down financially—if they had overextended by opening more stores too quickly. I had yet to talk with Luc about the bread or the Davis, Wilson, and Marks incident.

On Monday, my new day off, I got up late—hurray!—worked out, and went apartment hunting. And I scored! A cute complex that hadn't been showing previously was finally open, though all units weren't done yet.

"Next month," the building manager promised, taking down my name. I told him even a studio would do.

When I looked out the living room window of the unfinished studio he showed me, I could see the ferries gliding back and forth across the Sound.

I craved that apartment and everything it represented to me.

Sophie and I had developed a good rhythm now that things between us had warmed up, and between rushes we actually chatted. That was good for my social life, but not for my job life. I couldn't afford to work fewer than forty hours a week, and though Luc hadn't yet asked me to cut back, I still worried.

If I were the assistant manager, though, Luc could release some of his duties to me. I'd be busy forty hours a week, thus able to afford the apartment I'd found, and he'd be free to open new bakeries. We'd all be happy.

Sophie took care of the cash register, and I put pastries and breads on display. As he passed by, Luc tugged on the back of my French braid.

"If you have a little time when things slow down, can we talk for a few minutes?" I asked him. I thought I might as well get him while he was feeling magnanimous.

"I always have time for you, Alexandra," he said, smiling as he walked back into the bakery. I felt like butter on hot bread.

I focused on the pastries, hoping my face wouldn't give me away. Patricia made the most wonderful mocha mousses, but the tops looked a little plain. I took each one out of the case and shaved some dark chocolate over it before placing one small coffee bean in the center. I put them back into the case.

"How old is Luc?" I asked Sophie, trying to sound as casual as possible.

"I think he's twenty-eight," she said. "Why?"

"Just wondering."

She looked at me a little too long before turning away.

We got through the lunch rush, and Sophie cleaned up the café. I cleaned up the sandwich station and made a small salad for her out of the leftover greens, lettuce, and onions, with a vinaigrette of lemon juice and oil. I salted it and handed it to her.

"Go sit down for a sec," I said, breaking off a piece of baguette. "You look really tired."

"I am," she said. "I was out all weekend, and I'm still not caught up, even with the day off yesterday. Things don't look good for me and Roger. What did you do this weekend?"

"Hung out at home," I said. "Met a friend for lunch. Went to church."

"That's why you wanted Sunday mornings to be your late day."

"Yeah."

"You must be serious."

I shrugged and said, "I'm trying."

She took the salad, thanked me for it, and paged

142

through the Living section of the *Seattle Times*. When she was done, she ran her dishes to the kitchen and then came up front.

"Did you eat lunch?"

When I said no, she took half a leftover sandwich from the prep case and handed it to me. "I'll write it on the inventory list," she said. "You eat."

As I sat down, I thought, *It's so much nicer being at peace with Sophie.*

After we restocked the inventory, she pulled a business card out of her wallet. "Have you ever heard of this church?"

I looked at the card. *Barb's House of Miracles? Uh-oh.*

I shook my head. "But I don't know every church, of course."

"Someone told me that the minister started on TV," Sophie said, putting the card away. "I just wondered."

In her wallet I saw a picture of two younger teens, one who looked like Sophie in a cheerleading uniform.

"Your sister?" I asked.

"Nope, me."

My eyes widened. "You used to be a cheerleader?"

She looked at the picture again, pain in her eyes. "I keep this because it's the only photo I have of my friend Kim and me. She died a couple years ago."

"I'm sorry," I said.

"Me too."

The silence stretched.

"You know, Sophie," I said, "you could come to church with me sometime." I waited, ready for her to shoot me down. She did.

"I work Sunday mornings, remember."

"We could go to the meeting during the week," I said. "At night. The twenty-three- to thirty-year-olds meet then." I decided not to mention anything about it being called the Impact Group or Nonna's idea of ripe fruit.

Sophie tilted her head and thought about it. "I'd like that. It might be nice to mix a little Christianity onto my palette with the Buddhism and Hinduism, you know? Jesus must have been a very nice man."

Luc strode into the room. "Hey, is this a sorority party?"

Sophie winked at me and turned to clean the coffee machine.

"Alexandra, you wanted to talk with me?" Luc asked.

I nodded and wiped my hands on my apron.

"*Bon*," he said. "I've been wanting to talk with you, too."

I took a deep breath and chose the table farthest into the corner of the café. Luc came over with a cup of coffee. "Would you like one?" he asked.

I declined. I had enough jitters.

"*Alors*," he said. "We begin."

I folded my hands on the table to keep them from shaking. "First, I wanted to tell you how sorry I am that I messed up the Davis, Wilson, and Marks order," I said. "It must have been during a rush time, but I know how important they are to L'Esperance."

Luc kept his eyes on me. "They are a high-end client, Alexandra, and they order expensive trays. Their word of mouth is very important."

I had expected that, but it still deflated me. "Have they ordered again this week? Or last?" Luc asked.

"If they have, I haven't taken their order."

"Ah," Luc said. "Too bad." He drained his cup of coffee. "From what I hear, you have a Gallic temper."

So he'd heard about that. "Oh no, not really," I said. "I think everything was fine. Really, I'm not like that at all."

Luc's eyes twinkled. "I know, Alexandra, I've been watching you. I know what you're like. Was there anything else?"

Well, yes, actually. I'd like that assistant manager's job.

"Yes. I don't know if you know the church around the corner," I said, "but my grandmother goes there, and they have a soup kitchen each Saturday night. They needed bread, and, well, I paid for our leftover bread last Saturday night and took it over. I was wondering, if it was okay with you, could I buy it at a discount and do that each week?"

Luc looked at me, and I held his gaze. I felt like a jelly doughnut for so many reasons. *Okay, jelly doughnuts aren't French, but still. I am American,*

145

after all.

"Is that your church?" he asked.

"No, it's my grandmother's church. It's a very good one, though."

"Alexandra, you may take, free of charge, whatever we have leftover on Saturday night. And if there are day-old pastries, you may take those at the end of each night, too, and give them to those who need them. How much did you pay for the bread last Saturday night?"

"I think about ten dollars," I said. "We had ten baguettes leftover." Saturdays were big baking days, because people often bought bread to serve over the weekend. But it also meant we often had leftovers.

"Reimburse yourself from the till," Luc said. "*Je t'admire*, Alexandra," he said, using the familiar form of "you" to tell me he admired me. To go from a formal relationship to a familiar one makes quite a statement in French. A boundary had been crossed. Land had been taken!

"Thanks," I said. "I'd better get back to work."

"One more thing." Luc motioned for me to sit down. "I'd like to talk with you about your job."

Uh-oh. Here it comes.

"Sure." I folded my hands again, thankful I hadn't had any coffee.

"Things are slowing down up front, and I probably should have hired a part-time person when I hired you instead of a full-time one. But Patricia is busy in the back. Too busy to keep up. I wondered if you'd like to be half in the front of the house, during the rushes to help Sophie, and half in the back, to help Patricia. It might be the best for everyone."

I stood up and then sat down again. "What would I be doing? Could I bake?" My hands shook with a completely different emotion.

"Ah, *non*. Probably not. You'd do whatever Patricia wanted you to do. Dishes, errands, but maybe more, too, *par la suite*. I've noticed you have a way with the food, and maybe you like working with the food more than the customers."

My cheeks flushed, remembering the special order. Did he really feel I'd be good with the food, or was he telling me I wasn't good with customers?

"Is it okay with Sophie?" I asked. "She doesn't want to work in the bakery too?"

"Sophie has no interest in the food, as you know," he said. "*Le vegan*."

"Is Patricia okay with me helping her?"

"I don't know," Luc admitted. "You'll have to ask her."

"Me? Ask Patricia?"

"Only La Patricia will decide who she works with and if she needs help, even though you and I can both see she does. Can you handle that, Alexandra?"

Patricia hadn't said an unnecessary, kind, or conversational word to me since I'd left the walk-in door open. Since I'd started at L'Esperance, actually. Was this a challenge? A test? The more I learned about running the café, the bakery, and everything around them, the more valuable—and managerial— I'd be. They could hardly open more stores until the current ones were safely managed by others, and I knew that was Luc's goal.

And if Luc weren't here every day, it might be easier to get to know one another personally too. Without that fraternization issue getting in the way.

"*Mais oui!*" I responded. "I'd like that."

"*Voilà!* Talk with Patricia soon, at the end of her shift. Find an agreeable moment, if you can. I'm sure she'll let me know what she thinks about the matter." He laughed.

He could afford to find her funny. He wasn't the one about to risk his life asking if she needed help.

Luc went back to his office and shut the door.

"What do you think?" Sophie asked after I told her the plan. "Are you willing to work with La Patricia?"

"I need the hours," I said. If anyone's hours were going to be cut, Sophie had seniority. I was glad she had no interest in the food or special projects.

She wiped down the counter. "I understand. Did Luc say anything about that special order? I heard one of the croissant rollers telling him about the 'let them eat cake' comment. Auguste, I think. His mustache was waggling."

"Auguste! The snitch. I wondered how Luc found out. Luc was a little disappointed, I think, that there have been no more special orders from them."

"Sorry," Sophie said. "When do you start with Patricia?"

"As soon as I ask her for the job," I said.

"You have to ask her?"

I grimaced. "If she refuses to work with me, there's not much Luc can do about it."

"*Ooh la la,*" Sophie said, shaking her head.

"I thought you didn't speak French?"

"Lexi, *'ooh la la'* isn't exactly college-level French."

I blushed. "I'm sorry; you're right. That was stupid."

"That's okay," she said. "I haven't always been cool to you. Are you going to ask her in French or English?"

"French," I said. "She's been bullying me too long."

"Good luck," Sophie said.

"*Bon courage* is more like it," I said.

I peeked into the pastry room just in time to see Patricia scream at one of the delivery drivers. The *Trois Amis* ducked out of her way. *I'll ask her tomorrow,* I thought.

"*Be at peace with everyone,*" I heard.

Yes, Lord, thank you. I talked with Luc and Sophie, and it worked out great, didn't it?

"*Be at peace with everyone,*" I sensed again.

Oh yeah, no worries, Patricia will see things Luc's way. She's way behind. I can deal with her bluster. I have no choice. I need the hours; she needs the help.

"*Be at peace with everyone.*"

Like Samuel, three times hearing the voice caught my attention. As I walked past the catering area, I noticed the silver tray had not been returned.

I need to apologize, don't I? And get the tray back. I don't even know who he is, God. What am I supposed to do, call up the firm and ask for the cute young accountant who wears suspenders? I'd apologize if I could, and if he ever comes back in, I will. But otherwise, I have no way to reach him.

I washed my hands of the matter. I had enough to worry about.

I walked to the front of the café and wiped down the counter, thinking about where I could place the *produits de la France* rack. Maybe if Luc liked the idea, he'd put one in La Couronne too. It'd be my personal touch.

As I worked my way down the counter, I moved the fishbowl that held business cards for the weekly free-lunch drawing. I wondered if Sophie had drawn one this week. Maybe I'd ask if I could do it. Delivering good news would be fun.

I poked around in the cards, and one caught my eye.

Davis, Wilson, and Marks

Dan Larson
Copyright Attorney
Davis, Wilson, and Marks
6100 Pike Street
Seattle, WA *98000* 206-555-1212

As I stared at the card in my hand, I remembered seeing him flip it into the fish bowl while waiting for his order.

Not an accountant. Another *lawyer*!

Sandra Byrd

Ten

Nul bien sans peine.
No pain, no gain.

Oh great. Now I *had* to call him. The problem was I didn't want anyone listening to what I had to say.

I snapped my fingers. *Voilà.* I'd call from the walk-in.

"I'll be back in just a sec," I told Sophie, who was brushing the crumbs out of the pastry case.

I walked into the cooler, the only private place in the entire café, and shut the door. Luc had installed a handle on the inside so no one would get locked in.

I dialed the number on the business card and a woman's voice answered. "Davis, Wilson, and Marks. How may I help you?"

She sounded like someone whose pedicure polish matched her manicure. I resisted the urge to tug on a hangnail. "Hello. May I speak with Dan Larson, please?"

"Let me check if he's in..."

Blue veins started to rise to the surface of my

skin and I shivered. The walk-in must be chillier than normal.

Within seconds, a man's voice came on. "This is Dan."

"Hello, my name is Alexandra Stuart," I began. In the silence between us, I felt the vibe of someone expecting a telemarketer. I shuddered through a flashback from my marketing job. "I work at L'Esperance," I continued. "The French bakery that did your special order?"

"Oh yes, yes," he said. "How can I help you?"

"Well, two things. One, I was the person who messed up your order. I wanted to apologize for that."

"Thank you, Alexandra. The cake platter you designed worked out really well."

My chilled knees were practically knocking. I could hear Auguste and the other *Trois Amis* clattering about in the pastry room outside of the walk-in. *Please don't open the door,* I willed them.

"I also wanted to apologize for losing my temper," I continued. "It was my fault and nothing you did. I was having a stressful day, and I took it out on you. I hope you won't hold it against L'Esperance."

I heard him exhale in the silence. "No need to worry—but thank you, Alexandra. Did we ever return your silver platter?"

"No," I said. "I don't think so. If you bring it back," I infused my voice with cheerfulness, "we can fill it with another order!"

"I'll bring it back," he said in a softer voice. "And ask for you personally. I've got a client waiting, but I'll see you soon. Thanks for calling." He hung up.

All right, God. I did it. I'm at peace with everyone.

As I fled into the warmth of the café, I couldn't help thinking that Dan Larson had a nice voice.

I dressed with care the next morning, planning to talk with Patricia that day. Lord, if it's okay with you, it would be so cool to work with the pastries and the front of the house. To be prepared to know the entire restaurant operation.

I wanted to make Luc proud of me too.

Sophie and I handled the rush, and the morning went well.

"I guess I'd better go talk with Patricia," I said. She'd only been there a few minutes, as she spent most mornings at La Couronne. Luc switched places with her during the day, but I thought they already had an assistant manager over there.

"*Bon courage,*" Sophie whispered to me.

I tightened my apron and walked past the *Trois Amis*. Auguste crossed himself, as if I were heading into an oncoming train. Luc smiled and winked. "*Bonne chance,* Alexandra. Don't let me down."

I wouldn't. It was time I started going after what I really wanted.

"*Je m'excuse,*" I said, standing in the door of the

155

pastry room.

Patricia grunted. "Yes?" she responded in English.

"Do you have a moment to talk?" I persisted in French.

"No, but I suppose you'll talk anyway. Go ahead, Alexandra."

I stepped into the room. "I really admire the work you've done with the pastries; they look beautiful and sell well. I've always liked to bake."

"This is not the Betty Crocker home kitchen, Alexandra," she said, arranging flash-frozen apple slices in a tart shell. "These are not Easy-Bake Oven sets."

For a Frenchwoman, she was remarkably up-to-date on American toys.

"I know you need help," I said. "I've seen it, and Luc confirmed it. I could work half the days in the front, during the rushes, and half back here, helping you."

Patricia seemed unmoved, silently doing up one tart after another.

Summoning the *courage* Sophie had wished me, I made sure my voice was respectfully modulated but clear and strong. "If I were back here helping, there'd be candied lemon slices on the lemon tarts, as there should be."

She stopped shuffling the apples and pastry and looked me in the eye. She was only a couple of years older than me but seemed like she'd suffered one oven burn too many. She patted her hair net.

"*Bon,* Alexandra," she finally said. "You can start with me tomorrow. I'll leave a list of minor tasks and add to it during the day."

With extreme self-control, I stopped an ear-to-ear grin. Instead, I allowed a petite smile. "Thank you, Patricia. I will strive to be of great help to you."

"Make sure that you do."

Patricia would only be here until summer, Luc had said, and then she was heading back to France and her sister would come here to learn the family business in her place. I could deal with *anyone* until summer. I hoped the sister had more sugar in her makeup than starch.

The days passed, and soon I'd been working with Patricia for a couple of weeks. Patricia dirtied dishes, I washed them. Patricia laid out a recipe, I set the ingredients on the counter.

"Not vanilla *beans,* Alexandra," she'd shout. "Vanilla *sugar.*"

Bon. Then don't just write "vanilla" on the recipe. I ran back and got the sugar.

On her breaks, she smoked Gauloises, and I dipped coffee beans in deathly dark chocolate.

I was busy, and I liked it. Sophie and I ran the shop up front during the rushes at breakfast and lunch, and then I ran back to help Patricia for the hours in between. I was a go-to girl for a lot of things, but I knew I was getting experience in every area of the shop.

One day, Sophie and I took a quick break outside. Sophie lit a cigarette, and I tried to forget every dire warning my mother had told me about secondhand smoke.

"So why *do* you work here, if you're a vegan?" I asked.

"I think I'd like to open my own coffee shop or something. Some kind of business, and that's the only one I know right now. I'm thinking of applying for a small business loan. Roger doesn't think it's a good idea, though. He wants me to manage his band."

"Oh," I said. I'd lived long enough to know not to comment on someone's boyfriend at this stage in a friendship.

We chatted lightly about nothing, feeling our way from animosity toward collegiality, and then walked back inside together. On our way through the catering area, a silver platter caught my eye.

"Oh," I said. "Dan returned this?"

Sophie raised her eyebrow. "Dan?"

I ducked my head and rushed to explain. "I called to apologize, and he said he was going to bring it by."

Sophie smiled suggestively. "He did ask for you by name. He stopped by on Sunday before you came in."

"Oh, no big deal." It *wasn't* a big deal. So why was I disappointed?

"He's sending his assistant back on Tuesday to

get another special order," Sophie said. "Frankly, I was surprised he came to get it himself last time. Someone must have been sick. Do you want to prep his order?"

"Sure," I said. I'd do it first thing Tuesday morning. I enjoyed preparing the catering trays.

Tuesdays were really busy days now that the bakery was closed on Monday. Luc had begun delivering lunches to a few local businesses to offset the down times, and that added business—and work.

"Alexandra?" Luc came into the pastry room. He raised his eyebrows at Patricia, who nodded that she could do without me for the moment.

"Just a minute, I'll grab my paperwork," I said, thinking he wanted to talk about the special products rack.

"*Non,* Alexandra, there's someone here to see you," he said. He stayed back in the bakery, discreet, but watching.

Who could it be?

I walked into the café and saw the man in suspenders standing in front of the bread rack.

"Hi, it's Dan," he said. He held out his hand. "Remember me? I came by to pick up the special order."

Thankfully, I'd done it up that morning. He'd arrived fifteen minutes early.

I liked that he wore suspenders. "Oh, I'm sorry, I thought you were sending someone for it in a few minutes. Let me get it from the walk-in cooler."

"Wait," he said. "I came early on purpose. I

wondered if you might have time for a break?"

Sophie leapt in. "Yes, what good timing. It's exactly time for Lexi's break. I'll go make sure the tray is ready and bring it out in a few minutes."

She disappeared into the back. The *Trois Amis* pretended not to watch.

"Lexi," Dan repeated. "I like that even better than Alexandra."

"Would you like a *café crème*?" I asked. It seemed as good a thing to say as any.

"Sure," he said. "And one of those napoleons. Is that what they're called?" He pointed to the case. "Since I imagine I'm getting bread and cheese today and not pastry."

My face colored, but I could tell Dan was only kidding. I wasn't going to let him get the upper hand.

"Their official French name is mille-feuilles," I said, "not napoleons. I'd be glad to get you one."

I made coffee for us both, then plated a mille-feuille and brought it to the café table. I sat across from him.

He was kind of cute, but I was only being nice to him because his account was important to L'Esperance. *It's good business.*

He took a sip of his coffee. "I wanted to come myself today because I told you I'd look for you when I brought the tray back, and you weren't here."

"Yeah, I come in late on Sunday mornings."

"Your colleague said you were at church." He nodded toward Sophie, who was pretending not to

160

eavesdrop as she handed a cookie to one of the kids who came in every day. She eyed me over the little girl's head and winked.

"Yes," I said. "Thanks for placing another order in spite of my mistake last time. I personally prepared these trays and made sure they look good."

"Everything turned out fine," he said. He bit into his mille-feuille. "Delicious! Don't you like them?" He motioned to my lack of pastry.

"I do like them," I said. "They're my favorite. I just try not to eat them too often."

Like, any day I have a half marathon run planned.

He fiddled with his fork. "I can see how that'd be tough, working in a bakery. Do you work only in the front? Or in the back as well?"

"Both," I said. "In fact, I made that mille-feuille you're eating." I beamed. "Well, okay, I prepped it, even if I didn't make it."

I washed the bowls. But that *was* prepping. *No one can make food in a dirty bowl.*

Dan stayed long enough to make small talk about my work and his. I was glad we hadn't lost his company as a customer.

I was also glad because...well, it was fun to talk to him.

Finally Dan stood and Sophie waltzed out with the catering box. She placed it in my hands, then went to help a café customer.

"Thanks again," I said. "I'm glad this all worked out okay."

"I'll be sure to return the tray sometime other than Sunday morning, Lexi," he said, letting his voice linger on my name.

Something tingled inside me. He had a nice smile, I'd give him that.

But he was also a lawyer, and I had plenty of those in my life already; no need for another one.

Later that week, Patricia called from La Couronne and said she was ill and wasn't coming in. Could I please make sure all the pastries were out and looking good?

"*Mais oui!*" I told her, ecstatic. "Don't worry!"

"What's with the high-watt smile?" Luc asked me, playfully tugging on the back of my apron strings.

"Patricia wants me to put the pastries out for her today," I said. "She's sick."

"Good for you, bad for me," he said. "I'd better get over to La Couronne and make sure everything is okay. The manager there is a little..." He waggled his hand back and forth as if to say "iffy." "We're going to replace him soon," he said. "With a woman. Women seem to make better managers for bakeries."

I was a woman, a woman with managerial abilities wielding full control of the pastry case today. My smile grew. I was on my way.

Luc talked with Sophie, handed something to

her, and then left the shop. I felt bad for him, having to come back later and close up since Patricia wasn't here. He was running around a lot. I wondered if he ever had downtime or a night out. Or a date.

I took stock of the pastry case. "What do you think we need?" I asked Sophie.

"Lemon and fruit tarts," she said. "Apple tarts. Mille-feuilles and perhaps some of those mini opera cakes."

Sophie seemed so sure of herself, so in charge. The way she said it made me vaguely uncomfortable, like I was talking to my boss.

"Maybe a couple of chocolate mousses, too," I said, needing to add *something*.

She happily agreed, and things returned to normal. "When I get the register done, I'll come back and see you in your new home."

I went back to the pastry kitchen and pulled out the lemon tarts, topped with the lemon slices I'd candied the day before. I'd stayed late, off the clock. Luc had noticed.

I set out the rest of the pastries, and Sophie came back. "You look good back here!" she said.

"Who's up front?"

"Auguste."

Jacques, one of the other *Trois Amis*, put a tall chef's hat, a starched *toque blanche*, on top of my head. He and Sophie clapped, and Guillaume took a picture with his phone.

"*Voilà, le chef de cuisine*," Jacques said with a flourish. Then he and Guillaume returned to rolling

163

the day's fifteen hundred croissants.

Sophie sat on one of the stainless steel counters, and I bit back a comment. It was like someone wiping their hands on the frame of the *Mona Lisa*. Okay, not really, but the room was mine today!

"So what's with the hat?" she asked.

"Standard chef wear," I told her. "Each fold in the hat represents one way to cook an egg."

"There are a lot of folds on there," she said. "Several dozen."

"A hundred or more," I answered, dusting cocoa over the top of the mini opera cakes.

"Did they teach you that in college?" she asked.

I put on my most serious, academic face. "Wikipedia."

She laughed, and I did too.

"Don't you want to smoke?" I asked. She usually used this time as her smoking break.

"Nah," she said. "I'll hang with you for a while. You're different than I thought," she said. "I thought you'd be a spoiled little college girl who thought she was something special because she spoke French."

"I thought you were bossy because you were experienced. And blocking everything I wanted to learn just to be mean."

"I was," she admitted. "But when you had your meltdown I saw you weren't Barbie, so maybe I didn't need to hate you on principle anymore." She smiled.

I pulled the sheet of mille-feuille out of the cooler and slid the pastry off the huge pan and onto the chilled marble work counter. Patricia made them every couple of days and then froze them so they cut neatly.

"*Mille-feuille* means 'one thousand sheets' in French, and the flaky pastry and thick pastry cream make a mess if sliced when thawed," I said in my best professorial voice.

"Learn that on Wikipedia?" Sophie teased.

"I don't know if *crème pâtissière* is even on Wikipedia," I laughed. I cut along the edges to even them up, leaving fragments of crust on the counter.

Sophie checked her watch and jumped off the counter. "I'd still like to come with you to church sometime, if you give me a ride. No car. And Roger would definitely *not* be into driving me there. Might worry that I'll go moral on him."

I realized I should run the gauntlet once with the Impact Group before I took Sophie.

"Can I eat one?" Jacques strode into the room, grinning, and motioned to the cut-off crusts. I bet Patricia let him eat the ends.

"*Bien sur.*" I handed one over.

Jacques bit into the edge, now thawed enough that the crème pâtissèrie swelled out, pillowlike, onto the pastry. "*Magnifique!*"

Sophie winked at me. I snapped a towel in her direction as she left to relieve Auguste.

Alone again, I stared at the mille-feuille, then picked up one of the crusts and nibbled at the end. Flaky, buttery, light on my tongue. Then the soothing, vanilla-flecked cream hit. And last, tart-sweet lemon glaze with chocolate squiggles. I took three or four bites and then set aside another crust for later.

I sliced the mille-feuille, humming to myself. Maybe Patricia would be sick all week.

When I got home that night I looked up crème pâtissèrie on Wikipedia. Not there? Criminal! I got typing.

crème pâtissèrie

from Wikipedia, the free encyclopedia

A rich dessert "pastry cream" (crème pâtissière) made with a combination of milk or cream, egg yolks, fine sugar, and occasionally flavoring such as vanilla, chocolate or lemon. Crème pâtissèrie is a key ingredient in many French desserts including mille feuille (better known as Napoleons) and filled tarts.

My own little contribution to the civilizing of American desserts. By the next day, someone had redirected it to custard. [Sigh].

A few nights later, while trying to sneak out to the midweek church service, I ran into my mom in the kitchen.

"Where are you going all dressed up?" she asked.

"Church," I whispered. I tried to slip past her, but alas, it was not to be.

"Church!" she cried excitedly. "In the middle of the week!"

I sighed and gave up. "My friend Sophie works on Sundays, so if I'm going to bring her to the Wednesday service, I need to try it out."

"Oh, I'm so glad you're going." She hugged me.

She was happy, so why was I so reluctant? A few reasons, actually. First, there was the Desperation Factor, in which everyone in the room would spend the entire night sizing up every member of the opposite sex as a possible mate. Then there was the John Travolta Factor, in which a large number of single Christian men did not know how to dress themselves.

And I was going alone.

I walked into the church and felt like I had at college in Bellingham all over again. The new girl.

The annex they held the class in was nice. It had its own latte bar, and one of the group members acted as a casual barista.

There were leather easy chairs and small groupings of comfortable furniture.

I looked around the room. The only person I recognized was Jill, whom I went to Sunday school with in junior high and high school. Back then, she was like a drill sergeant about activities, constantly prepared with sign-up sheets galore. I hoped she hadn't brought her clipboard and whistle.

"Hi." A guy about Luc's age approached me. Funny how I now judged all men against his standard. The guy held out his hand. "Have we met?"

It didn't seem like a come-on, just genuine and nice. His clothes matched, and he hadn't flipped the collar on his shirt like a frat boy. I felt embarrassed that I had labeled these people with my obviously erroneous assumptions before I even met them.

Except Jill. I was right about Jill.

"I don't think we've met," I answered. "I'm Lexi. I went to this church growing up, but I've been away for a few years, so I'm basically new."

"I'm Brett. Let me introduce you around."

He introduced me to a few people, and I recognized a few more. Then we got to Jill.

"Well, Lexi, you're back," she said, eyeing me. "I thought you'd left Seattle in your dust! Off to France, wasn't it?"

"By way of Bellingham," I said.

"Did you get there? I'd love to hear all about it." She still pulled her hair back in a ponytail and wore no makeup, but she had a furrow between her brows now.

"No, I didn't. But I work in a French bakery downtown."

"How quaint," Jill said. "A bakery. I'm working for a lobbyist downtown. I'll have to drop by sometime."

The group talked as everyone drank coffee, then

broke up into discussion groups. Actually, it was okay. The discussion was good—kind of stilted, but the church had always been that way, so what had I expected? A tent revival?

I still didn't feel right here. Maybe because I was new again.

"Next week we're off for Easter," the leader, Bill, said at the end of the night, "but the week after that is our mixer. If everyone would sign up to bring or provide something, we'll have a good time. We're going to have a game night."

"Is it okay to bring a guest?" I asked.

"Yeah, definitely," Bill said. "A good time for that."

Jill's clipboard started to circulate. I suppressed a smile. I'd known her since seventh grade, and she obviously hadn't changed. Definitely a Type A personality.

By the time the clipboard reached me, all the "bring food" places were filled in with names. I chewed on my lip. Food was what I did best, but the only open spaces were for providing icebreakers. Because it was a game night, the icebreakers were supposed to be based on games everyone has played.

Lovely. I signed my name and handed the clipboard to the woman next to me. The simple act of looking me in the eye brought a deep blush to her face. She hadn't said a word the entire night.

It had been a lot easier being at church group things when Tanya had been with me. *I wonder if she's been going to church with Steve?* We'd have to talk about it.

I dove back into the present. "Hi, have we met? I'm Lexi."

"Michelle," the quiet girl said. "Nice to meet you."

I left that night not feeling all that bad. I could bring Sophie here without worrying. Finding someplace for myself was another matter entirely.

I went to work early the next day and helped Sophie set up. With a little help from my friend *café crème*, I dealt with the morning rush and then went back to help Patricia.

"Alexandra, here," Luc called as I passed. He waved me in front of one of the machines he used to bake bread.

"I want you to learn to roll dough," he said.

The only person I'd seen him teach to use the massive dough roller was Auguste, whom Luc was mentoring. *This could not be better.* I was learning all aspects of L'Esperance.

"Move here," he said, positioning me right in front of the machine. "Now, take a *morceau de pâte,* a piece of the dough, and run it through the rollers, like this. You see?" He reached around me from one side and ran it through, then reached around me from the other side and ran another blob of dough through.

It had been a long time since a guy stood so close

to me. Since Greg, and Greg and I had been really cautious about not getting too physical.

Luc didn't touch me, nor I him, but I was intensely aware of how close he really was. I couldn't breathe without smelling his cologne. It wasn't spicy-smooth like Greg's, just smooth. Really, really smooth.

Luc ran a few more dough balls through the automatic kneader, then stood back and let me do it on my own. He'd moved away, but I still felt that presence, like an invisible touch. And the scent of that cologne.

"*Bon.* You really do deserve to wear *la toque blanche,*" Luc teased. "I saw the photo."

I looked over his shoulder at Guillaume, the naughty tattle-tale who had snapped my picture. I hoped my hair looked good in it.

Everyone got a big laugh out of Luc's comment except Patricia, who glared out the pastry room door in my general direction.

I stepped back from the dough machine to see Sophie motioning in my direction. I met her halfway.

"There's a cute guy here to see you," she said.

"The lawyer from Davis?" I asked.

"So you think he's cute, huh?" Her eyes twinkled at me.

Ouch! She'd caught me.

"No, it's not him," she said. "It's some guy named Steve."

The only Steve I knew was attached to Tanya. I

ignored Patricia and Luc and quickly walked to the café, convinced something was wrong.

Eleven

La vérité se cache au fond d'un puits.
Truth hides at the bottom of a well.

Steve waited at the table closest to the door. As soon as I approached, he stood up to shake my hand and introduce himself. He looked exactly how I thought he'd look—blond hair, which I noticed was thinning a bit, and the build of someone who plays volleyball a few times a week. Cute, but not in a call-attention-to-me way. Pants pressed on the crease. So Tanya.

"Tanya told me you worked here...I hope it's okay to drop in."

"No problem," I said, knowing that there *must* be a problem or I wouldn't be meeting him for the first time without Tanya.

"I've been making sales calls, and I was in the area," he explained awkwardly.

"Can I get you something? A coffee?"

"No, no. Look, Lexi, I'm concerned about Tanya." My heart beat faster. "Why?"

"Well, we were getting along really well, enjoying

ourselves, and then all of a sudden, well, the trail went cold. Maybe she's just not interested in me anymore, and if that's the case, then I won't like it, but I'll deal." He rubbed his chin and pushed his hair back. He had shallow circles under his eyes.

"I just don't feel like that's it," he continued. "I think I've offended her somehow, but I don't know how. I tried talking, but while she insists nothing is wrong, I feel that nothing is right. And now we aren't talking at all. Which is why I'm here. I hope I'm not being pushy."

Oh, Tanya. Don't crawl back into that shell, I thought. *It's not protective anymore. It's isolating.*

"I—I think I might know what's going on," I said. "I hope you'll give it some time and patience. I'll talk with her and encourage her to talk to you."

"Okay," he said, "but at some point, it's only gentlemanly for me to pull away from her if that's what she wants."

I nodded. He was right.

Tanya would be at our house for Easter. I'd talk with her then. There was no better time than Easter for a new beginning, and she needed one before Steve withdrew, too.

We always got up early on Easter morning, even if it was too cloudy in Seattle to see the sunrise, and it usually was.

"Sleeveless dress, eh?" My mom tweaked the

flesh on my upper arm.

I flexed my bicep. "I'm not doing all those workouts for nothing."

"You look very pretty," Mom said. "I'm sure everyone will notice."

"You look pretty too," I said. She'd recently tossed out most of her stretch pants and had started wearing regular slacks and even some skirts.

"I don't want to look like a haystack compared to Leah's mother," she replied.

Ah. Now I understood the recent wardrobe makeover.

A barrel of family fun lay ahead of us that day. Leah's mom was coming for dinner, along with Nonna—and her date!—and Uncle Bennie, the human resources guru. *Please don't let him bring up the failed job in Bellingham,* I silently begged.

Tanya planned to come for a little while. I don't think she'd talked with Steve since I'd met him at the café the week before, and she'd been so "busy" that I hadn't been able to pin her down to talk.

"Are we going? Or are we going to celebrate Easter at Christmas?" my dad bellowed from the garage.

Mom beamed. For the first time in a long while, my dad was coming to church. I'd asked him last night, telling him it was my last Easter at home and I wanted him to come. But I really asked him for Mom, and he knew it.

We drove to church, and I think even Dad was impressed by how many people stopped to talk with

Mom. He rarely went with her, so I don't think he realized how connected and cared about she was. It felt cozy to be between them in church. This is what other families must feel like all the time.

I want my kids to feel like this, I thought. *Kids? Oh, no no no. First they have to squawk. No thanks.* But celebrating the Resurrection felt more real and less rote to me than it had in a long time.

After the service, the three of us drove home. Nonna had already commandeered the kitchen. I pinched a piece of cooling Easter egg sweet bread, and Nonna tapped my behind with her hand.

"That wasn't ready yet!" She tugged me into the family room. "I'd like you to meet Stanley Jones. Stanley, this is my favorite granddaughter."

"Oh yes, Mr. Jones," I said, smiling. "I remember hearing about you. You subscribe to *National Geographic,* don't you?"

Stanley stood up to shake my hand. "Why, yes. I do. How did you know?"

Nonna gave me the evil eye. "Stanley is enjoying a little relaxation. Why don't you go and mix a Bellini for him, and we'll show him some hospitality?"

I laughed to myself all the way to the kitchen. Easter was the one holiday we did all Italian in honor of Nonna. I always thought it was weird to eat lamb on Easter. Lamb of God and all that. I wondered if my mother had always wanted Italian on Easter, or if Nonna had ever asked her.

Leah was trimming asparagus for an antipasti

platter, but her hands were a little unsteady.

"Okay?" I asked.

She nodded. "My mom is bringing her new boyfriend. I'm hoping they don't decide to get married the same month as Nate and I. I'm afraid she's going to make a big announcement."

I bet she also hoped her mother didn't wear something that left nothing to the imagination, but she was too kind to say it.

After giving Mr. Jones his Bellini, I walked into the dining room where my mom was putting the final touches on the table.

She smiled. "What do you think of Nonna's date?"

"He smiles and nods at everything Nonna says."

She whispered, "He turned down his hearing aid."

The doorbell rang, and Mom peeked out the window. "It's Tanya. Want to get it? I don't really need your help. Since you made dessert, that is!" she quickly added.

I opened the door. "Hey, girl," I said, hugging Tanya. I scanned the driveway and the street. "I don't see your car."

Tanya pointed at the sea foam blue VW Beetle convertible sitting in the driveway.

"Is that yours?" I screamed.

Tanya nodded and smiled, dimpling up. "It was time, and the teaching contract is good. I think I'm going to sign with them again rather than go to the Christian school."

"Oh, I am *so* jealous," I said. "Does it smell like a new car?"

She jingled the keys in my face. "Want to find out?"

"Well, let's go sit in it!" I said, excited.

I pulled the front door shut behind me and raced down the driveway.

Tanya opened the driver's door and waved me in. "I'm always going to be in this seat. You sit here and see what you think."

What did I think? It had a six-CD changer and an MP3 hookup. It had blinkers in the side mirrors. It was perfectly new. Unlike a car I knew and loved, the backseat was not quilted with duct tape or sporting permanently pebbled carpet.

"Let's go for a ride," I said. "We can drive down along the beach at Alki. That'll be quick and fun."

We switched positions, and Tanya took off down the hill. While I had her trapped, I asked, "So, what does Steve think of the new car?"

She sighed. "Gee. You've given me five minutes. Thanks."

"If I don't push you, who will?"

"Who says I need to be pushed?"

"Look how nice it is," I said. "Let's walk the beach for a few minutes."

She parked the car, and we took our shoes off and walked on the cool sand.

"Have you talked with him?" I asked.

She shook her head. "No."

"He came into the café and asked if I knew why

you might be pulling away. I told him he needed to talk with you, but that involves you actually talking."

"I know," she said. "It's just what you and I talked about in high school. Why get serious with a guy if you can't marry him?"

"Hello! That's because we were young. You're old enough to get married now. We're a year older than Leah, and she's getting married in two and a half months."

She kicked the sand. "Christian guys want virgins."

"You are a virgin," I said quietly. "You are perfectly clean. You are pure."

"No, I'm not." Tears slipped down her face. Tanya did everything quietly. Even grieving. Tears slipped down my face too.

I pulled her down to sit next to me on a retaining wall. "Tanya," I said softly. "You were date raped; that is not engaging in consensual sex. You were a victim."

"I don't want to engage in consensual sex with anyone, which is what has to happen if I marry someone, which is often the natural outcome of dating," she said in a flat tone. She wiped the tears away with the back of her hand.

"Has Steve asked you to marry him?" I asked, forcing her to face where things really were rather than where they might go.

Tanya lightened a bit and smiled. "No, but he wanted me to visit his family over Easter."

"Ah. More serious. And that's what triggered

this?"

She nodded.

"Not all Christian girls are virgins. We knew plenty in college who made mistakes, and they moved on to good marriages. Even so, your situation is totally different. You don't even know if *Steve* is a virgin, do you?"

She shook her head.

"But this isn't about being a virgin, is it?" I asked quietly, knowing the answer already.

She shook her head again. "Why did this have to happen to me? I did all the right things, and then this."

"Do you feel like you need more counseling? It'd be okay."

"No," she said. "I'm mostly okay. I haven't had to face this part of it though, really. The wanting trickling back and the not-wanting still there."

"I'd hate for that jerk to ruin the rest of your life. Wouldn't you?"

I saw anger in her face. *Good.*

"How about this," I said. "You at least give Steve a chance—tell him what happened. Not all the details, but enough. See how he responds. If he responds poorly, we'll know he's not the one."

"I told Jared, remember?" Jared was the guy she got kind of serious with about a year after the rape. "And he backed way, way off."

"Ugh, Jared." I made a face. "He had skinny little earthworm lips. Would *anyone* want to cozy up to him?"

180

Tanya giggled. "Now that you say it, he did have earthworms for lips."

"Just give Steve one chance. Deal?" I asked.

"Deal," she said.

I wouldn't ask about Steve again. I knew she'd tell me soon enough.

We got back just as Uncle Bennie pulled up. "Alexandra!" he said. "I've been looking forward to talking with you!"

Nonna opened the door and pulled the still-smiling Stanley outside to meet her only son. "Bennie!"

"A little later?" I told him, hoping that "later" never arrived. I let the current of people carry me inside and away from Bennie. Tanya's mom and dad had already arrived, as had Leah's mom, alone and with red eyes. I brought her a loaf of Easter bread wrapped to go.

"For home," I whispered. Life wasn't easy for anyone.

At dinner, the conversation turned, naturally, to the wedding in just a couple of months.

"I always wanted my daughter to marry a lawyer," Leah's mom said.

"I always wanted my son to marry a lawyer," my mom joked back, holding her own.

"I insist on hosting the wedding shower," I said, seeing my chance to wrest one thing away from Leah's mom. "I won't take no for an answer, since Leah's the only sister I'll ever have."

Leah shot me a grateful look. *I may not be able*

181

to do much, but at least there'd be two opinions.

"Maybe you'll marry a man who has a sister," Tanya offered.

"First she has to *find* a man," Nonna said sweetly. I pretended to shoot her an angry glance. I knew she was paying me back for the *National Geographic* comment.

After dinner, my mother served dessert on the patio. At the last minute, I'd decided to make a coconut cake—layers of decadent white cake perfumed with coconut milk. Buttery vanilla frosting separated each layer, and toasted nuts and coconut draped across the top. I loved it. Apparently others liked it too, because it earned more raves than the rest of the meal.

"This is delicious!" Uncle Bennie said. "Peggy, you've outdone yourself. This is even better than the tiramisu you've been making for years. You should have changed long ago."

My mother slumped but forced a smile. "Alexandra made dessert today, so she'll have to take the credit."

"Everything I know about cooking I learned from my mom!" I said cheerfully.

Dad cleared his throat. Stanley smiled.

I was confused. I knew my mother wasn't happy my cake had been a success. Wasn't it okay for both of us to be good?

I followed her into the kitchen to help clean up. "I like the traditional tiramisu too, Mom."

"I know you do," she said stiffly. "And I liked your coconut cake." Then she turned her back to me.

I moved a few things from the sink closer to her. A brochure lay on the counter.

Two Wonderful Weeks in Italy

Come away to Italy for two grand weeks. Sun yourself on the famous Amalfi Coast, hob nob in Genoa, the Italian Riviera. Meet God in the spacious, famous cathedrals of Siena, and when in Rome--do as the Romans do! *Mangi!* **All tours are escorted and planned with nothing left for you to do but enjoy.**

"Whose is this?" I asked.

"Mine," Mom said, brightening a little. "Teresa and I are thinking about going. She's offered to pick up most of the expense using the commission she made in the sale. We won't see each other as much after your father and I move. Of course, Dad wouldn't go. He's been once and doesn't like traveling. I've never traveled on my own. There's my asthma to worry about, and I'm not sure if it would be that much fun."

She looked at me, wanting my encouragement.

"Sounds fun to me," I said, a little woodenly. My desire for her to be happy wrestled with the unwanted entitlement inside that felt it should be my turn, since she'd already been to Europe once.

We both had envy and insecurity issues. I saw that now.

"You think?" she asked, perking up.

"I know you'll have fun!" I answered extra cheerfully, wishing I felt as enthusiastic as I sounded.

She smiled and relaxed a little, I thought, from the cake issue. She was looking for her place in the world again, just like I was.

In the other room, I could hear people preparing to go home, and I went to say good-bye. Nonna hadn't left Uncle Bennie's side the whole afternoon, for which I was extremely grateful. She had no idea how much she was helping me.

"You just let your old uncle know if you need my help," he said to me on the way out. "They don't call me Chief Headhunter for nothing!" He slipped a piece of paper into my hand and guffawed at his own joke.

"I'll let you know," I said, hoping to rush past this conversation. "I'm pretty happy where I am."

"You haven't been fired yet, so that's something," he said, his eyes twinkling.

He knew I'd been let go in Bellingham! But did my parents? They'd freak if they knew I'd been fired from two jobs.

"I need to say goodbye to Tanya's parents," I said and left the room as quickly as I could.

Once everyone had left, I opened the paper he'd slipped me. It was an industry column on finding and keeping a job.

<u>Ask Jerry.</u>

Dear Jerry,

I'm twenty-seven years old and I've bounced from job to job, quitting them, mostly, because they were boring. I mean, where is my career?

One of the issues I see a lot with people your age is that they expect way too much early in their careers. Expectations of promotions, excitement, raises, and work-life balance put a lot of pressure on the self and a lot of pressure to move on if things aren't moving quickly.

I always look for people who buy into what we do, not just those who have the skills we need and just want a job. What is it you want to do? What is important to you? What are you good at? Start by answering these questions to get a better idea of where your career is, or should be, headed.

First Nate, now Uncle Bennie. Was the world trying to tell me something?

Monday I drove past the new apartment complex—hopefully *my* apartment complex. I'd left an application, but the manager wasn't taking deposits yet.

At L'Esperance, Patricia now at least spoke French to me in her tobacco-hewn voice. I still washed her dishes and did her errands and repetitive prep work. She did all the supply ordering.

She let me arrange everything in the cases up front, though, which was enough to keep me happy. First I slid in little strawberry tarts—fresh for the new spring season, tucked under coin-sized kiwi slices. Next, chocolate mousses, whipped into light peaks and dusted with bittersweet cocoa. Last, creamy *crèmes brûlées* in white ramekins that looked like upside-down chef's hats. I loved biting through the brittle caramelized layer on top, thin as ice on an October pond.

After I helped Patricia, I made sure Sophie had everything stocked for the next day. On my break, I munched a crispy madeleine cookie—spongy on the inside, crisp on the outside, and perfumed with lavender honey and lemon. I offered one to Sophie.

"Can't have it," she reminded me. "Butter. Eggs."

"Oh, I'm sorry," I said. "Sometimes I forget. What are those?" I nodded at the heavy set of keys in her hand.

"They're Luc's. Since Patricia is gone tonight, I'm closing up."

I'd never seen him give the keys to anyone before. Suddenly the half-eaten cookie in my hand didn't look so appetizing.

"Oh, okay," I said. "Cool." *Not cool.*

The next day my mom came in to have lunch with me.

"*Eh bien,* it's Margaret *la Magnifique,*" Luc said, sweeping over to my mother and kissing her hand. Irritation prickled up my spine. He was flirting with someone as old as his *maman.*

My mother giggled and blushed.

"Ready?" I asked, taking off my apron.

We strolled down the street, the day sunny and beautiful.

"See that building?" I pointed out the apartments being developed. "I'm hoping to get an apartment there. They're taking deposits in a few weeks, and I should be able to move in just before the wedding, when you guys are getting packed up."

"Oh, Lexi, it's beautiful," Mom said. "Is it affordable?"

"I hope so," I said. "I don't know the exact price, but I asked for a studio. I've saved almost everything I've made since I moved back in with you guys."

"I'm sorry we can't help you out more," she said as we entered the little bistro I'd picked out. "With both Dad and I retiring..."

"I'm fine," I said. "Really."

I think we were both a little nervous about me

being solely responsible for me.

We sat at a table next to the window, and I ordered for us in French, since I knew the waiter from L'Esperance.

My mother sighed. "It's so nice to hear you speak French, both at work and here. I envy you that, Lexi."

"You've never wanted to speak French," I reminded her. "And aren't you going to Italy?"

Mom's face lit up. "I think we are. Right after the wedding."

I grinned and dug into my purse. "Here," I said. "I got this for you."

\$25 Gift Certificate

Seattle Language School

Ciao, caro allievo!
Welcome, dear student!

Want to leam Travel Italian? We have just the thing for you. In our six week course, native speakers will guide you through the phrases and customs necessary to make your trip a complete and fulfilling success. And when you're ready to travel, we'll be the first to say, "*Arrivederci!*"

"For me?" Mom's eyes filled with tears.

"Unless you know anyone else going to Italy," I

said, smiling.

"Oh no, no. I don't think I can take lessons. I'd be too embarrassed to speak out in class."

"Well, then, you'll have to let the gift certificate go to waste."

She grimaced. My mom hated wasting anything. She had started composting when most people still considered it stewing garbage.

I clapped. "Gotcha!"

When I stopped being obsessed with myself and started looking out for the benefit of others, a lot of the differences I had with them melted away. Sophie. My mom. God.

Mom leaned across the table and kissed my cheek. The waiter stood back discreetly for a moment, then delivered my all-time favorite sandwich.

I nibbled the corner of the sandwich and then closed my eyes, letting the soft brie melt into the salty ham and sweet powdered sugar. Every possible taste bud was included. Life was good.

Except for the image of Sophie holding Luc's keys.

Croque Alexandra

Ingredients:

8 slices very fresh, soft white bread, crusts removed
8 ounces thinly sliced ham
4 ounces brie cheese, no rind, softened

Dijon mustard
Nonstick spray with flour added
3 eggs
1/4 cup water
3 Tbs flour
Dash salt
1/8 C Powdered sugar

Directions:
Lightly spread Dijon mustard on one side of four slices of bread. Equally distribute brie on top of mustard. Equally distribute ham on top of brie. Top with remaining slices of bread, making four sandwiches.

Spray nonstick skillet, turn on medium high heat. Turn oven to warm, 250 degrees.

Whisk eggs, flour, salt, and water in a small bowl. Pour into a shallow pan. Dip each side of one sandwich, quickly, into egg mixture. Place into skillet and fry each side till crisp and brown and Brie melts. When done, place sandwich on cookie sheet and place into oven to keep warm.

Repeat with other sandwiches till all four are ready to serve.

Just before serving, shake powdered sugar over each sandwich with small

mesh strainer.

Serves 4.

Sandra Byrd

Twelve

A toile ourdie, Dieu envoie le fil.
God sends the thread to begin the web.

Saturday afternoon, we had three leftover Tartes
Tatin that we wouldn't be able to sell the next day.
I'd take them to Pete that night with the bread. Even
Nonna would be impressed, although she and
Stanley now attended church on Sunday. Saturday
night was her new bingo night. Or maybe she just
didn't want Pete and Stanley to meet.

Sophie found me cleaning in the back. "Lexi,
someone's here to see you."

"Okay."

"Also," she asked, "could you give me a ride
home tonight? To my parents' house?"

Alarmed, I looked up. "No Roger?"

"Not tonight," she said, shaking her head. "I
moved out."

"I'm sorry."

She waved her hand, making it clear she didn't
want to talk about it.

"We have to stop by my grandmother's church on the way home, to drop off the bread," I said.

"That's okay. I'll help."

As I walked to the café, I passed Luc in the bakery. I heard him grumble under his breath about how my friends and family certainly visited a lot, and he hoped they were making purchases too. He'd had another stressful week at La Couronne, so I decided not to take it personally.

When I stepped into the café, I saw Dan. He had on jeans and a T-shirt, no suspenders. He looked younger. Less lawyerly.

Why hadn't Sophie mentioned it was Dan?

"Hi," he said. "I brought your platter back, and I have another order to place." He smiled an infectious smile. I couldn't help it. I smiled back.

"Can you take a minute to sit down with me and fill out the order form?" he asked.

"Sure, sure," I said. I mean, it was a part of my job, after all.

We sat in the café, and I filled out a catering order—a rather large one this time, for both bread and pastry.

"Make sure those napoleons are on there," Dan pointed out. "So, do they lock you in here to bake all weekend? I hear bakers have awful hours."

Was he teasing me?

"I'm not a baker," I admitted. "I wish I were. And I work far fewer hours than most of the lawyers I know. Most of the lawyers I know don't have time to have fun." I batted my eyes, wondering what had come over me. Flirting with customers was Luc's area of expertise, not mine.

Dan didn't seem to mind. "Well, you must know the wrong kind of lawyers. Lawyers like me like to have fun. We go...snow-boarding."

He waited for a response. I didn't give one.

"And we like to go to movies," he tried, "when something good is playing."

I was softening, and I could tell by his face that he knew it.

"Some lawyers, like me, really break out of their shells sometimes and enjoy nature. A partner at our office today said the cherry trees in the U District are blooming right now. Would you like to walk through and see them?"

It was a novel thing to suggest, and walking was a comfortable way to get to know someone, because the pauses wouldn't be too awkward. Before I knew it, I'd agreed.

"Sure," I said, suddenly shy.

"Good! Then it's settled," Dan said. "Next Saturday afternoon I'll come by to get you."

I wavered, uncertainty rising within me. If I wanted out, I had to do it now. I hadn't expected this...him. It felt disloyal to Luc, somehow.

Sophie nodded her head as vigorously as she could behind Dan's back.

"Okay," I said finally. I scribbled my address on a piece of paper.

"See you then," Dan said. "Four o'clock?" I shoved the pen into my back pocket. "Sure. Four o'clock."

When he'd left, Sophie hugged me, and I managed, with a little effort, to match her big smile with one of my own. Luc, on the other hand, turned his back and disappeared into the bakery.

That night, Sophie and I drove the loaves and the Tartes Tatin to Nonna's church, and I introduced Pete and Sophie.

"Nice to meet you, Saint Sophia," Pete said. Sophie blushed, the first time I'd ever seen her do so.

"I'm not a saint of any kind, Lexi," she admitted in my car on the way to her house.

"You're softer than you let on," I told her.

She was quiet for a moment. "Is that your church?" she asked.

"No, mine is further downtown. Still coming with me next week?"

"Yeah." She elbowed me playfully. "A few days before your big date."

I blushed. "I don't know if it's a *big* date. I was kind of surprised, actually. I mean, I don't know that I have anything in common with him. And he's a lawyer. I have a life full of them already. I have more in common with guys who are into restaurants and food and the other things I'm into."

In other words, Luc.

Sophie's face darkened, but she turned away

196

before I could read any more into it.

Does she like Luc? I wondered. *Does she think it's inappropriate for me to build a relationship with him?*

Neither of us spoke for the rest of the drive.

A few nights later, my mom sat in my room chatting with me while I got ready for the Impact Group. I had to leave in a few minutes to pick up Sophie.

"We made our reservations for Italy." Mom beamed. "And my classes start next week. I'm so glad you suggested them."

"Me too," I said. "What does Dad think?"

She shrugged. "He thinks it's fine. He generally supports whatever I want to do, but you know he's not a real emotional person. Nonna thinks it's silly."

"*What?*" I brushed my hair. "Why?"

"I don't know. Learning Italian when her mother—my grandmother—made a point not to speak it her whole life, seems silly to her."

Maybe mothers and daughters weren't completely at ease at any age. Yet my mother always called Nonna first with good news or bad. Except when she called me.

I checked to make sure I had my icebreaker and headed for the Jetta.

I hope Jill doesn't say anything stupid about my icebreaker. I hope Sophie feels at home at the church.

197

I was halfway down the street before I realized I'd called it "the church" instead of "my church." I'd never really decided on my own if it was my church. I'd assumed I'd just go back there when I returned to Seattle, but maybe that wasn't where I was supposed to be.

I know I put my faith in you, Lord, but the structure is all pulled away now. If it's me and you, it's because I make it me and you.

No one's driving me to church anymore. If I'm going to get there, I have to drive myself.

Sophie lived in Magnolia with her parents now that she and Roger had broken up. When I pulled in front of the house, she stepped out the door. She'd been watching. It was thoughtful of her.

"Ready?" I asked as she climbed in the car.

"Yep."

"Hey," I said, looking at her as I pulled away from the curb. "What's with the piercings? Or should I say, lack thereof? You don't have to take them out, you know. You don't need to change yourself."

"I took them out just for the night," she answered. "I thought some Christians might be put off by them. Some people are." She flipped down the passenger-side visor to look in the mirror. It came down crookedly.

I really liked that about Sophie. She didn't push herself on others to accept her as she was. It showed consideration of what made others comfortable. I wanted her to know she'd be accepted as she was, though.

"You have to hold your head at a right angle to get a good view," I apologized. "Sorry, my car's old."

"At least you have a car," she said, cocking her head. "It's got character."

"Yeah, it wheezes like Patricia running from the café to the bakery to the Gauloise cigarettes."

Instead of meeting at the church that night, the Impact Group met at a park. The weather, for once, had cooperated.

The group had claimed an area of lawn in front of the lake, and a few people whizzed Frisbees back and forth while Bill and a buddy manned the grills. I introduced Sophie to as many people as I remembered, whispering to her that I was still new there too. Thankfully, everyone was kind, and even Jill refrained from the subtle church quiz, trying to probe someone's spiritual state.

Once everyone had food, Bill stood up. "As you know, it's a game night, and all our activities have to do with games. You'll notice the *checkered* tablecloths."

Jill smirked, appreciating the cleverness. Bill and Jill. I could see it clearly now. Could Bill?

"Michelle and Lexi have prepared some game-related icebreakers for us to get to know one another better. I'll let them take over."

I gestured to Michelle, who had sat next to Sophie and me. "You can go first."

Michelle stood and handed out several stacks of Cranium Whoonu cards, then asked each person to rifle through and choose a card that best described them and their interests, but might be a surprise to others.

"I like your icebreaker idea," I said. I liked her, too, as did Sophie. Michelle had relaxed, coming out of her quiet shell, and she and Sophie were laughing a lot.

"No way!" I said as Sophie showed us her country music card.

Michelle flipped over her card on the table, and Sophie and I asked, "Really? Roller coasters?" at the same time.

"Uh-uh," Sophie said when I showed her my American cheese card, sounding scandalized. "Not Miss Gourmet!"

We laughed and chatted with the others at the table.

All around me people talked about their jobs and their apartments. Jill had a new apartment downtown. I thought about asking if she needed a roommate.

Nah.

Then Bill asked me to explain my icebreaker.

I brought out a half dozen stubby pencils my mother had loaned me from her preschool, and a small sheaf of papers. I handed a paper to one person at each table.

"Has everyone here played Mad Libs?" I asked. I explained that the person with the paper should ask for a noun, verb, or whatever was needed to fill in the blanks, then read the story aloud to the table.

I filled in the blanks for my table as they called out answers.

Happily Ever After

Once upon a time there was a (positive adjective) _____ single person who attended the Impact Group. This person was (adverb) _____ confused, because he or she had expected to be at a (positive adjective) _____ job right now instead of the (negative adjective) _____ one she or he was working.

One time Single Person was talking to a (noun) _____ about her (negative adjective) _____ personal life.

"You think that's bad?" the friend answered. "I have a friend who is dating a (animal) _____ ."

It could be worse, Single Person admitted.

Instead of constantly (verb ending in -ing) _____ , Single Person decided to (faith-related verb) _____ instead. Besides, Single Person thought, what I really

want to do is (positive activity).

You just never know, (positive well-known phrase)

_____ •

It got a lot of laughs. Now, I'd always been a fan of quizzes, but I just didn't feel like I fit with this group. I said nothing, though, because Sophie was in a fantastic mood all the way home. She looked so young without her piercings: nose, earrings, and the recent eyebrow bar included.

"I liked your game," she said.

I was relieved. They'd seemed a little young to me but I'd had no idea what else to do.

"I never play games anymore," she continued. "It wasn't really an icebreaker like Michelle's, but it made me realize that a lot of people have the same problems I do. And it made me laugh. I don't laugh as much as I should for someone in the so-called prime of her life."

"Me neither," I admitted. "I miss it."

I pulled up in front of her parents' house. I hadn't asked why she'd moved out of Roger's place, but I'd seen her take the bus every afternoon.

"Do you want me to pick you up before work?" I asked. "It's no problem."

"No thanks," she said firmly. "The bus is really easy."

I understood. I didn't want help either, and it was hard enough living in your parents' home.

"You opened, you should leave early," Sophie said on Saturday as we packed up the sandwich supplies after lunch. "Besides, don't you have a big date to get ready for?"

I wished she'd keep her voice down. I didn't want Luc to overhear. I glanced toward his office and saw I needn't worry. He was speaking softly in French, to someone on the phone.

He caught my eye, smiled, and firmly closed his office door. He almost never closed that door. *Weird.*

"Okay," Sophie continued, "I've bagged all the leftover bread and pastries for you to take to the church on your way home. Now go!"

I stacked the baguettes in the front seat of the Jetta and took off. Thankfully, my parents had gone to Whidbey to choose the cabinets and carpet, which meant Centurion Dad wouldn't be on duty, waiting for Dan to pick me up. When I'd first brought Greg home, Dad had met him at the door in marine full-dress uniform.

I chuckled, thinking of it, and was halfway through my shower before I realized I'd thought of Greg without causing a little paper cut on my heart.

I got out of the shower and debated clothes. I called Tanya for help. "What do you think I should wear?"

"How about that frilly white shirt you bought a

couple weeks ago?" she said. "You thought it was romantic."

"Oh. I have other plans for that," I said. "Besides, I'm going for fun, not romance."

She and I brainstormed and finally came up with jeans, boots, a short-sleeved peach shirt, and a jean jacket. Silver hoop earrings, no necklace, and long, sophisticated ponytail.

"Want me to help plan *your* outfit for tonight?" I offered hopefully.

"No...but I am having dinner with Steve."

I knew my happiness came through my voice. "Good!"

"I'm afraid. And heavy-hearted." I could hear it through the phone.

"Hang on." I set the phone down, tightened the towel turban on my head, and grabbed the Bible off my nightstand. I picked up the phone. "You know I've been reading my Bible without anyone kickstarting me for, like, the first time in my life."

"Yeah."

"So here's what I just read in Matthew." I turned to Matthew 11:29, where I'd left off a couple of days ago, and read the passage out loud to her. "'Come to me, all you who are weary and burdened, and I will give you rest. Take my yoke upon you and learn from me, for I am gentle and humble in heart, and you will find rest for your souls. For my yoke is easy and my burden is light.'"

"Yeah," Tanya said, her voice lighter. "I need to give up the burden."

"You do," I agreed. "And you can."

"Have fun tonight," she said. "Let's talk tomorrow afternoon. I've got some prep work to do for school, but I'll call you when I'm done."

"Okay. You have fun too," I said, glancing at the clock. Dan would be here in twenty minutes, and my hair was still wet.

By some miracle, I got ready with five minutes to spare. I saw Dan pull up and suddenly felt dizzy. What was I thinking? This was practically a blind date!

I took four deep breaths. Now I felt like I was going to hyperventilate. Deep breathing was supposed to help, not hurt. I didn't want to end up breathing into a paper bag.

I looked out the window—discreetly, of course— and watched as Dan poked his head under the hood of his truck. Then he tried to start it. It turned over and over but didn't start. He lifted the hood, fiddled with something, and tried again. Nothing.

He wiped his hands on a rag, closed the hood, and walked toward the door. Watching him—no suspenders, no power suit, dead truck—he looked more like a dejected boy than an up-and-coming lawyer. My anxiety faded, and I felt sympathy and friendship instead.

I opened the door. "Car trouble, eh?"

"Yeah," he said. "I called Triple-A. They'll be here in a few minutes to tow it back to the dealer." He sighed. "I don't have time to deal with this, really. There's a lot going on. That's why I bought a new truck instead of used."

I squinted at the truck. "A Ford?"

"Yeah."

"My dad always said Ford stood for 'Found On Road Dead.'" I tried to lighten the mood. "Or 'Forever On Repair Dock.'"

Dan seemed to relax a bit. "I guess that means your dad drives a Chevy or an import, huh?"

"Dodge." I lifted my keys. "I can drive, if you don't mind my asthmatic vehicle."

"Sure. I mean, if you still want to go," Dan said.

"Worried about my driving?"

He laughed a really rich laugh, one you wanted to laugh along with, as he followed me to my car. I brushed about five pounds of baguette crumbs off the passenger seat, and Dan sat down without flinching.

"Spend the day making croutons?" he teased.

"No, I deliver bread on Saturdays."

"I didn't know L'Esperance delivered bread. Don't you have a delivery person?" Dan asked as we headed toward the U District.

"I take leftover baguettes and pastries to the soup kitchen at my grandma's church on Saturday," I said. "Sorry for the crumbs."

I noticed I'd left the icebreakers and pencils from the Impact Group on the passenger floor. An empty water bottle rolled around in the back. Dan graciously ignored the mess. I wondered if he was truly a pressed-pants kind of guy.

"Sharing your bread. Like the little boy with the

loaves and fishes," he said.

I looked at him. He'd referenced a story from the Bible! Tanya would be extremely impressed.

We parked, and he leaped out and came around to open my door. "No excuse not to be a gentleman just because you had to drive," he said. I could tell he felt embarrassed about the whole thing.

"No worries," I said.

Ribbons of walking paths spooled throughout the campus, some of the prettiest winding around old brick buildings and gardenlike corridors.

"Did you go here?" I asked, waving my arm to indicate the university.

"Yeah," he said. He talked about his college years, and they sounded like mine—a lot of fun, friends, and painful lessons.

The cherry trees were perfect. Delicate clouds of pale pink blooms swirled around the trunks of each tree. When the wind blew, a delicate shower of petals drifted down on and between us. It felt as sweet as it smelled.

We talked about my brother and Leah, about law school, and what Dan did now.

"I went into copyright law for two reasons. One, because the firm offered me a job," he said. I appreciated his candor. As a long-term job seeker, I knew what he meant. "Two," he continued, "I love reading. Almost anything, but especially history, which leads to a lot of old books, which leads to copyright things. However, that's not how my job's worked out so far."

"What do you mean?" I asked.

"I don't even work with book and literary issues," he lamented. "I'm spending all my time on illegal download issues for rap groups. Big Dog and the Hedge Hog," he smiled. "The Ping-Pong Sisters. Doctor Drivel."

I laughed out loud. "No way."

"No," he admitted, "but almost. It's definitely not why I went to law school."

We'd walked the entire loop, and dusk was settling in as we headed back toward my car. "Did you go to cooking school?" Dan asked.

"No. I have a degree from Western in French studies."

"Oh," he said.

"Yeah," I answered. "Oh. So I looked around for a while, tried a few things that didn't work out. What I really love to do is bake and cook and be in an environment that allows me to do that."

"So you made a good fit at L'Esperance."

"I think so," I said, answering the questioning tone in his statement. "I should know in the next month or two for sure."

We got back to the car, and I unlocked the door. We stood for a while, still talking. He was easy to talk to, and I wasn't ready for the afternoon to end.

"Would you like to get a bite to eat?" Dan asked. "Or rather, would you like to drive us for a bite to eat?"

"Sure."

We drove to a nearby sushi bar, a kaiten-sushi

bar, where the food went round and round the restaurant on cooled and heated conveyer belts. It felt like *The Jetsons* meets Tokyo.

"So how does this work?" Dan said. "I have to admit, I'm more of a steak-and-potatoes guy."

Just like my dad. I suppressed a sigh.

"Well, the plates go around on the conveyer belts," I explained. "Each plate has a colored edge, and each color represents a price." I pointed to the price guide on the wall. "You just stack your plates when you're done eating, the waitress adds them up, and that's how much you owe."

"You're going to have to tell me what these all are," he said as strips of fish circled us like airplanes waiting to land.

I grabbed some easy food first. "California rolls," I said.

"Even I know what those are." He relaxed. "Rice, crab, and cucumbers. *Cooked* crab, right?" he asked.

I assured him that it wasn't raw and poured soy sauce into each of the tiny dipping dishes. I dipped the roll into the soy sauce and put it in my mouth in one bite, Japanese style. Next, I chose some *edamame,* green soybeans zipped up in fuzzy cases, and showed Dan how to pop them out.

I snapped open a set of chopsticks.

"Do I have to use those?" he asked.

"You don't have to," I teased. "They have trainer pairs up front for the kids."

"Maybe you can show me." He handed over his pair.

209

I placed a stick in his right hand, slipping it into the soft pocket between thumb and forefinger. I noticed how nicely manicured his hands were. Clean, but not fussy or metro. Then I slipped the second stick in.

"Now, you use them like pincers," I said, my hand over his as I tweezed a piece of salmon with them.

I withdrew my hand so he could lift it to his mouth, but I could still feel the warm imprint of his hand in mine.

He mastered them in five minutes, and we joked about his quick progress. Part of me wished he'd needed my hand over his just a while longer.

I went as far as to get flash-seared tuna, my favorite, because it wasn't truly raw but was pretty close.

"What's this?" Dan asked.

I told him.

"I like it!" he said. "I've never eaten sushi before. In my family, raw fish is bait."

After dinner, as we walked to my car, Dan said, "That was really good, Lexi. An adventure. Thanks for suggesting it."

Maybe he wasn't as much like my dad as I'd thought. Dad wouldn't have tried the seared tuna, much as I loved him.

"Can I pay you back?" I asked. "We didn't spend *that* much in gas money."

"No," he said firmly.

We chatted comfortably on the way home. He

noticed my blood donor card sticking out of the visor and seemed genuinely touched when I told him why it was there.

"My truck should be done by Monday, I hope," he said. "I can't afford to miss any time off next week. We're preparing for a big case."

We pulled up in front of his home in Ballard. He lived in a very cute condo complex near Tanya's school. Window boxes everywhere, secured entry. I reminded myself I'd be putting down my own deposit in two weeks at *l'appartement de luxe.*

"Thanks for a great evening," Dan said, not rushing out of the car. His eyes were brown and warm, like cinnamon chocolate. "I'm really sorry about the truck breaking down."

"No problem," I said. "I'm sorry about the state of my car."

We sat in silence for a minute or two. "You know, I have your address but not your phone number. If I want to reach you, should I just call the shop?"

"I'll give you my number."

"I don't have any paper."

I pointed to the pages and pencils on the passenger floor. "You can use one of those. It's garbage."

He snagged a piece of paper and scribbled my number as I dictated it. Then he got out of the car, walked toward the entrance to his condo, and waved good-bye before walking inside.

I waved back and drove away, replaying the night in my head—smiling, then worrying, then wondering why I even cared if I liked Luc so much. And I did.

Dan hadn't said he'd call. He asked how to find me if he wanted to call. Like there was a decision to be made.

Maybe he'd prefer someone like Leah, a lawyer like himself. Maybe he was way out of my league after all, like Greg had been.

Still. We'd laughed a lot and had an awfully good time.

I wondered what the future held.

Thirteen

Ce que trois personnes savent est public.
It is no secret that is known to three.

"You first." I sipped my latte and leaned back into the soft coffee-shop armchair. The room buzzed with the happy hum of the after-work and after-school crowds and the trainlike whistle of the espresso machines. Tanya and I were trying to get some girl time before Steve came by to go to dinner with us.

"Well, we talked, and it went okay," Tanya said.

"Yes, I *know* that much, but you said I'd get the details in person. I'm here. In person. Give me details."

Her relaxed smile reached her eyes, and I knew she was going to be okay.

"We went for a nice drive. I packed a picnic. Nothing like *you* would have packed," she teased, "but Subway. And that was okay."

"I eat Subway!" I said, defending myself against food snobbery.

"Oh right. Let me remember when I saw that." Tanya tapped her chin. "Oh yeah. On a field trip in eighth grade." She swirled the coffee in her cup, returning to the more-serious subject matter. "So I explained all about the situation, and...uh...the healing and counseling."

"And he said..."

"His face got kind of weird, and I thought, 'Oh great, Jared all over again.'"

"Nah," I said. "Steve doesn't have earthworm lips."

"Right!" Tanya blushed a little. "He said it made him really mad it had happened, and he was glad I told him, and it made me seem, well..." Her voice dropped. "Incredibly strong in his eyes."

"See? I hate to say it—no, I don't. I told you so. He's a good guy." I sighed happily and savored the last drop of my drink.

Tanya leaned in toward me. "Do you think I'll ever want to make love? Even when I'm married to a good guy?"

"Yes," I said. "I believe it. I do."

"I hope so," she said.

"Women's sex drives don't peak until thirty-five or something," I said. "I think we have some time to work it all out. Although I myself am hoping for less than a decade to a marital resolution."

She didn't answer or joke, but she didn't flinch either.

"Why do sex issues have to be so hard? So constant?" I asked, picking at the rim of my empty cup with my fingernail. "It's one of the reasons Greg and I broke up."

"Really?" Tanya said. "You didn't tell me that."

"You weren't in the frame of mind to talk about it," I reminded her.

"What was the issue?"

"He wanted it, and I didn't," I said. "Well, that's not really true. We both wanted it, but I kept saying no. Eventually, it got tiresome and corroded all the good times. It bugged me that he kept making me say no over and over instead of using some self-control on his own. Frankly, he kept making it harder and harder for me to say no because he had some good arguments. I loved him and wanted to, and he knew it."

"Oh," she said. "I didn't know."

"It's okay. Why didn't God make the sex drive turn on at the slipping on of a wedding ring and not before?" I asked.

After a few seconds of silence, Tanya shared some more news. "Speaking of weddings, I asked Steve to escort me to Nate and Leah's. Your turn."

"What do you mean?"

"You know what I mean," she said. "The date with Dan."

"Dan, Dan." I pretended to rack my brain. "Oh! *Dan!*"

She laughed. "You liked him, didn't you?"

I let my mind wander back to that day. "I did. More than I thought I would, actually. We laughed a lot."

215

"You're pink," Tanya said.

"It's hot in here."

"Did he ask for your number?"

I continued playing with my cup. "Yeah, he took it."

"So what's next? Are you guys going out again?" She smiled expectantly.

"He hasn't called yet."

"Oh." Her voice grew quiet, then brightened with forced joviality. "Well, I read someplace that when guys say they'll call you, a girl thinks he means before he gets home that night, whereas the guy means before he dies."

I thought back again. "Actually, he didn't say he'd call me. He just took my number."

Tanya had a confident look. "He'll call. Probably this week. It's only been a few days."

"Yeah."

She stood up and waved, and I turned to see Steve standing just inside the door. I also saw his face as he spotted her, and she moved to greet him. I could see where this was going to end up, even if she couldn't. But then, maybe she could.

They chatted for a minute, and suddenly I felt cranky. I really didn't want to go to dinner with the two of them.

I opened and closed my purse twice, our secret signal to head to the bathroom together. Once we got there, she asked, "What's up?"

"Is it okay if I don't go tonight?" I said. "I've got to open in the morning, it's Sophie's late day, and

I'm feeling kind of PMSy."

"Sure, sure," she said. "We'll find another day soon. You're not mad that I asked him to come, are you?"

"No," I said, but I was.

Besides the PMS, it didn't help that my best friend had a date to my brother's wedding—as did my *grandmother*—but I didn't. Tanya also had a great job and a great car. But it was the date right now that bugged me.

I knew deep in my heart that it was representative of something else. Was I dateable? Was I desirable as a companion and a partner and a friend?

Right now it sure didn't seem like it.

When I got home, my parents were out with friends. I checked my Allrecipes.com status and found good feedback on my recipes. I realized then how desperate I was for affirmation.

Maybe if I'd given in to Greg, it would have solidified our relationship, and we'd still be together. Maybe making love early wouldn't have been all that bad.

I paced my room, trying to think of something to do to distract myself. Suddenly I had a great idea. I knew at least one other woman who wouldn't be on a date tonight. Someone who needed kindness as much as I did.

I zipped up to the Metropolitan Market and bought a small cartful of ingredients to bake something new and a small Swiss dark chocolate bar for myself.

At home, I put some music on, preheated the oven, and started mixing ingredients. As I did, I nibbled on my chocolate, one piece at a time.

Our black Lab, Ruby, sat at my feet, begging. Pleading with her eyes.

"No, Ruby, I can't give you any," I told her as I popped another piece of chocolate in my mouth.

She kept staring. "*Why not?*" she seemed to ask.

How could she know? She thought everything I ate must be divine; all her "people food" treats were. She didn't know that dark chocolate—even though it looked good, even though her "equals" ate it—would cause her great harm.

I got her a pig's ear instead, which she begrudgingly took. "You're going to have to trust me when I say it's not good for you, whether you understand or not."

"*Just like sex.*" The thought came from within my heart and mind.

I turned back to the mixing bowl and sighed resignedly. "Okay, Lord, I get it," I said.

I'd heard it said that sex was like chocolate. While I wouldn't know about that, I understood the lesson. I might not comprehend all the reasons it wasn't good for me right now, but I could trust the One who'd asked me to wait. Just like Ruby had to trust me for what she didn't fully understand.

I blasted my music and kept my phone close and the volume turned up loud. It was getting late for someone to call, but you never knew. He might have had to work late.

When the cookies were cool, I ate one as a taste test. Not bad for a first try and a recipe tweak. I found the nicest tin I had in my collection and packed them. I'd take them to work in the morning.

Sophie's Vegan PB and J Cookies

Ingredients:

**1 1/2 cups creamy, full fat peanut butter
1/2 cup vegetable shortening
1 cup white sugar
1 cup brown sugar
1/2 cup vanilla almond milk (in health row of most supermarkets)
1 Tbs lemon juice
1 tsp vanilla
2 1/2 cups all purpose flour
1 1/2 Tbs baking powder
1 1/2 Tbs baking soda
1/2 tsp salt
1/2 cup jam or jelly (Montmorency Cherry from Trader Joe's is recommended)**

**Directions:
Preheat oven to 375. Lightly mist pan with oil-based spray.**

In mixing bowl, fully blend peanut butter, shortening, both sugars, almond milk, lemon juice, and vanilla.

In separate bowl fully mix flour, baking powder, baking soda, and salt with a fork.

Add flour mix to peanut butter mix. Blend till just mixed.

Drop by teaspoonful onto cookie sheet about 2 inches apart. Lightly press thumb into cookie, and fill with 1/2 tsp jam.

Bake till just underdone, about 10 minutes.

Let sit on pan for 1-2 minutes, then slide, using spatula, onto racks to cool.

An hour later, I settled in bed and opened up Matthew. I started reading, really getting into it. After a few minutes, I got to the part about the boy sharing his lunch.

I forgot to tell Tanya that Dan knew a Bible story, I thought. I stopped reading for the night and tried to fall asleep, but I kept thinking about Dan.

Maybe he'd call tomorrow.

I had a surprise lined up for Leah that week, and she took off work two hours early so we could preview some condos together—supposedly for her and Nate.

"Hi, be right with you," I said as she walked into L'Esperance. I took off my apron and hung it on the peg in the back. When I entered the café again, Luc was serving my almost-sister-in-law.

"Eh *bien,* here is a gift from me to you." Luc handed her a fresh cup of coffee.

"*Merci,*" Leah replied.

"She speaks French too!" He winked and went back to the bakery.

No, she doesn't, I thought, strangely irritated. But I said nothing. I was sure he knew.

"Is he always that charming to your friends?" Leah said, giggling, as we walked to the curb.

"I haven't noticed," I said lightly. Maybe I should start paying closer attention.

"How are you, anyway?" I asked, changing the subject. "End of April...not too long until the Big Day."

"I'm jittery!" she said. "But things are busy at work, for me and for Nate, so that keeps us occupied. And Nate's had some headaches too."

"Oh, nothing new," I said.

"You know, I'm just guessing here," Leah said, frowning thoughtfully, "but sometimes I think that so much is expected of Nate all the time, that when he's sick, it's the only time he has a reasonable excuse to be imperfect."

I thought about it. "Maybe you're right," I said.

"He always was expected to be the golden boy."

"And you the golden girl." Leah turned to me. "I'm not dissing your parents—I really like them— but all parents have these expectations. Look at my mom."

"Yeah," I said. "Detaching from anything leaves wounds."

"And on *that* cheery note," she joked, "let's go find a condo."

I stopped next to my car. "Leah, I hope it's okay, but I just heard today that the building I've been waiting to get into is taking applications and deposits. The manager called me because I've been mooning around the place for a month or more. He'll only hold one for me for today. Do you mind if we do that too? Plus," I said, suddenly kind of shy, "since you're going to be my sister, it'd be fun to share."

"Totally," she said. "Let's do yours first!"

We drove the few blocks to the building. Its secure garage was open, and I parked on the second floor. We took an elevator to the manager's office. I pushed the button, and he opened up.

"I knew you'd be back," he said. "Ready to sign?"

"Yes. Then can I show my sister the studio?"

He had pulled out a sheet of paper but paused in the act of handing it to me. "Studio?"

"Yes, a studio," I reminded him.

"Uh-oh." He rubbed his eyes underneath his glasses. "I have no more studios. I thought we were talking one bedroom. I must have made a mistake.

I'm so sorry."

I sank into the chair in front of his desk. Leah put her hand on my shoulder.

"How much more is the one bedroom?" I asked quietly.

"Three hundred dollars a month," he said. "Because we had a misunderstanding, I'll make it two hundred a month for the first six months. If you still want it."

I took a deep breath. "Can I think about it for a while?"

He shook his head. "Unfortunately, no. I had a line here earlier. I only saved this one for you because I feel like we've gotten to know each other."

I hit my forehead with the palm of my hand. "See?" I said to Leah. "I've been here too much."

"Why don't you show your sister the apartment?" he said. "Here's the key. Then let me know what you'd like to do."

We walked out of the office, and I glanced at the number on the key. Seventh floor. I hit the elevator button, and it glided to the seventh floor. There we found two potted plants that held post on either side of the elevator, and hallways carpeted with new maroon carpeting. Downright regal.

"Nice elevator. Nice hallways," Leah said.

We walked down the hall looking for number 710.

"There it is," Leah pointed.

I slid the key into the lock, turned it, and pushed the door open.

"It's better than the studio," I said. The blinds were open, letting in the late-April sun. Ferries glided across the smooth water of the Sound, and the Olympic Mountains glimmered in the distance.

"Wow, Lex," Leah said. "You should be a real estate agent. You know how to find a place."

"Look in here," I called from the kitchen. New appliances, none of them stainless, which I loved. Stainless seemed cold to me unless it was in a commercial kitchen. Double convection oven. Sub-Zero fridge. Cherry floors.

"This is a bargain," Leah said. She peeked into the bedroom, next to the living room. They shared a common fireplace and the view. "I can understand why you want to do this instead of something bigger but not as nice in West Seattle."

We sat cross-legged on the living room floor. The warm afternoon sunlight streamed down on us.

"Should I sign?" I asked.

"Only you can decide that," she said. "Can you afford it?"

"I have no idea what the assistant manager's position will pay," I said. "But it's got to pay more than I make right now, for sure. If it were just like, thirty percent more, and I was careful, I could swing it. I have some savings I've been putting away for about three months." I'd bought a few clothes, paid my car off except for two payments, and the rest I'd saved. Thanks to my parents, I had no student loans.

"I think Luc will be fair," I said.

"Lex, what if Luc doesn't offer you the job?"

"I know," I said. "I've thought of that. But he's been making sure I do a lot of things all over the shop. I love every aspect of working there. I can speak French with the family. I know baking. He thinks I have a good heart. And he likes me," I ended. "I know he does."

"It does seem right," Leah said. "I just don't want you to be disappointed."

"If it doesn't work out," I said softly, "I'll still have tried everything I can do to do what I love and make a living. Then I guess I'd have to move on."

"To do what?" Leah asked.

I shrugged. "Real estate agent." I tried to be lighthearted. The truth was, I had no guarantee of ever finding a really good job, much less in the next two months.

We walked to the elevator and glided down to the office again.

"And?" the office manager asked.

"I'll take it," I said.

"I knew you would." He beamed. "Here's the rental agreement."

We left the complex, and I turned and blew a kiss at it, neatly folding up my lease agreement. I felt like framing it. I slipped it into my glove box, and Leah and I went to look at several other cute options for her and Nate to make their first home. She showed enthusiasm, but secretly, I think she liked mine best. I loved her and I loved Nate, but I didn't want my big brother as a neighbor at my first place on my own. Thankfully, it was a choice I didn't need to offer. Raphael had made it clear that he was leased up.

After bleaching the food-service stations at work a few days later, Sophie and I took a break. Patricia had left the bakery to me today while she worked on a special order for a cancer-center fundraiser over at La Couronne.

"What are you going to do this afternoon?" Sophie asked me.

"Bake cookies," I answered. "Patricia left the dough mixing to me today, which is a miracle, since normally she just lets me pull them in and out of the ovens."

"Those ovens scare me," Sophie admitted. "They're huge and really hot."

"Yeah, they are, but I'm careful."

"Speaking of cookies..." She walked back to the employee coat area and returned with my cookie tin in her hands. "Thanks for the PB and J cookies you made for me. No one has ever made me vegan cookies before. Not even my mom."

"You're welcome," I said. "It was fun."

"Did you post the recipe on Allrecipes.com like your other ones?"

"No."

"I wish you would. Vegans have a hard time finding good stuff."

I promised I would, and she said she'd post a

review and tell her vegan friends.

I cleaned out the pastry racks while she served croissants and *cafés crèmes* to a man and woman who'd just come in. They sat in a far corner, heads almost touching, voices low and intimate. I tried to avoid them.

Sophie noticed their obviously romantic bent too. "Did you ever hear back from that Davis, Marks guy?" she asked.

We'd talked about the date the day after, and she'd noted how much fun I'd had, even though I'd tried to downplay it to her. *And myself.* I knew she was just being nice, but I didn't need a reminder of my rejection.

"Nah," I said, shrugging it off. "It's okay. We didn't have all that much in common."

I thought about people like Bill and Jill, future pastor couple extraordinaire. Nate and Leah. Even Steve and Tanya. They just seemed to fit in so many ways.

"I think I need someone more interested in the stuff I'm interested in," I said. *Someone who is in my league and preferably French.*

We could both hear Luc's voice streaming in from the oven room. Sophie looked at him, then at me, and turned away.

She knows.

"Alexandra," Luc called, on cue.

"You got things here?" I asked, glad for the chance to excuse myself.

"Oh yeah," she replied, back to her normal self.

"Go on."

I slid down the glass on the pastry case and stood back to examine it. "*Voilà,*" I said. "Perfection."

In the bakery, the *Trois Amis* were rolling croissants.

"I want to show you how the ovens work," Luc said. "If I'm not here and Patricia isn't here, someone should know what to do."

I agreed, pleased and excited.

"The heat of the oven has made your face like a rose," Luc teased.

He showed me the oven's different settings and the proper procedure for turning them on and off.

"See how they swivel?" He reached in with a gloved hand and a pole and spun the racks inside the oven. "The bread is then baked evenly on all sides."

"I see!" I said. I liked everything about it: the tools of the trade, the smell of the bread, the baker himself. I understood him and his passions. And he, mine.

My lesson completed, he headed into the office to do paperwork, closing the door behind him, and I went back to *my* bakery. *All right, Patricia's bakery.* But mine for the day, the first day I was really in charge of any baking.

First, I rolled out the puff pastry for the *palmiers,* delicate flowers shaped like the palm of a hand. After forming them, I skillfully brushed on the glaze, like a Moroccan woman painting henna on the hands of her clients. I popped the cookies into the huge, floor-to-ceiling oven, rolling the baking cart in and shutting the door behind it.

Then I mixed up dark chocolate-chunk cookies, a favorite among our patrons. French foodies didn't like change; some people ate the same thing day after day. Or, if we did make a change, they expected it to be among the most traditional offerings. The vegan recipe might need to find a different bakery outlet. *Maybe when Sophie opened her coffee shop!*

A few minutes later, I realized the oven timer was going off. Had it been beeping for a minute or two already? I slid another huge tray of chocolate chunk dough balls onto the waiting oven rack and raced back to the oven room.

I grabbed an oven mitt, but in my rush, I grabbed a short one and not the one that reached all the way up to my elbows. I opened the oven door and wheeled the six-foot baking rack out of the oven. As I slid the tray of cookies off the rack, the most virginal part of my forearm bumped up against the rack's metal framework.

"Ahh!" I screamed. With great restraint, I managed not to drop the rack of palmiers onto the floor but onto the stainless steel counter next to the oven. Auguste heard me and raced into the bakery.

A livid red welt at least three inches long sprang up across my forearm. I pulled off the glove, gritting my teeth and trying not to cry while Auguste hovered over me, murmuring comforting things in French, like one would to a hurt child. Jacques and Guillaume arrived with Luc, who carried a first aid kit. He led me into the office and waved to the *Trois Amis* that things were okay. I walked quietly, in deep, throbbing pain, not wanting to disturb the few café customers.

"Sit, sit," Luc cooed in French, leading me to his chair. "Eh bien, this was not a good way to start your baking today," he said, but with more tenderness than reprimand.

He very gently spread ointment across my forearm, then covered it with a bandage. When he was all done, he said, "Now you have begun to gather the tattoos that mark true bakers."

"Yeah," I said. "I need to finish the cookies."

"*Non,*" Luc said. "No more by the ovens today. Give this a day to be still."

"But Patricia expects them to be done tomorrow," I protested.

"I will come in early tomorrow, and you can too, and we will have a *café crème* and you can bake before the rush. How about four?"

I smiled. "Thanks."

"*Voilà,* problem solved!"

I saw a small stack of confiture, the jam Luc brought back from *la belle France* each year. "Maybe this is a good time to talk about the rack of goods we can sell in the front of the store," I suggested.

Luc pulled a chair up next to me. "Maybe it is," he said, but his voice was somber. "I don't think this is a good time to start a product rack sales project right now, Alexandra. I'm trying to decide if we're going to open another store. I'm managing two stores at once, really. Patricia is getting ready to go back to France, and Margot, her sister, is preparing to come here very soon to learn how to work at the bakeries for the next six months. She'll bring others with her. I'm going back to France in July for both personal and professional reasons. And"—he held my gaze as he dropped the final bomb—"I talked with Sophie, and she's not convinced it would be a moneymaker."

Sophie! Since when did Sophie get to decide if things would be moneymakers? She hadn't said anything to me. Was she talking about this behind my back?

Luc must have read my face. "I asked her opinion, Alexandra, and as much as she knew you liked the idea, she had to tell me her own thoughts. So, *regrettablement,* the product racks will have to wait."

"*Je suis désolé,*" he continued to apologize, "because I know how important it is to you, and I care very much about that."

I was still trying to process this. "I understand." What else could I say?

The phone rang, and Luc turned to answer it. I stood up, preparing to head back to the bakery to do what cleaning I could with my right hand.

Out of the corner of my eye, I noticed a sheet of paper. It was the closing schedule that Luc and Patricia used to determine who would close the store on what days. It listed the schedule for May.

Luc and Patricia's names filled half the boxes. Sophie's name filled the rest.

Fourteen

Il faut savoir saisir sa chance.
You must take opportunity by the hand.

My face must have shown my general discouragement, because my dad started being really nice to me. Or maybe he realized he would miss me when they moved. I don't know. I had enough trouble trying to figure out my *own* emotions, much less anyone else's.

"If you give me a hand, I'll buy you a Red Mill burger for dinner," Dad said, walking past me on his way to pack some things in the basement. Most of them were going to the Salvation Army.

"You bet," I said. I pulled my hair back into a French twist so it'd be out of the way and headed downstairs. I scanned the basement, taking in the thirty years' worth of memorabilia. "You want to get this all done *tonight*?" I asked.

"No, but a lot of it, while your mother is out of the house. She's so sentimental, she'll coo over every little toy and blanket down here and nothing will get

233

done. She told me to do it while she's at Italian lessons."

Mom was blossoming under the twice-a-week lessons, and her friend Teresa had signed up too.

I dragged a box over and began to sort through the piles. Nate's Rollerblades! After he'd fallen at the rink during a church event and broken his wrist, Mom wouldn't let him go again. He wouldn't sell the Rollerblades, though, so here they sat. I put them into the Salvation Army box.

I flipped through my yearbooks. Tanya looked so young, a little pumpkin face before she thinned out as a teen. I set them aside to put with my things.

Oh! My kiddie kitchen utensils. I picked up the little pink spatula. I'd drawn a smile under two of the holes to make a face. My Mini Maddie measuring cup. My Easy-Bake Oven.

"Remember this, Dad?" I held up the pink oven. "Remember when I made you cupcakes and brownies?"

"Yes," he said, his gruff voice softening a little. "I remember how gummy those cupcakes were, with the messy white frosting and those little sprinkly things. But they were the best things I ever tasted because they came from my girl."

"And," I said, flashing the burn on my forearm, "I distinctly remember burning my hand on the light bulb. It must have been a sign!"

The Easy-Bake Oven reminded me of Patricia. She was nice to me for one whole day after I burned myself, then went back to snarling. She hadn't let me make anything new, but I was still in charge of cookies. And errands. And taking dictation on her product orders. The cookies, at least, were a step in the right direction.

An hour or two later, we'd made good progress and hauled everything to the end of the driveway for the Salvation Army to pick up the next day.

"Dad?" I asked. "How about if I drive, and I'll take you past my new apartment?"

He smiled. "Sure, honey, I'd love to see it."

We drove to Red Mill and ate our burgers, then headed downtown. When we pulled up in front of the building, I could tell he was genuinely impressed.

"This is a nice place, Lex."

We parked the car around the block and stood in front of the building.

"Secure entrance twenty-four hours a day," I said, proudly pointing out the thing I knew he'd think was the most important.

"And is it affordable?" he asked.

Okay, second-most important.

"I think so," I said. "If I get the promotion to assistant manager."

We walked around the building, and he looked at the flier. I pointed out the one bedroom I'd contracted.

"And what if you don't get the promotion?" Dad asked.

I know, I know. I'm banking quite a bit on something that has never been mentioned between

Luc and me, and that's looking even dimmer after seeing the closing schedule.

"If I don't, then I lose my deposit, and I find something small in West Seattle," I said. "I don't have many other options."

"A roommate?"

I shook my head. "I don't know anyone. And it's a one bedroom. I shared a one-bedroom place in college, with twin beds, and I don't want to do that again."

He seemed to understand that, and we drove home. "It's a terrific place, honey, and I hope you get it. But maybe you should think about a few other options. That's a lot of money to lose."

"I know," I admitted. It was half my savings. "But what other options?"

"Well, I met with Mack—my friend at Peterson's—the other day. He didn't mention a job, but it might be worth a follow-up."

I knew he was right. If that schedule meant what I thought it meant, I might be running out of options. "I'll call him tomorrow."

When we got home, I made white cupcakes with frosting and sprinkles, and left them on a plate in the kitchen with a little card that said, "Dad." Then I logged on to Allrecipes.com to see if there was any new feedback on my recipes. On a whim, I scrolled to the bottom of the page. At the very bottom, in tiny black letters, one phrase caught my eye.

Jobs

Inaction Designer
Licensing Coordinator
Sales
Recipe Writer

Recipe Writer!

I read the job description. I wouldn't create recipes, but I'd be figuring out how to make them work for the readers and making sure the ingredients were correct. And they were located in Seattle.

I quickly uploaded my résumé and grinned. I'd tell no one.

A recipe writer!

Sophie and I overcame our unspoken discomfort about the special products sales rack, and I didn't say anything about her closing the store several afternoons a week. I still didn't know what to make of it, but when I'd talked with Tanya about it, she'd agreed that it didn't look like a good sign. I was trying to share my faith with Sophie, though, and I truly liked her. I didn't want to burn that bridge.

After we cleaned the café on Sunday evening, I went back to clean the bakery section too.

"*Voilà, c'est le Phoenix,*" Patricia said gruffly, as I walked into the back.

I smiled. It was the closest she came to being

friendly. "Come on now, no more ashes since my one accident," I said, pointedly looking at her burned hands. "And I baked all last night." I lugged some large mixing bowls to the sink.

Luc came into the kitchen to chat with Patricia before leaving, as he usually did. "And just what did you bake, mademoiselle?"

"Rhubarb crisp," I said.

"*Buerk, la rhubarbe,*" Luc said. "*C'est une mauvaise herbe.*"

"It's not a weed!" I insisted. "It tastes wonderful. And rhubarb is listed in *Larousse.*" I trumped them, knowing a mention in *Larousse,* the bible of gastronomy, would end the discussion.

"What do you expect from a culture that uses cake mixes?" Patricia teased. "And thinks that a box of Jell-O qualifies as dessert? *Mais non.*" But I could tell she was impressed I knew rhubarb was in *Larousse.*

I strode past them, imitating their haughtiness. My culture did just fine with desserts.

When Luc and Patricia had finished their conversation, Luc said, "Well done, Alexandra. I'll see you tomorrow and taste what you can do. My money is on you, as Americans say."

He winked, and I recalled the smell of his aftershave and the closeness of his forearms leaning near mine as he helped me knead dough. He left the room, and my eyes trailed after him until Patricia called me.

"*Attention,* Alexandra," she said.

"*Oui?*"

"I'll be at La Couronne the entire day tomorrow getting the shop ready before *la famille* arrives from France. I do not have time to make the crème pâtissèrie before I leave. We have a special order for mille-feuilles. Can you make it in the morning, flash freeze it, and have it ready for the customers by tomorrow afternoon?"

I tried to maintain a competent, professional demeanor in spite of my joy. "I can." It's not like it was pediatric neurology or anything.

"*Bon,*" *she* said. "Save me some of the crème pâtissèrie so I can tell you how to adjust it for next time."

That was it. Nothing more. But it was enough.

The next morning I arrived early. Luc and Sophie and I had a cup of coffee, Luc and I lingering a bit longer than Sophie. I mixed the crème pâtissèrie and rolled out the pastry dough before I had to help Sophie with the morning rush. I tossed the mille-feuilles into the freezer, assembled and glazed with lemon and chocolate, just as the first customers arrived. I'd slice it when it was frozen, after the rush.

I'd been wrestling with my feelings since I'd seen the schedule. Sophie had no idea I'd been counting on getting the assistant manager's job, and it still wasn't a for-sure thing for her. Maybe Luc had simply asked her to fill in since I was busy in the bakery. Sophie wanted to open her own coffee shop soon. She'd be moving on.

I hadn't heard anything from Allrecipes.com in

the few days since I'd applied either. Most of their candidates had probably gone to culinary school.

I ran up front to help Sophie, who seemed totally discombobulated. She kept making eye contact with a scruffy guy in the back of the room.

"Are you okay?" I whispered after the rush.

"I'm taking a break," she said. She grabbed a cup of tea and sat with Mr. Scruffy.

I wiped down the counter and checked the clock. I could cut and plate the mille-feuilles in an hour. I wondered who had placed the special order. I hadn't looked, as it was one of our most popular items, but now I was dying to know. I couldn't leave the counter and register, though, until Sophie came back from her break.

Sophie toyed with her tea but didn't really drink it. Mr. Scruffy leaned away from her rather than toward her. Finally he left without giving Sophie any money for his pastry and coffee. She came back to the counter, sighed, and paid for it out of her own money.

"New friend?" I asked.

"Maybe," she said.

"I thought vegans didn't do animals," I teased.

Sophie cracked a smile and then laughed out loud. "Yeah, he doesn't have a lot of potential, does he?"

I shook my head. "Not good enough for Saint Sophia."

"Right," she said softly, thoughtfully. "Saint Sophia. No, he was a friend of Roger's. I think I'm done with that whole crowd."

I'd asked her back to church, but she hadn't wanted to come. She said she was busy, and she looked like she was being honest. Of course, I didn't want to go back either. I felt awkward. Constrained. Maybe I'd try again. I probably should, for Sophie's sake.

"You'd better get going on the special order," Sophie said. "It needs to be delivered. Since the day's deliveries have already gone out, I said you'd bring it by."

"No problem," I said. "Glad to help. Where's it going?"

She continued restocking the shelves like nothing was out of the ordinary. "Davis, Wilson, and Marks."

I stepped back. "And to *whom* is it being delivered?"

"Not Dan, if that's what you're asking. But it's being delivered to the same floor, so if you wanted to take a chance and stop by..."

"You're evil. Evil personified," I said.

"Yep," she said. "That's me. Better get going. It has to be there in an hour."

I walked back to the bakery and looked at myself in the big oven windows. Not too bad. Hair was okay. I needed to touch up my makeup.

Lexi! Get a hold of yourself. It's been weeks and the guy hasn't called you.

Yeah, but maybe he wanted to be pursued, like Nate said. *Guys want to feel wanted too.* Maybe he felt since he'd asked me out the first time and stopped by the café, that I should show some interest.

You know, go for it, I thought.

I readied the pastry trays and then took a few small pastry rounds and spread them with the crème pâtissèrie I'd made. That would be my excuse: I'd finally made my own, as he'd mentioned, and I wanted him to try it.

Auguste and I loaded everything into my car, and I drove to Dan's building, which was right across the street from Leah's office. I pulled into the loading zone and let the security guy know what I was doing. Then I brought box after box up to the twenty-seventh floor and set up the trays in the conference room. I'd brought some flowers to scatter around the tables, and I told the receptionist to call and we'd come and get the trays in the next week.

Then I went down to my car, took off my apron, and looked in the mirror. I opened my purse and slicked on some peach lipstick; I knew it looked good with my golden skin. I grabbed the little pink box with the special mille-feuille inside and headed back to the twenty-seventh floor.

"Can I help you? More to deliver?" the receptionist asked.

"Oh no, I'm bringing this by Dan Larson's office," I said. "Can you point me in the right direction?"

"Yes, about three-quarters of the way down that hall." She pointed to a long corridor carpeted in rich blue with stainless-steel-framed art hanging on the walls.

I walked down the hall, peeking into office windows. Lots of high heels and shiny hair. Lots of smart-looking people.

You're smart, I reminded myself. *Your hair is shiny.*

I tried to look like I knew what I was doing, but I still had to look into each and every office. Maybe she'd given me the wrong hallway.

Then I saw him. Actually, I didn't see his face first; I saw the suspenders, the cherry wood desk, and his strawberry blond hair nearly touching the brunette hair of a woman poring over a document with him.

His office was a mess. Stacks of paper squatted on every available surface. A tower of stacked Starbucks cups rose in the corner. A Nerf basketball hoop was hooked over the corner of one of the barrister bookcases. I liked that.

Dan and the woman stood on opposite sides of the desk, but the way they worked together looked...intimate. The woman laughed and pointed to something on the document, and Dan hit his forehead as if to say, "of course." She touched the back of his hand. The two of them bowed over the document again, and despite the circles under his eyes, he was smiling.

He didn't see me. Maybe there was nothing going on between them, but I wasn't up for an embarrassing confrontation if there was. After all, he hadn't called.

I looked at the pastry box in my hand, turned around, and walked back toward the receptionist.

"Did you find Dan?" she asked.

"Yes, I did," I said, not trusting myself to look at her. I took my miniature mille-feuille and headed toward the elevator.

The security guard seemed to sense my despair. "Anything I can do for you, miss?"

"No, thank you," I said and handed him the pink box. "Enjoy."

I got into my car and drove to L'Esperance, where I parked in the back. I sat in my car and let silent tears roll down my face for a few minutes, then pulled myself together and went back to work.

I always heard bad things came in threes. First, no e-mail from Allrecipes.com. Then Dan and The Brunette. And as I walked into the café, I saw Jill of the Eternal Clipboard.

She and Sophie were chatting.

"Lexi!" she trilled as I walked into the room. "Sophie said you were doing errands, but I wanted to wait. What a cute little shop you work at." She emphasized the word *little*. "If I come by this week for some lunch with my coworkers, maybe you could be our waitress!"

"Maybe," I said as sweetly as I could. "Sophie, I'm going back to make the pastries." I emphasized *make*. "Hope to see you soon," I told Jill, asking God to forgive me for the lie.

I ignored the questions in Sophie's eyes and took sanctuary in the pastry room. After a few minutes, I heard the bell over the door tinkle as Jill left.

Sophie cast me concerned looks for the rest of the day, but she didn't say anything until closing time. "Okay?" she asked after we finished cleaning.

"Yes."

"Did you see Dan?" she asked.

"Yes."

"Did you talk?"

"No. Here's the deal," I said. "Lawyers like lawyers. I've seen it in my own life. I don't like law. I like cooking. End of story."

"Okay," she said. "Your friend Jill asked me to come back to the Impact Group."

"What'd you say?"

"I said I'd love to," Sophie said. "I'm going to see when I can go."

I blinked. I had no idea she truly wanted to go back. And she hadn't asked if I was coming too.

So much to deal with in one day. Good for Sophie. Bad for me. Or was it?

When I got home that afternoon, I pulled the romantic white blouse out of my closet and looked at it.

I *was* supposed to make a move; I just made the wrong move. The wrong move with the wrong guy. I wouldn't make that mistake again.

"You don't mind coming with me, right?" Tanya asked, nervousness evident in her voice. We'd put the top down on her convertible, and I had a hard time hearing her. Not that I was complaining.

"To the counselor?" I asked.

She tightened her grip on the wheel. "I just wanted the moral support of someone sitting in the waiting room. My mother would completely panic, and Steve and I aren't really there yet."

Yet.

"What's your best friend for?" I said.

I sat in the office waiting room reading women's magazines while Tanya talked with her therapist. I'd come with her for the six months or so after it had happened, and I'd hoped never to be back. It was an unpleasant déjà vu.

After fifty minutes, Tanya emerged, wrote a check, and we left.

"How'd it go?" I asked.

"Good," she said. "I told her what brought all this back up, and we talked about how I could move past it."

"Are you coming back for more sessions?" I asked.

"If I need to," Tanya said. "One of the things that bugged me was the thought of another man—my husband, whoever he may be—touching me sexually in the same places that I was violated. The thought of it made me sick. I never wanted anyone to touch the same places."

"Hence, when things got more serious with Steve…"

"Yeah, when I thought he had potential, I backed

way off. But my counselor gave me a great fact to think about. Every year, ninety-eight percent of the atoms in the body are replaced. Every cell is renewed. Every three months, you have a new skeleton. Every six weeks, you have a new skin. The skin, the body that he raped, isn't there anymore. I'm a new me."

"You are a new you," I agreed, "inside and out."

We drove toward my house. She was going to drop me off and go on a date. I was going to read a magazine in my brother's old room.

"So, no future with Dan?" she said.

I shrugged. "He looked pretty tight with that other woman."

"Could you have been mistaken?"

I considered this. "Maybe. But it's not like he's called either." *Out of my league.*

"So I guess that leaves French Hottie, eh?" Tanya teased.

I laughed. "The only French hottie I've been in close contact with is the oven. But that might change soon." I paused a moment. "I forgot to tell you that Dan knew the story of the loaves and fishes," I said. I could see her mind scrambling to catch up. "I mean, on our date, he knew it."

She heard the sorrow in my voice. "That's nice, Lex," she said and laid her hand over mine for a minute.

"So, does Steve pass the test?" I asked. The sun was setting over the Sound, and I cheered at the thought of how awesome it would look from my new apartment. I was already planning my open house.

"Hmm," she answered. "Not sure yet if he passes the test or not."

I smiled, remembering when we'd decided on "The Test." One day when we were teenagers, we came upon her mother shaving the hair out of her dad's ears. We were totally grossed out.

"Older men grow hair in their ears," her mom had said, laughing. "If you're going to get married, you're going to end up doing this someday."

From that point on, it became our test. Would we be willing to shave this man's ears in twenty or thirty years? If the answer was no, he wasn't someone to spend a life with.

"He isn't particularly hairy," Tanya noted, hope in her voice.

"Yet." I wiggled my eyebrows at her suggestively.

"Speaking of weddings," she said, shifting gears on the Beetle as we went uphill, "how are things going with Nate and Leah?"

"All right. I never see Nate. He's so busy working on a case that they haven't even put money down on a place to live yet. He's had migraines for two weeks. Leah and I are going shopping for shower stuff soon, though."

"Sounds good," she said. "Steve set the date aside so he could escort me."

"Yeah," I said. "I know. I—I think I'm going to ask Luc. I know he's planning to go back to France for a while this summer, but I don't think he'll be gone by then."

"Are you going to start with him at the wedding?" she asked dubiously. "I mean, as the first personal thing you do together?"

"Nope. My parents are going to Whidbey next weekend to move some stuff into the new house. I'm going to ask Luc over for dinner. *A deux.*"

Sandra Byrd

Fifteen

Les apparences sont souvent trompeuses.
Appearances are deceiving.

Before going to work early the next morning I quickly checked my e-mail, expecting nothing.

I was wrong.

In my inbox, received sometime during the night, was an e-mail from Allrecipes.com.

I prayed before opening it, voice trembling. "I'll take what you give me, Lord," I said. I'd just read the section of Matthew where Jesus taught the vineyard workers to be content with whatever work they'd been assigned and the pay they'd agreed to work for.

I felt peaceful but resigned myself to the e-mail being an auto response saying they'd contact me if something was available.

Instead, it was a personal note.

From: Allrecipes.com

To: Stuart, Lexi

Subject: Job Application

Dear Ms. Stuart,

**Thank you for your application. We
would be very interested in meeting
you in person to discuss the recipe
entrée job. Please call me at your
earliest convenience to schedule an
interview. We'll be interviewing all
through the week.**

"They want to interview me!" I shouted.

My father ran into the room in his slippers.
"What's the matter?" he asked, scalp pinking up.

I pointed at the screen. "I'm going to have a job
interview at Allrecipes.com, the place that I post my
recipes!" I jumped up and down like a teenager, just
as Mom entered the room.

Dad looked proud, Mom hugged me, and I
hugged her right back. At my first break this
morning, I'd call. After a round of congratulations, I
headed out to the garage. That's when a troubling
thought hit me.

I'd made a six-month commitment to Luc.
Although that was before I'd begun to doubt the
assistant manager's position. But Luc didn't know
that, and I'd promised.

I almost ran several red lights on the way to
work. At work, we were preparing for the visitors
from France, coming over Memorial Day weekend
and staying a bit beyond. Luc seemed kind of wired,

252

so I pretty much stayed out of his way. I realized that the clock was ticking if I was going to have a date for the wedding, and I still planned to ask him to dinner. If I'd had another option, I'd have taken it and not pushed things with Luc, but I had no other option. *Sometimes,* I told myself, *when you're out of options, you do things you might not have done otherwise and it all works out for the best. In theory, anyway.*

I snuck away for a break in my car—the only private place I could think of besides the walk-in—and called Allrecipes.com. I hoped no one on the street honked or made a ruckus. I asked for Cameron, as I'd been instructed. He answered, a warm Caribbean lilt to his voice.

"Hello," I said. "This is Alexandra Stuart. You e-mailed me this morning about the recipe job?"

"Ah yes, Ms. Stuart. So nice to hear from you. I loved the enthusiasm in your letter and the fact that you already use Allrecipes.com. When can you come in for an interview? I am interviewing every afternoon this week between two and four."

I'd opened early today, so I could leave by three. Tomorrow and the next day I'd have to stay later.

"Would today be too soon?" I asked. "Four o'clock?"

"Not at all," he said. "I look forward to seeing you then."

I hung up, nervous, not knowing what I'd do if he offered me the job.

I helped Patricia scrub down the entire bakery. It took hours, and my hands were red. She didn't notice or even make polite conversation.

"Margot will be here in a few days," she barked. "Everyone from France is coming next week. I want things to look perfect!"

I looked forward to Margot's arriving. She had to be easier to work with than Patricia.

Once we'd finished, Patricia took two small, identical stainless steel bowls of cream out of the walk-in.

"Before we wash these, I want you to taste something," she said. She dipped a clean spoon into each and bid me to taste them, which I did.

"This one," I said, pointing at the first, "is sweeter. And maybe not as evenly blended."

I tasted the second one again. "Not as sweet, but creamier."

"*Bon,*" Patricia said gruffly. "Which cream would you use with the mille-feuille?"

"The second, less-sweet one," I said, "because the mille-feuille has a sweet glaze."

"Correct," Patricia said. "And what would you use the other one for?"

I ran through some options in my mind. "Cream puffs?"

She gave a stiff nod. "*Oui.* The first one, the sweeter cream, was the one you made last week. It was adequate."

Adequate was high praise from Patricia.

"But I shouldn't have used it in the mille-feuille," I said. "Too sweet, right?"

"Too sweet," she agreed. "Hopefully, you've learned something." She pursed her lips, indicating her doubt.

I felt almost honored that she was teaching me something. "Thank you."

She wordlessly handed me both bowls, and I went back into the kitchen to wash them. I had a lot to learn.

Even taking the stress of the French visitors into account, Sophie seemed weird to me. She avoided me all day, not meeting my gaze and making excuses about why she had to be at the other end of the restaurant whenever we worked together. I offered to drive her home, and she politely refused.

"I'm going to look at an apartment after work."

"Sophie, how great!" I said. "Tell me all about it."

Reluctantly, it seemed, she told me it was a studio near L'Esperance, so that she could walk to and from work. "It has a peek view of the Sound too," she said.

"I'm so glad!" I told her. "I know how much that view of the Sound means to me at my new place. We'll be neighbors! Within a few blocks of each other."

"Cool!" she agreed, but she seemed sad. After finishing her work, she went to the back to talk with the *Trois Amis,* and I opened the cash register to count out the bulk of it and give it to Luc for the afternoon deposit.

Under the cash drawer were this week's pay envelopes. I grabbed mine to put into my purse. Below mine lay Sophie's. The wording on her envelope caught my eye.

Sophie Straccia, Assistant Manager, L'Esperance

I picked it up. *What?*

Sophie came back to the front.

"What's the matter?" she asked. I probably looked as malarial on the outside as I felt on the inside.

I still held her pay envelope. "I wasn't snooping," I said, trying to find my footing. "I was just getting my paycheck."

"Oh, I'm so sorry, Lexi," she said. "The accountant brought the checks before lunch. I know Luc has been meaning to talk with you. He asked me not to say anything until he told you himself, but he's been swamped. And he just asked me a day or two ago."

"Oh," I said. "Well, congratulations."

How could she? Didn't she know I was hoping for that job?

Well, no, she didn't. We'd never talked about it. Luc had never mentioned it to either of us. I'd just assumed...and she was probably hoping for that job too.

Luc walked in. He must have guessed from my expression and general confusion what had happened. "Alexandra? Could we meet in my office for a moment?"

I wordlessly handed Sophie her pay envelope, then followed Luc into the office. He closed the door.

"Alexandra," he said, "Please let me express my deepest regret for not talking with you about this sooner. I have been so busy preparing for our guests from France that some things got away from me."

"No worries," I mumbled. "You certainly have the right to do what you need to do here."

Luc nodded. "Yes, but you are very important to me, and I didn't want you to find this out in this way. Sophie has been with us for almost a year, and I felt she needed to have the opportunity to be the assistant manager, if she wanted it."

"She doesn't speak French," I said miserably, trying to point something in my favor. As soon as it was out of my mouth, though, I realized how petty it sounded. "I'm sorry, that wasn't nice."

"*Non, non,* it's fine," Luc said. "*C'est vrai,* she doesn't speak French. But, in reality, she doesn't need to speak French to do a good job as an assistant manager. And she is a good organizer."

He paused. "You have many talents, Alexandra. And someday you may find yourself managing the front house of a bakery too. Although, I doubt it."

He, too, thought I was an underperformer. I sighed deeply.

Since seeing that closing schedule, I'd been thinking in the back of my head that he might ask Sophie to be the manager. She was there first. But then, I thought, he might train me to manage the next bakery his family opened. But now he was saying that wasn't going to happen either.

"I think very highly of you," he said, taking my hand in his. "Very highly. And I do think you have a future." He looked deeply into my eyes. "One that is becoming more and more clear to me."

"What do you mean?" I asked, heart pounding. I tried not to focus on his hand holding mine. *Is he suggesting that he and I might have a future together?*

"First, I must check on some details. I promise to speak with you soon." The telephone rang. He chatted for a minute, and it was clear it was something that needed his immediate attention. "We will talk more later, Alexandra, I promise," he said, covering the mouthpiece of the phone. "Do you need to go home for the rest of the day?"

Although I didn't need to, he was offering me an opportunity. I could go home, shower again after working in the bakery all day, and put on some clean clothes before the Allrecipes.com interview.

"Maybe just a little early," I said. He looked sympathetic. It made me feel worse. He was letting me off early so I could go to a job interview that might result in my leaving before the promised six months.

I exited Luc's office and found Sophie in the café.

"I've got to help in the bakery," I said. "Is everything under control up here?"

"Oh yeah," she said. "It's fine."

I started walking toward the bakery—shuffling, really—then turned back. "Sophie?"

"Yeah?"

"I really am glad for you," I said. "You earned it."

She walked over and hugged me. "Thanks, Lexi. I wasn't sure how you were going to take it. I thought maybe you'd be interested in the position, but then I thought, *Nah, she'd rather work in a bakery than run a café!*"

I wouldn't be running anything except my car engine. If it even turned over this afternoon.

She went back to work, a bounce in her step, and I squeezed back tears. There was no way I could afford to move into my apartment now if I kept working here.

I left work a bit later, called Tanya, and left a message on her voicemail. She was probably in an after-school meeting.

"I didn't get the job; Sophie did. Please pray for me. I have another job interview this afternoon, and I'm really confused about everything."

Then I turned my phone all the way off and drove home, passing my apartment building. I looked longingly at it, not knowing what to do. I drove down I-5 and onto the West Seattle Bridge, but instead of heading up the hill, toward home, I went down, toward the beach. It was a weekday, and cool and blustery. I'd probably have the place to myself.

I parked the car, took a blanket out of the trunk's emergency kit that Dad had packed for me, and walked toward the sand.

I kicked my shoes off and dug in my heels. I closed my eyes and let the tears course down.

God, what am I going to do now?

I'd meant what I'd said to Sophie. I understood that she'd been there longer than me and had paid those dues. But hadn't I paid some dues, too, working hard through college?

I let the tears dry on my face and the wind whip some pink into my golden skin. I liked the windburn. It made me feel on the outside how I felt on the inside.

I needed to pull myself together. I had a job interview for a job I'd really like, that might get me out of the dead end in which I suddenly found myself. But if I got it, and I took it, I'd be breaking my agreement with Luc and letting him and Sophie down when they needed me most.

When I got home, my mom was in the family room, packing photo albums and scrapbooks. "Come on in, honey," she called. "So much to do! Are you sure you don't want to come to Whidbey with Dad and me next weekend?"

I didn't answer. She didn't look up.

"Then the shower, the wedding, Italy, and oh my, moving in," she continued. She finally looked up and saw the expression on my face. "Lexi! What's the matter?" She set the scrapbook down.

"Sophie got promoted to assistant manager," I said. "And Luc said he couldn't really see me in that position anytime in the future."

"Well, why ever not?" Mom asked.

"I don't know; it wasn't the time to ask."

She pulled me to her, and I folded into her arms like I did as a girl. *You never outgrow the need for a hug from your mom.*

"What are you going to do?" she asked.

"Go to the Allrecipes interview at four," I said.

"That might be just the place for you. Do you know how much they pay?"

I shook my head. I'd find out soon, I hoped.

I showered and wrapped my hair in a towel, then sat on my bed and thought about what to wear to the interview. I had to leave in half an hour. I spotted my Bible on the nightstand and picked it up on impulse, searching for the verse I'd read a couple weeks ago.

"Are not two sparrows sold for a penny? Yet not one of them will fall to the ground apart from the will of your Father. And even the very hairs of your head are all numbered. So don't be afraid; you are worth more than many sparrows."

I closed my eyes and prayed. *I'm not a sparrow, Lord, but I feel like I'm falling to the ground. Please catch me. And put me in the nest in which I belong.*

By the time I'd located Allrecipes on Third Street, I

was starting to get excited. It was really close to my parents' house, but I'd been commuting to Seattle every day, anyway, and if I took the cool apartment, I could certainly drive here. I felt pretty good about things.

"I'm here to see Cameron," I said to the receptionist.

She seemed very kind and asked me to sit while she paged him. A few minutes later, he came forward.

"Alexandra?" he asked in that deep voice with its lovely lilt.

I stood, getting a good vibe already.

He showed me into his office. "Tell me about yourself and the kind of job you're looking for."

I told him about my college degree and lifelong love of food and recipe experimentation, from Jell-O cube salad as a girl to Boyfriend Bait Beef Stroganoff.

He laughed aloud. "Who named that?"

"My roommate said it was boyfriend bait so that's what I decided to call it. Boyfriend Bait," I said proudly.

"Let me tell you about the job," he said. "It's entry level, inputting recipes when needed, organizing our online files, sometimes checking things out if something seems wrong with an entry. You'd be technical support, but there would be some chance to interact with the food now and then."

Entry level. Well, as Nate said, I wasn't going to be vice president out of the chute. "Is there room for advancement?" I asked.

"Definitely."

We chatted for a few minutes longer, and then the interview was over. I'd flunked enough interviews to know when one had gone wrong, and this one had not!

Cameron shook my hand. "I'll be contacting people in the next few weeks," he said. "Thank you for coming in."

"Thank you for interviewing me," I said. "I appreciate your time."

On the way home, I felt hopeful. The job had a lot of promise, and if I did leave L'Esperance, it would make it easier to date Luc.

But there was still Sophie. I truly didn't want to leave her in a pinch when she was getting her first crack at management. Plus, Luc seemed pretty set on heading back to France this summer.

Despite my new hope, none of my questions were easier to answer.

At home, I changed into some jeans and sat in the hammock in the backyard. I'd brought my Bible outside. After reading a bit of Matthew earlier, I decided to get chapter twenty-two done as well. Only six more chapters and I'd have read the whole thing.

I opened the Bible and nearly closed it again. A chapter about a wedding and a bridegroom. I couldn't escape weddings and romance no matter where I turned, even in my Bible, for heaven's sake. *No pun intended.*

Who *was* I going to invite? Maybe this was encouragement to ask Luc. *Yeah!*

I read further. "'Love the Lord your God with all your heart and with all your soul and with all your mind.' This is the first and greatest commandment. And the second is like it: 'Love your neighbor as yourself.'"

God, I've been trying, trying, to love you with all my heart and soul and mind. I just don't know what else to do, and I'm not feeling good about church.

I should try another church. Maybe that little Church on the Hill in Ballard. I went into the house, looked them up online, and smiled. I'd go Sunday.

A few minutes later, I heard some commotion in the house and realized Nate and Leah were here. I went into the kitchen and saw them sitting with my parents.

"Hey!" Leah stood and gave me a big hug. She looked so happy.

"What are you guys up to?" I asked.

"Oh, we're just getting ready to sign a lease on an apartment," Nate said. "Nothing like yours, according to Leah, but okay for now. We'll live there for a few years until we buy something, and that will be fine."

"Oh good! I'm glad you found something," I said with forced cheerfulness, wondering if I could even

264

keep my apartment.

"I can't wait for my wedding shower," Leah said. "My mom isn't bugging you, is she?"

I chuckled. "Nope. I'm screening my calls. But seriously, she's handled almost everything by herself and taken all my suggestions. She's been good."

I stayed and chatted for a few more minutes, then made up a reason to excuse myself. Everything was going perfectly for Nate and Leah, and the comparison to my own tattered life was more than I could handle after my day.

The next morning I arrived at L'Esperance early, like every Saturday. Sophie was already there.

"Hey, it's my early day," I said.

"I'm trying to come in early every day now," she said, blushing. "Anyway, you'll never guess who called me last night."

"Who?" I asked, wiping down the coffee machine. "Roger?"

She made a face. "Nah, we're kaput. I don't think I'm going to date anyone for a while until I get my head straight about the job and why I keep picking Rogers." She shook her head. "No, it was Michelle."

"Michelle?" I asked, not able to place the name.

"From your church group. She asked if I was going to the barbecue tonight, and I told her you'd already asked me weeks ago. If it's still okay with you, I'd like to come."

I sighed inwardly and fixed on a smile before turning to her. "Oh, I'm sorry. When you said no, I made other plans. I promised my mom I'd bake a cake with her tonight. I know that sounds crazy, but they're moving soon, and this is her preschool class's graduation cake…"

Sophie held up her hand. "Say no more. It's fine! I'll go another time."

"No, no, you can…borrow my car," I said. I wanted her to go, but how would I get to church tomorrow?

Sophie stopped wiping down the mirrors. "Really?"

I nodded. "Really. Take me home tonight. We'll bring the bread over to Pete's and then you can have the car until the morning. I'll get a ride to work after church, and we'll be set."

"Thanks," Sophie said softly. "If there's any way I can help you, here at work or anything, let me know."

"I will," I said.

Later that night, after Sophie had dropped me off, my mom and I packed some of the kitchen and then baked several cakes. We took a break to let them cool before frosting them, and I heard her talking with my dad in the next room.

"I guess Nate and Leah won't take that apartment after all," she said. "There's going to be bridge construction nearby for six months, and Nate doesn't think he could handle the noise."

It's too bad they couldn't find someplace nice like mine...

"*Maybe they could,*" came the voice inside of me.

It was so clear, I dropped a pan on the floor.

"You okay?" my mom called from the other room.

"Yes," I answered.

No. Don't ask that of me too. It's too much.

I heard nothing else, but the second half of a verse came back to me.

"*Love your neighbor as yourself.*"

"Who *is* my neighbor?" I muttered. I refused to consider the thought further. Why would God suggest such a thing?

We frosted the cakes, wrapped them, and put them into the freezer in the garage. My mom looked sad, and I felt it too. We'd come a long way from our Easy-Bake days. We were transitioning, both of us, and we knew it. Our unspoken thoughts filled the kitchen loud and clear.

I went into the living room while my mom cleaned up. "Dad? Can I borrow your truck in the morning?"

He gave me a quizzical look. "Why? What's wrong with your car?"

"I loaned it to a friend so she could go to church tonight, but I need to go to church in the morning."

My mother came in. "But we can go together, honey!" she said, smiling.

267

"Well...uh...I think I'm trying a new church."

She stopped. My dad turned off the television. "Which one?" Her voice sounded hesitant. She was always afraid we were going to fall in with some cult.

I couldn't resist. "Have you ever heard of Barb's House of Miracles?"

They both looked dumbstruck.

"No, I'm kidding," I said. "Well, that's where Sophie wanted to go, but I brought her to your...er...our church. But I feel like I might want to try somewhere new. And since Sophie has my car, and Dad won't be going in the morning, I wondered if I could use the Dodge."

"Where are you really going?" my mother asked, looking relieved it wasn't Barb's.

"Church on the Hill, in Ballard."

She smiled resignedly. "Enid's daughter goes there." That made it acceptable.

The next morning I drove to Ballard and parked in the small church parking lot. Candles burned on the altar, and there was a large, simple cross in the middle of the back wall. Late-spring light flooded into the room, catching the dust motes in a stained-glass dance. Most of the people were in their twenties. There were a few young families, but for some reason, the squawking kids didn't bother me today.

We started with worship, and partway into the

second song I felt the desire to lift my hand in worship. I was sitting next to a woman and didn't want to smack her with my hand, so I kept it to myself. But then she stood and raised her arms, and soon half the congregation had stood and lifted their hands in worship. The other half didn't, but they didn't seem pressed to do so either.

I stayed seated, but I lifted my hands, closed my eyes, and felt the Spirit of God electrify me from the inside out.

I'm home.

After church, I shook hands with the pastor, who looked about thirty-five, and his wife. I would have stayed to chat, but I had to get to work. I revved up the truck and headed out of Ballard, toward home.

I turned the corner of a familiar street. And then I saw him jogging.

Don't look up, don't look up, I pleaded, but he looked up anyway, right into my eyes.

Dan.

Sandra Byrd

Sixteen

Chaque route a une fourchette.
There's always a fork in the road.

"How'd it go last night?" I tied my apron behind my back.

"Really nice," Sophie said. "I left my piercings in, and no one even stared."

"Not even Jill?" I asked.

"All right, Jill did." She laughed. "But she wasn't snotty or anything."

Luc rushed around in the back.

"What's going on?" I said, noting the dramatic change from the lazy Sundays we usually had.

"*Lay Francays* are coming today," Sophie said. I giggled at her mangled French, and she laughed with me.

"Alexandra!" Luc called. I headed back to the bread room, where he pulled me over to the croissant table. "Look at this," he said. He pointed out a few batches of dough that were proofing too fast due to the unusual heat and the fact that

Jacques hadn't taken the dough out early enough. I bent over the dough with him, nearly touching heads, measuring.

"You want me to help roll?" I asked. Normally, that wasn't something I did, but I could, in a pinch.

"*Oui,*" he said. "Go tell La Sophie what you'll be doing and come on back here."

I went up front and noticed someone striding out the front door.

"Was that Dan?" I asked Sophie.

She nodded.

"Did he buy anything?"

"Nope," she said. "He just came in, looked around, and left."

"Did he ask for me?"

"No," Sophie said softly. "He didn't say anything."

Oh.

I helped roll the croissants and went over and over in my mind the words I'd use when asking Luc to dinner. I'd have to catch him before the guests arrived, and I hoped he wouldn't be too busy with them to have dinner. *But you can't eat with your cousins every night, right?*

At lunchtime, I saw my chance. I'd been helping in the back, keeping it clean for when Patricia arrived with her sister, *Le Monstre,* as the *Trois Amis* sometimes jokingly referred to her. I heard Luc walk in the front door and went to meet him. I took off my floury apron and set it aside.

I stood right outside the office door. "Do you

have a minute?" I asked.

"*Mais oui,*" he said. "Come on in. I have just a moment."

I went into the office. "You know how interested I am in cooking," I started.

"*Oui,* of course. You're a fine emerging cook."

"Well, I've been working on some new recipes," I said, "and there are some professional things I'd like to ask you. I wondered if you might be free to come over for dinner on Friday night this week."

I held my breath. He looked like he was holding his too. For once, he seemed at a loss for words. I couldn't tell how, but from his face, I could see that I'd completely misread the situation.

"It's a lovely invitation," he said hesitantly, "but I have guests in town."

"Oh yes, your cousins."

"Yes, my cousin Margot," Luc said, pausing slightly. "And my fiancée, Marianne."

His *fiancée?*

With the facial self-control of a politician, I held the smile on my face and groped for the right words. I had to do something to rectify the situation. I had just invited an engaged man to dinner. Not that I'd known.

"I...uh...they'd all be welcome at dinner," I choked out. What else could I do?

His face relaxed into that grin I used to think was foxy and now thought might actually be wolfish. He kissed both my cheeks. "I think everyone will think it's divine to eat at an American home. Thank you.

May we bring some wine?"

"Yes, please," I stammered.

"Let me know the menu when you've figured it out," he said, "and I will bring something appropriate."

With forced dignity I got a fresh apron, tied it around my waist, and walked back to the café. I mindlessly wiped down the counter.

"Did you know Luc was engaged?" I asked Sophie.

She shook her head. "No, but I suspected he might be seriously involved, based on something I'd heard Auguste say once. Why?"

"No reason," I said. "I've just invited him and his fiancée and the two evil stepsisters over for dinner next Friday night."

"Oh, I'm sorry, Lexi. Were you...were you interested in Luc?"

"Not a good idea to date your boss," I said by way of a nonanswer. "But," I added with emphasis, "I never did think it was cool that women wear engagement rings and men don't."

Friday night came soon enough. I had no date for my brother's wedding. I had no way to afford the one place I had picked out to live, and it seemed like God was urging me to offer that peach to my brother, who already had everything. I had no job that would lead anywhere.

I decided to have a good time that night. What else could I do?

I opened the door precisely at six, as the four of them arrived. In spite of having almost every reason not to, I liked Marianne. She was kind and petite and fashionable in a nicely cut teal blue suit, but all in a way that made you feel she was being herself and not trying to compete with anyone else. She kissed both my cheeks as she came through the door and took off her shoes, obeying the polite sign requesting them to do so, even though I could see them looking at one another, puzzled. We spoke French all evening, a treat for me.

"Where do I set these?" Margot barked, holding out two bottles of wine.

"Here, let me take your jacket," I answered sweetly. I hung up their jackets and then took the wine from her and carried it to the kitchen. They trailed along.

What had I gotten myself into?

Luc opened the bottle of wine and divided it among the five crystal glasses my mother had left out. She was a little disappointed too, when she'd found out that Luc was taken.

"Make the best of it," Mom had said before leaving for Whidbey.

"I don't seem to have much choice, do I?" I answered. I wasn't going to be a martyr, though. I did have one piece of wickedness planned for dessert.

I served fresh Washington clams steamed in

their own liquor with drawn butter and sea-salted sourdough. Next was a light spinach salad and then, of course, salmon. "Washington is known worldwide for its salmon," I said. This one I had poached Japanese style with tamari, and I served it with cucumbers dressed with rice vinegar and jasmine rice.

"You are the proverbial thorn among the roses, as my father would say," I said to Luc, noting that there were four women and one man. I couldn't help it: I meant a thorn in other ways too.

"Too bad Philippe couldn't be here," Margot said. It was clear from the way her face relaxed that she doted on him.

"Philippe is our younger brother," Patricia said. "Also a baker, of course. He's at home, in France."

"He's a Protestant, like you, Alexandra," Luc filled in helpfully.

"A rabid Christian Protestant," Margot grumbled.

Luc looked at her out of the corner of his eye and quickly changed the subject. He pushed his plate away. "Absolutely delicious."

"*C'est formidable,*" Margot agreed, and Patricia looked at me a little appreciatively, although giving no ground. I think the burn put me in another league in her mind, and for that I was glad.

We moved to the living room.

"May I help you with the coffee and dessert?" Marianne asked.

Luc beamed, and I felt so mixed up. I had been

attracted to him in a physical kind of way, but that was before I knew he was engaged. Had I misread his French flirtatiousness for real interest? Or had I simply labeled it what I wanted it to be?

I still felt something for him, but the more I got to know Marianne, the more I felt that recede. Of course, that left a void in my heart.

Or maybe it just made the one already there seem even more painfully empty.

"*Mais oui,* please help me," I answered Marianne. Once in the kitchen, I shared my secret with her.

"I've planned a special dessert. Something very American, but that will surprise both Patricia and Luc." I told her the story behind it, about their disdain for cake mixes, and she laughed along with me.

I think, under different circumstances, we could have been friends.

I cut the dessert into pieces and plated them on the fine Belleek china my mother had unpacked from the new house just for this occasion. Marianne and I carried the plates into the living room and served dessert. We each took a small bite, watching Luc and Patricia for their reaction.

"*Délicieux!*" Margot proclaimed. "And I should know."

"Is there a secret ingredient in this recipe?" Luc asked, eyes twinkling in a friendly manner. I think he was on to me.

"*Mais oui,*" I said. "But first, please tell me, do

you like it?"

"You win," Patricia said begrudgingly as she scraped the crumbs from her plate. Marianne and I laughed together, and when I shared the joke with the others, Luc laughed too, though Patricia and Margot barely smiled.

After dessert I cleared the dishes and left them quietly chattering, satisfied, I hoped, that they realized Americans weren't complete culinary barbarians.

As I approached the living room again, I heard Patricia ask Luc, "Have you asked Alexandra yet?"

"*Non,*" he answered. "I haven't found the right time. Maybe after the week's vacation."

"Maybe," Margot sniffed. "I'm still not sure it's a good idea."

What could *that* mean?

Let Them Eat a Perfectly Divine Coconut Cake

(with a Cake Mix!)

Ingredients:

**One box butter recipe yellow cake mix
One small box coconut cream instant pudding
3 eggs
1 1/3 cup coconut milk (not coconut cream). You may have to emulsify this as it comes out of the can separated.**

1/2 tsp coconut extract
1 stick of butter, softened

Frosting:
1 stick butter, softened
4 cups powdered sugar
1/8 cup milk or cream
1 tsp coconut extract

Shredded Coconut
Chopped Pecans (if desired)

Directions:
First, mix together the cake mix and the instant pudding till completely combined. Then add the 3 eggs, the coconut milk, the coconut extract, and the butter.

Blend for about 3 minutes in standing mixer or 5 minutes with handheld, in order to give the pudding time to develop.

Spread into two 8" round greased/floured cake pans. Light aluminum works better than dark or glass. Bake for 30 minutes at 350 until the cakes are just set and barely beginning to pull away from the pans. Don't overbake till edges are brown or pulling away from pan. Let cool completely.

Whip the frosting ingredients together

until completely fluffy. Frost the cooled cake, placing the first cake layer, round side down, on a plate, then spread frosting across the middle. Put the flat side of the other layer down on frosted center. Frost sides and top of cake.

Toast some coconut till golden brown (not dark brown) in the oven. Chopped pecans, too, if you prefer. Sprinkle on top of cake.

The next week at work was busy, as Luc and Patricia were in and out. They spent most of their time entertaining the guests or looking for property for a new bakery, maybe on the east side of town.

"Guess you really get to be the manager this week, eh?" I teased Sophie. "Don't fire me."

"Ha ha, Lexi," she said. "I wouldn't fire you, ever, but that doesn't mean you won't quit. I desperately hope you won't! Have you decided what to do after your commitment is up?"

"Not yet. I might have an option."

Sophie stopped counting cash into the deposit bag. "Why not wait just a little bit longer to decide, until all the brouhaha from the visitors is over?"

"Why? Luc has made it clear I'm not manager material in his eyes." I tried to keep my voice positive, but I knew my disappointment and anxiety leaked out. Because we'd had guests at dinner, I never had the business one-on-one with him I'd hoped for.

"You'll see your uncle at the wedding," Sophie persisted. "No sense rushing things."

"Yeah, but I have to decide really quickly what to do about my apartment. I can't afford it on my L'Esperance pay."

Sophie only said, "Just don't rush." I had the feeling she knew more than she was telling, but I couldn't get anything else out of her. Everyone seemed to know something I didn't—Patricia's comment the other night, now Sophie.

I decided to walk down the street to a cake bakery on my lunch hour that day to check out a show cake for Leah's wedding shower. Her mom didn't want homemade.

Halfway there, my phone rang. It was a number I didn't recognize, but I answered it anyway.

"Hello?"

"Hello," came a lilting Caribbean voice. "May I speak with Alexandra?"

"This is Alexandra," I said, my head starting to buzz.

"This is Cameron from Allrecipes. I'm calling to tell you that the job is yours, if you'd like it."

"The job is mine?" I said excitedly before calming into a more professional mode.

"The job is yours."

I walked and talked at the same time as he explained the position and the pay—not great, but it would allow me to keep the apartment if I tightened my budget everywhere else.

"I'll need your answer within a week," he said, "so I can get back with the other candidates. By the way, Alexandra," he added with a grin in his voice, "I made your Boyfriend Bait Beef Stroganoff. It was fantastic."

I laughed out loud, thanked him profusely for his time, and hung up. I walked a bit farther down the street and sat on the bench outside "my" apartment building.

The job was mine! But what about Sophie? She'd made it so clear she wanted me to stay. And I *had* made a commitment until July, at least, longer if I wanted to help out Sophie.

What should I do? I asked God. *What is the right thing to do?*

I now knew he wasn't going to make every decision for me. Like my parents. On one hand, it irritated me that they were still trying to make decisions for me or my life, with their values. That they still thought of me as the mythological Pan, except half woman, half girl.

On the other hand, the idea of making all these decisions on my own and living with the consequences scared me.

The same was true with God, I realized. It was time to make some choices on my own.

A clutch of preschool kids hopped by, chirping with their teacher. Enjoying life.

I was too young to give up my dreams. I wanted

to enjoy my life too.

I stood up, walked down to the cake bakery, and placed the order for Leah's shower Friday night. Then I headed back to L'Esperance.

I was in another world when cooking and baking. I could see new recipes emerging from old. I could smell when a cake was done without looking at the timer. I could taste the subtle difference between baking with vanilla sugar as opposed to vanilla extract. I knew which vegetables needed to be blanched and which did not.

Yes. I've found my place.

I walked into L'Esperance and got ready to prep tomorrow's pastries. Sophie came skidding into the pastry room. "Here," she said, thrusting a card at me.

"What is it?" I took it from her hand.

"He asked for you," she said. I read the business card. *Dan Larson.*

"I'm sure anyone can fill out his order," I said. I just didn't feel up to this right now.

"He didn't leave an *order*, Lexi! He wanted to talk with you. He said he had a meeting tonight, but would stop by tomorrow morning. I told him you'd be here early with the *Trois Amis,* getting ready to bake. I bragged on you, told him you've been doing quite a bit of the baking lately." She grinned.

"Oh okay," I said. "Maybe he simply wants me to place the order since I took all the others."

Sophie rolled her eyes. "Oh yeah, guys do that all the time. They come in to place an order at five in the morning. Right."

I caved. She had me there. But was I interested in an in-and-out kind of guy?

After work I thought it through. Maybe the zing I felt with Dan was like what I had felt with Luc. Physical attraction. Desire to date. Not wanting to be alone. But nothing serious or long-lasting.

Dan was probably like that. Just a step as I moved past Greg and into a new life. Nothing personal.

The next morning I tried not to care how I dressed. I did wear a salmon-colored shirt, because I knew it brought out the best in my skin and eyes.

"You are so weak," I said to myself in the mirror as I made sure I looked my best.

The birds called to me as I left the house before even Dad was moving around. I got into the Jetta, turned over the engine twice before it started, and spurted down the road, toward the bridge and toward L'Esperance.

He probably won't even show. It's been several weeks. Maybe he was seeing someone else and it didn't work out, so he decided I was worth a second look. Or maybe I was right and he simply wants to place a new order and to make sure things are comfortable between us. You know, live at peace with everyone.

I hated that my self-talk sounded like that so often. I looked up at my blood donor card on the rearview mirror.

Be positive, Lexi.

Quiet hopefulness was the most I could muster.

I arrived a little before five. Jacques was already rolling croissant dough so the morning delivery could go out by eight. Auguste tossed a *toque blanche* at me. Normally, I'd have goofed with him and put it on, but today I didn't want to mess up my French braid.

Just before five, a light tap came on the glass bakery doors.

Dan.

I looked at him, hair not at all tousled at this time of day, pants neatly pressed. Suspenders. He smiled, and I felt a surge of joy inside me, unlike, honestly, anything I had felt with Luc. Maybe our time together *had* been personal.

Auguste raised his eyebrows at me, and Jacques whistled under his breath. I shot them a warning look and unlocked the bakery door.

"Hi," Dan said. "Sophie said you'd be here early, so I hope this is okay."

I nodded. "Come into the café. No one is there yet, and I can make you a cup of coffee."

He looked longingly at the racks of almond croissants as we walked by.

"Have you eaten breakfast?" I asked.

He shook his head.

I took one of the warm croissants off the rack and put it on a plate. I turned the café lights on, warmed up the coffee machine, and drew two cups of coffee. Sophie wouldn't be here for another half hour.

We sat across from each other at a small table.

"Your coffee is great," he said. "So is the crescent roll."

"Croissant," I corrected. "I'm glad you like it." I wasn't going to let him off too easy. I mean, he had ignored me for weeks.

"Well, Lexi, I guess it's my turn to apologize. I had a really good time with you at the U gardens and at that sushi place."

"Me too," I answered quietly. I tucked a strand of hair back into my braid, but it fell forward again, so I just let it stay there.

"The week afterward, I spent some time getting my truck fixed," Dan continued. "I planned to call you after a few days, but my boss sent me on a business trip that lasted for over a week."

"In the African bush?" I asked.

"No," he admitted. "I had phone service, of course. But, well, honestly, I'm not used to splitting my time with anything other than business. New lawyers get all the dirty work, and if they want to work their way up in the firm, they have to buckle down, shut up, and get their work done."

At least I understood where he was coming from. "Yeah, I know all about that. My brother is a new lawyer." I paused. "I did stop by your office once," I admitted. "You were working with a woman."

I had no reason to be jealous. We'd been on one date. He owed me nothing. But he was here at five in the morning, and I wanted to make sure everything was clear and upfront.

"A new attorney in our firm," he said. "We're working on a copyright infringement together. I hardly know her."

"My brother is marrying another lawyer in a couple weeks," I said. "I think they enjoy talking shop together."

He was no idiot. He caught my vibe.

"I don't like to talk shop after work," he said emphatically. "In fact, I know I need to balance my time better. I've been jogging. In fact, after I...uh...saw you drive by my house the other day when I was jogging—"

"I was coming home from church," I said quickly, not caring if I interrupted. I didn't want him to think I was stalking him.

"Oh yeah, of course..." His mind seemed to wander for a minute. "Well, anyway, I stopped in here later, just, you know, to see if you were here. But then I thought you'd probably be mad, so I left. I almost called you maybe a hundred times, but it's been so long that I thought it would be better to talk in person. Later, I decided I really wanted to see you again no matter what. I'm sorry for all that. I feel like a jerk. If you'll accept my apology, I'd like to take you out again this weekend. I'll drive."

He offered a tentative smile. Cute dimples. I hadn't noticed before.

"I don't know," I said. "My future sister-in-law's shower is Friday night."

"How about Saturday?" he asked. He reached into his leather briefcase and drew something out, then handed it to me.

It was a menu for Tango, a very cool Spanish tapas restaurant in town. I'd been dying to go, but it's a date place, and I'd had no date. I knew he'd chosen something he thought I would enjoy. I took the bait.

"All right," I said, forgiving him. After all, he'd been gracious enough to forgive me once.

"See you at seven," he said. He looked back at me as he walked out the door and flashed a full-on smile, dimples and all. I thought I felt my heart skip.

I went back to the bakery whistling.

 Seventeen

Il ne pleut jamais mais il verse.
It never rains but it pours.

Friday I left work early, and so did Leah. We met at the other bakery to pick up the cake for her shower.

We'd decided to have the shower at Leah's mom's house since my mom's house was nearly all packed. It looked a little forlorn. Everything personal had been taken down, and we were eating on paper plates. Even my stuff was mostly packed.

I'd thought it through. First, I would talk with Sophie, then with Luc. Then I was calling Allrecipes back to accept the job.

We entered her mom's house, me carrying the cake, Leah opening the doors. Her cheeks were the pink of a happy bride. I was happy for her.

Nonna met us at the door. Leah's mom stood behind her, unsure, I think, what to do about Nonna taking over.

"My girls!" Nonna said, reaching a big arm around us and around the cake.

"*Le mie figlie!*" My mom echoed Nonna in her shiny new Italian.

"Listen to her," Nonna snorted. "She's more Italian than the pope now."

We bustled into the house. "Nonna," I said. "The pope is German."

"Yes, well, the other pope."

"The last pope was Polish."

Nonna waved her hand. "Yes, yes...that just proves my point!"

I winked at my mother, who beamed. She didn't seem to mind. She was enjoying her life.

We set everything up, arranging lots of peonies in vases. Peonies were Leah's wedding flower. I loved them. Several crowded together in each of the crystal vases looked like *Petticoat Junction* with their frilly crush of petals. Their delicate perfume smelled best up close—light, inviting, but not pushy. Just like Leah.

I went to the living room in enough time to greet Tanya, who arrived well in advance of any of Leah's friends.

"I'm not too early, am I?" she asked a little worriedly. "I didn't want to risk going against the traffic and being late."

"Not at all." Leah embraced her. Because Tanya was my best friend and Leah my almost-sister, they saw each other quite a lot. I looked at the two of them hugging, both settled in jobs and in love, and I knew it wouldn't be long until we were all gathered again for Tanya's wedding shower.

"I think I'll get the cake ready," I said, excusing myself.

I walked into the kitchen, dodging caterers, and lifted the cake out of the box—three lovely layers of almond cake with delicate apricot mousse spread between each layer and enrobed in apricot-tinted marzipan. On top were delicate, peach-colored flowers and tiny ivy. I put it on an antique crystal plate and lit some tea lights around it, then arranged a few flowers and greenery at the base. Nearby was the translucent bone china Leah's mother had set out to serve on. Nonna's silver service was there too. I knew Nonna planned to give it to Leah for a wedding gift. I loved her generosity. I knew she had special things set aside for me too, if I ever get married.

As I sat down in the semicircle around Leah, I began to daydream about my wedding and what it would be like to be the bride.

"You next, Lexi." I snapped out of it. Oh—she meant my gift, not my marriage! The shower had progressed to the gift-opening stage, and Leah opened my present, a gift certificate for newlywed massage lessons.

"Oh! How perfect!" she said, grinning at me. I knew I was the only person she'd told about her secret dream to be a massage therapist.

After lots of talking and laughing and eating the terrific meal—and cake!—the women began to drift out one by one. Nonna, my mom, and I stayed to pick up. Nonna snoozed in the recliner in the family room while my mom ran the vacuum. I packed up the leftover cake in the kitchen.

Leah came in, swiped some mousse, and licked her finger. "You do know how to pick a cake," she said. "I suppose that's only natural." She broke off a piece of baguette leftover from the dinner.

"This bread's not as good as at your bakery," she noted. "So how are things between you and Luc, anyway?"

"You mean since I found out he's engaged?"

"Yeah."

"Okay," I said. "I guess I misinterpreted his flirting to mean what I wanted it to mean. Although...I don't know. I might have misinterpreted the degree, but maybe there was something there. Loneliness? I think maybe being away from his fiancée for a long time wasn't good. Maybe once he saw her again, though, it all came back to him. I hope they get married soon. Too much absence makes the fond heart wander."

"So are you over him?"

"Oh, I think so," I said, swiping my own finger into the frosting and licking it. "Almost. For me, I think he was like...cake. Fun. Dessert. But I think I've come to realize that you couldn't live off it long term, you know? Maybe I liked the idea of being with a Frenchman. Maybe, subconsciously, I thought I'd get to France that way."

Leah looked thoughtful. "No more cake for you, then?"

I tilted my head. "I've been thinking about it.

Really, his fiancée being here saved me from making a big mistake. I think wanting to date your boss is the grown-up equivalent of having a crush on your teacher. I've got to move past that now. I need to think about my future and get serious. No more cake jobs, no more cake men. I liked what you said about settling in your groove, buckling down, and making a commitment. No more fluff. I need bread."

Leah chewed another bite of baguette and swallowed. "You don't think you can have your cake and eat your bread, too? I mean, in a guy? In a job?"

I packed up the last of the cake and put it into her mother's stainless steel fridge. "I don't know." I grinned. "Maybe French bread?"

Late that night, long after everyone else was asleep, I headed out to the back patio on my own. It was sad, in a way. The patio furniture had already been moved to the garage of the new place, and Dad had thrown my hammock away. Moldy edges, he'd said. Time to move on.

Yeah, time to move on.

I sat on the grass with a blanket and my Bible, remembering the campouts Tanya and I had here growing up and the secrets we'd shared. I thought about the birthday party where I'd eaten too much cake and thrown up in the bushes. I remembered talking with Mom and Dad on this patio about failing my first class. I remembered Nate and Leah's first date and my high school graduation party.

After a minute, I cracked the Bible open to Matthew 25 and read.

Partway through, I got to something that stopped me in my tracks, because it seemed to talk so very much to me, exactly where I was. What had God given *me,* Lexi Stuart? And how was I supposed to use those talents, for his pleasure and mine?

Again, it will be like a man going on a journey, who called his servants and entrusted his property to them. To one he gave five talents of money, to another two talents, and to another one talent, each according to his ability. Then he went on his journey. The man who had received the five talents went at once and put his money to work and gained five more. So also, the one with the two talents gained two more. But the man who had received the one talent went off, dug a hole in the ground and hid his master's money.

What had God given *me,* Lexi Stuart? And how was I supposed to use those talents for His pleasure and mine?

The next day was Saturday. To be more specific, the

next day was "I Have a Date at Tango" Saturday. I'd made up my mind to talk with Sophie and Luc tomorrow too. I needed to get back to Cameron about the job offer.

I sat in my room and tossed darts. *Allrecipes. L'Esperance. Allrecipes. L'Esperance.* Most of the time it came up *Allrecipes.* The last throw, I promised myself I'd get the right answer and live with it no matter what.

The dart fell to the floor. What did *that* mean?

"Are you going to be home tonight?" I asked my mom before leaving for work.

"For a little while, yes," Mom said. "Then we're going to dinner with a few of Dad's old marine friends who are in town. Why?"

"Well, someone is picking me up for dinner, and I just wondered," I said.

"A date?"

I nodded. "I guess you could call it that."

"With..."

"Dan," I said. "The guy I went out with a few weeks ago."

She looked pleased. I'd told her before about my believing that Dan was a Christian. "We'll try to be here to meet him," she said.

It still mattered to me what they thought, but maybe, in doses, that was okay.

I headed to L'Esperance in a good mood and got right to work. Sophie was already behind the counter; we were busier than usual this morning. With blue sky, people ventured outside much earlier on the weekends than when they had to curl up against the rain.

After a couple of hours, the rush was over, and Patricia was shouting at Margot in the bakery room about the proper way to prepare pastry crisps with orange-caramel sauce.

I helped the *Trois Amis* prep the raspberry filling for the croissants and then manned the café while Sophie ordered supplies for the next week.

"Alexandra?" Luc asked.

"*Oui?*" I turned to face him.

"May I speak with you privately?"

I nodded, blood pressure soaring into the blue sky.

Luc led me into his office and closed the door behind us.

I sat across the desk from him, where he'd bandaged my arm and where I'd proposed our dinner date. There was still a warm sense of camaraderie between us, and I'd noticed that he still flirted with the women customers, though lightly. But something had changed. He was more subdued, and I was too. I think he was more aware of what was good for him now that Marianne was in town. And I knew what was more appropriate now that I knew Marianne existed.

The temperature had definitely dialed down between us. He felt almost brotherly, and I was pretty much fine with that.

"We haven't had much of a chance to talk since your wonderful dinner last week," he said. "The food—*c'est délicieux!*"

"Thank you," I replied. "I enjoyed getting to know Marianne. And," I said with a bit less enthusiasm, "Margot."

He laughed out loud, knowing what I meant, and I laughed too.

"Well, as I mentioned at the time, when La Sophie was made manager, I thought I saw another future for you."

I blushed a little, remembering my interpretation that maybe he'd meant something personal. Just like Nate had said. Women often assumed the guy was talking about them.

"*Oui, merci,*" I answered.

"Do you still like your job here?" he asked.

"*Mais oui,*" I said. "I enjoy it, but..." Before I could say anything else, he continued.

"What if you had to do more dishes or prep work or even kitchen laundry?"

Laundry?

"I'm a hard worker," I said, noncommittally and slightly confused. Maybe adding laundry duties was just what I needed to get out of my six-month commitment.

"*Bon.* Here is what I am thinking, Alexandra," Luc continued. "My sister is going to come to the United States next month, in July. She's going to work at La Couronne for a little bit, and perhaps do some scouting with me as we look at a new shop. My family likes to rotate us between France, where we get a solid education in baking and cooking, and the

U.S.A., where we'd like to continue to do business."

"Oh, that's a good plan," I said. "I'd like to meet your sister when she's here."

Luc held his finger up. "*Un moment,* I am not finished."

I tried to focus on what he was saying.

"So, when my sister comes here, that will leave our family bakery short-handed for a few months. Six months, until she returns home. Would you like to take her place there?"

Involuntarily, I stood up and shrieked with joy. "In *France?*"

Luc smiled. "*Oui.*"

I sat down again and tried to gather my thoughts. Had he really just offered me a chance to work in France? Paid for? Cooking? Baking? In a bakery?

After a minute, I stopped hyperventilating, looked at Luc, who was obviously bemused, and asked, "So, exactly how would it work? When would I go? For how long?"

"Ah yes, The Ever-Questioning Alexandra. You'd travel this summer, perhaps after your brother's wedding, to our village outside Paris. That is where my family's main bakery, café, and hotel are, although we have one other nearby. You'd stay with my family, but technically in a small stone cottage behind the main house. That's where my sister lives, usually, but she'll be here, rooming with Margot or Patricia, whoever stays in the U.S. You'd have to be the everything girl. You'd help out anyone and

298

everyone. But you'd also get time to work in the bakery and to go to the training school in the nearby town. It would be like...uh...how do American's say it...uh...work study. Some days in the school, some days at the bakery. But we'd be training you for a future with us."

"How long would I stay?" I asked.

"You can earn an apprentice certificate in six months," Luc said. "You'd be well qualified to bake or even cook commercially after that. It's not the Culinary Institute of America"—he shrugged—"but you'd be working in a real French bakery every day. One that has been in business since before the time of Napoleon." I could hear the Gallic pride.

"And then?"

"And then you could come back to work in the U.S. You would have no problem finding a good job. I had to approve this with my family before proposing it to you, but they all agree—even, reluctantly, Margot and Patricia. Alexandra, I think you enjoy the cooking and the baking more than the café management."

And you know, he was right.

"Or," he continued with a mischievous grin, "you might just find that you fall in love with France, or a Frenchman, which would be understandable. And perhaps you'd stay in France and become a true Frenchwoman and live happily ever after. France, after all, is the place where Cinderella began."

It was true. France was the original setting of the Cinderella story. Pictures of myself as Drew

Barrymore in *Ever After* came flashing through my mind. Unfortunately, one or more of the evil stepsisters, Patricia and Margot, would be there too.

"May I—may I think about it?" I asked. A month ago there would have been no question, but now there were complications. A future with Allrecipes.com. An apartment I loved. A potential new church home. And a guy I was beginning to like quite a lot.

"*Oui,*" Luc answered. "But not for too long, because my *maman* will have to find someone else to help if it does not appeal to you. And if it does, she will have to begin to get a work permit for you."

"Okay," I said. "Can I let you know right after my brother's wedding? In about ten days?"

"*Oui.*" We both stood up. He kissed me on each cheek, and it felt nice. Then we walked out to the café, where he greeted a long-time customer.

"It's the world's most beautiful hairdresser," he said. "She's returned."

Flirting Frenchmen. *I guess some things never change.* But I did know how he felt about Marianne, and that was reality.

I tightened my apron.

"So?" Sophie said. "What do you think?"

"Did you know about the offer?" I asked.

Her eyes didn't leave my face. "Yes. He asked me what I thought, after having worked with you every day. And to make sure that I'd be okay here at L'Esperance if you decided to go. I told him you'd be great there, but that I'd miss you of course. What are you going to do?"

"I don't know," I said, still a little dazed. "I don't know. But thanks for recommending me."

I told her about the Allrecipes.com offer. "If I took it and remained in town, would you be mad at me for leaving you but not going to France?"

"No," she said. "Follow your heart." Then she nodded toward the counter. "Those came for you while you were in with Luc."

I followed her gaze to a lovely bouquet of field flowers purchased from Pike's Market. I opened the card and read it with a pounding heart, then sighed. It made things even more complicated.

> **Looking forward to spending time together tonight.**
>
> **Dan**

Sandra Byrd

Eighteen

Plus on desire une chose, plus elle se fait attendre.
The longer you wait for something, the more
desirable it becomes.

I knew Type A Dan would be exactly on time, and he was. My mother popped her head into my room. "I think your friend is here."

Type B Lexi wasn't quite ready. I was standing in front of my bed with my bathrobe on, trying to decide between two outfits.

Outfit No. 1: khakis and a light sweater.

Outfit No. 2: a slim-fitting jean skirt and the romantic white blouse. I ran my finger along its edge, deciding what kind of mood I wanted to cast.

"I like that one best too," Mom said.

Yes. It felt right.

Mom closed the door behind her, and I finished getting dressed, slipping in some small pearl earrings and running a light gloss over my lips before heading out to the living room.

When I got there, my parents stood at the front

303

door with Dan. Dad had probably opened the door before Dan even rang the bell. Dan looked attractive and kind, but now that I knew him better, mischievous and fun too.

"Hi," I said. "I see you guys have met."

"Would you like to come in?" Mom asked Dan. With most of the furniture gone, there was no place to sit.

"Oh no," I said. "I think we'd better get going. You guys have plans too, right?"

"Yes," Dad said.

Dan shook their hands and held the screen door for me. Dad—*my father*—winked at me. I blushed, which made me feel like a teenager, and I quickly turned away as he grinned. *May he be cursed with eating fish for a week.*

We walked to Dan's truck, making small talk, and he opened the passenger door and let me in.

"Truck runs fine now," Dan joked. I thought of something salty to say, but bit it back. *Sometimes humor is better left unsaid.*

We drove across the bridge and downtown, near Pike's Market, and parked in front of a Volvo dealership up the road. Dan came around and opened my door, which I appreciated.

We walked down the street—close enough to be together but not close enough to touch—to the restaurant. We were shown to our table, an intimate setting for two by the window. Yellow twinkle lights cast a romantic glow, as did a candle between us.

The waiter took our beverage orders and brought

us some bread. Dan pointed to the basket, indicating I should go first. The bread had a rustic, grainy feel, like cornbread, only smoother. A tiny pot of honey butter cozied up alongside the basket.

I glanced at the cubist art on the wall and then at Dan. It was sweet of him to try to find a place that felt intimate and romantic and that would still satisfy my desire for unique food experiences.

"What would you like?" Dan asked.

I scanned the menu: cold tapas, hot tapas, cheese, ceviche, meats, fish. *So many choices.*

"What do you like?" I asked.

"A cheap date," he said, teasingly. Then he pointed at the menu.

I laughed. Cheap dates—dates wrapped in bacon and served with marinated eggplant—were a tapas offering.

"I think you've chosen the wrong girl, then," I said, playing along. We picked a few items to share, and an entrée each, and the conversation continued to flow. In spite of our joking and lighthearted topics, the date felt like it was going somewhere; we were connecting on a meaningful level. I think we both felt it.

The waiter came back and took our orders. Shortly thereafter, he brought a wooden plate of Spanish cheese.

"So, how has your week been?" Dan asked, slicing into some cheese and popping an olive into his mouth.

"Eventful," I said, not willing to share the France

305

opportunity yet. Maybe later tonight. I wanted to see how the evening went. "How about you?" I asked. "Busy at work?"

He nodded. "Yeah. We're finishing up the case I've been working on for the past month. My boss was ready to set me on another huge commitment, but I negotiated with him to have a little more free time. Like I told you I would."

I liked a man who could follow through. "The new Relaxin' Man Dan?"

"Well, I wouldn't go that far," he said. He flipped open his wallet and withdrew a card. "Here."

I read it. "'Daniel Larson. A Positive.' It's your blood donor card!"

He laughed that infectious laugh. "After I saw the vampire card in your car and how you were using it to remind yourself to be positive, I thought that was clever. So mine is A Positive. As in, 'make A Positive change.'"

I handed it back to him. "I'm glad you're not type B Negative."

"Me too," he said.

The waiter returned with our Cheap Dates, which we laughed over, and a small white plate of blue cheese soufflés drizzled with cranberry preserves. It was all I could do not to lick the plate.

I reached for my water glass at the same time as Dan reached for his. Our hands bumped and stayed touching for a moment.

I felt the vibe travel through my fingers and up my arm like an emotional artery right to my heart. It wasn't like the heat of my crush on Luc, but it wasn't sisterly, either. I couldn't put my finger on it, but I didn't hurry to take my hand away.

I looked up at him, and he held my gaze for a minute. I saw it in his eyes. He'd felt the vibe too.

"Well," I said, quickly withdrawing my hand. "The food is great so far. Amazing restaurant choice."

Spanish music strummed in the background, and I looked across the room and into the open kitchen like any foodie would.

Dan noticed the direction of my eyes. "You like the kitchen as much as the food, don't you?"

I laughed. "I do. I feel at home when I'm cooking and creating. As much as I like to eat," I waved my hand over the terrific offerings, "I like to cook even better."

The waiter brought our rum-glazed salmon and tenderloin with truffles.

"So tell me about the church you take bread to," Dan asked as we began our main courses. "Do you still do that?"

I nodded. "I did tonight. It's my grandmother's church. A soup kitchen."

"What church do you go to?" he asked.

I told him about my mom's church, but that I was looking.

"Oh, I know that church," he said. "I've never been there, but I know of it."

I put a steamed bun on my plate while I casually asked the next question. "Do you go to church?"

"I'm a Christian," he said firmly, answering my real question.

Tanya would really be jazzed at this. And, honestly, so was I.

Dan continued. "I've been kind of in and out lately, because I've been so busy at work. But the new 'Relaxin' Man Dan' has decided to sign up to teach the sixth-grade boys' Sunday school class for the summer. I need to get my life balanced, you know, and this is a part of it. If I have to be there every week to teach the boys, it will be good accountability for me to make sure I'm actually in church myself. I go to a church in my neighborhood. Church on the Hill."

"I just visited there," I said, astonished. "I didn't see you."

He nodded. "I've been skipping church to get my work done or work out or whatever. I had a feeling when you said you'd visited a church in my neighborhood that it was that one. There aren't too many in that area that attract...well...younger people."

I tasted the rice buried under my salmon. What was that spice? Smooth, hot, tomato-flavored, all at once. "That's great, about the Sunday school."

"Thanks," he said. "I wish I didn't need some outside mechanism to make sure I get to church, but I do."

"I know what you mean," I said. "I've just begun driving myself to church too." When he looked quizzically at me, I explained what I meant about taking responsibility for my own relationship with God and how, more often than not, it had been parked or stalled.

We ate dinner and talked about the bakery. I showed him my burn scar, and he seemed appropriately impressed and concerned.

"What are you working on now?" I asked.

"It's actually print copyright," he said. "I'm pretty excited to work on it. I think that in another year, I'll have paid enough dues to pick more of my own work within the firm. It'll be time for the newly enlisted to do the heaviest lifting."

The waiter came by and asked if we wanted dessert. "I have a plan for that," Dan said to me. "If you don't mind waiting."

I shook my head. "No, I'm full now anyway."

He paid, and we headed outside. I was almost sad to leave the restaurant—its warm smell, the laughter, the music. It would have been nice to dance together, and when I mentioned this to Dan, he agreed.

"Would you like to walk on the beach?" Dan asked as we got into the truck. "I know of a place kind of close, and if you want, we could start a fire and roast marshmallows."

It sounded perfect. Just what I needed.

We drove a couple of miles, the windows down and the early summer air blowing through my hair. He turned on a country music station, and we chatted on the way to the beach about the time he and his buddies tried to start a band of their own.

"Never made it past the basement as far as the garage," he joked.

When we arrived, he opened the door for me again. No wonder Dad liked him. Dad had made a mental X through Greg's name in college when Greg let me open my own door.

Hey, I'd said then. *At least he turned the engine off until I got in.* But now, well, I could see the difference.

Dan opened the back of his truck and handed me a blanket and two roasting sticks as well as a bag of marshmallows. He grabbed some wood and a pack of matches, and we hiked down toward the water. The wind puffed lightly, whisking up the sand, which rose and curled like steam above some nearby driftwood. The waves crashed an early lullaby.

There were enough people that I didn't feel creeped out, but not so many that we couldn't have our own spot.

The sky went from blood orange-red to eggplant purple, sun dunking into the water like a cookie into coffee.

"Hey, want to see something fun?" I asked.

"Yeah." He followed me closer to the water. I bent over in the dark and drew my name in the sand. As I did, each letter lit up and then died out before I wrote the next letter.

"How did you do that?" he asked.

"It's bioluminescence," I explained. "The same organisms that pollute the clams glow in the dark for a few seconds when you touch them."

He drew his name, and each letter glowed and died as he did.

I drew a glowing smiley face next to each of our names, and then we walked back to the blanket.

He lit the fire, and we talked. I was surprised how easy it was to make conversation; I never had to think of topics to fill an uncomfortable void. He told me about his parents, who lived in Enumclaw, and his sister, who was on her year abroad in Belgium.

Belgium is right next to France.

We roasted marshmallows in silence for a few minutes. I was glad I'd worn the white frilly shirt. When I'd bought it, I'd intended to wear it with Luc. That seemed a lifetime away, sitting under the stars now. But the thought of Luc and of Dan's sister living a year abroad brought France to mind. I needed to be honest with Dan.

"Speaking of living abroad," I said, "I had something interesting happen this week."

He handed me a toasted marshmallow. "Really?"

"Yeah," I said. "Luc offered me a chance to live in France and work at his family's bakery."

"Oh." Dan sat a moment in silence. "I'm sure it's a great opportunity for you." His flat tone told me both what I did and did not want to know. "How long would you be there?"

I had to be honest. "At least six months. I'm not sure after that."

He looked crushed. "What are you going to do?"

"I'm not sure yet," I said, though I had a growing suspicion. "I need to pray about it for a few more days."

"I'll pray too," he said, lifting his chocolate eyes to meet mine. He smiled, his eyes twinkling slightly as another thought occurred to him. "Although we might be praying for different outcomes."

I smiled back and took a small bite of the marshmallow.

"When do you have to answer him?"

"After my brother's wedding, in a week or so," I said. It was time to address the other thought I'd had in the back of my mind all night. "And about that wedding: I am, of course, a bridesmaid. But I haven't yet decided on an escort."

I loved how that sounded, like I had an army of guys waiting for me to call them up and give them the nod. "I wondered," I continued, "if you might be free. I know it's really short notice."

He said nothing for a moment. I had the feeling he was absorbing the fact that, despite considering moving away, I still wanted his company.

"I'd like to come," he said. "Thanks. Let me know the details."

"Sure."

"Say," he said, changing the topic, "in my new quest for recreation, I agreed to sign up for a summer Softball league."

"I used to play softball," I said, as we packed up the blanket and he threw sand on the fire. "Catcher."

"Well, if you're here this summer, maybe you can join."

I agreed, and we drove home in a comfortable

silence.

When we got to my house, Dan spoke first. "I'll wait to hear from you about next weekend."

"Of course," I said. "Thanks so much."

"No problem at all," he said. He reached toward me, and for a second I thought that he was going to kiss me goodnight. Instead, he opened his glove box and took out an envelope.

I wasn't sure if I was disappointed or relieved about the kiss. *Well, that's not* exactly *true.*

"I thought you might enjoy this," he said. "Open it later tonight." He put it into my hand, and I felt that soft and strong touch. He came around to open my door and walked me to the porch.

"Goodnight, Lexi," he said as I opened the door.

"Goodnight, Dan. Thanks for one of the best nights I've had in a long time."

He smiled, looking both strong and vulnerable at the same time.

Once inside, I sat on my bed and opened the envelope. I pulled out a piece of paper. Where had he found this? Of course. It was the piece of paper I'd grabbed off the floor of the Jetta in order to give him my phone number on our first date.

As I read it, I smiled and then laughed out loud. The job. The apartment. The church. And now the guy! This decision was getting much harder than it might have been.

Happily Ever After

Once upon a time there was a

POSITIVE single person who never attended the Impact Group. This person was TOO BUSY TO BE confused, because he or she had expected to be at a LITERARY COPYRIGHT job right now instead of the HIP HOP one she or he was working.

One time Single Person was talking to a CUTE BAKER about her LACK OF personal life.

"You think that's bad?" the friend answered. "I have a friend who is dating a LAWYER."

It could be worse, Single Person admitted.

Instead of constantly WORKING, Single Person decided to PRAY instead. Besides, Single Person thought, what I really want to do is GET TO KNOW SOMEONE BOTH DEEP AND FUN, WHO KNOWS HOW TO MAKE A NAPOLEON AND LAUGH.

On my day off, I helped my parents box up nearly everything left in their house. I explained Luc's offer to them. Mom was excited and a little nervous. Dad felt it would be unsafe for me to be there alone. Neither pushed their agenda, though. *A great step for all of us.*

I boxed up most of my stuff too. I'd e-mailed Cameron and asked if I could have one more week to decide on the job, and reluctantly, he'd agreed.

Tuesday I went back to work. Sophie was there early running a cash report. She took to the business side of things with particular glee: coming up with new reports and order forms, and interviewing suppliers. Luc was in and out, and Marianne was often with him. On my lunch hour, I took Marianne for a walk down the street to do a little shopping. It was fun to chat with another woman in French. One didn't chat with Patricia and Margot. One didn't shop with Patricia and Margot. *Mais non.* Marianne was a lot like me—and Tanya and Sophie. Though she didn't understand why anyone would chose to be a vegan.

My phone rang while we walked. The number looked familiar, but I couldn't quite place it, so I let it go to voicemail. When I got back to the shop, I listened to the message.

"Hey, this is Dan, just checking on Saturday night. What time, what to wear, et cetera. Also, should I put your name down for softball? Give me a call back when you get a chance."

"Gotta make a call, *boss,*" I said to Sophie.

She shook a finger at me. "Make it snappy, *peon.*"

I giggled and went back to the walk-in. No one was in the pastry room; Patricia had already left for La Couronne. The *Trois Amis* were prepping dough for tomorrow. I pulled the door shut behind me, sat on a closed crate of lemons, and dialed Dan's number.

The memory of my first call to him, in this very same place, brought back warm—and cold—memories.

"Dan Larson," he answered.

"Hi, it's Lexi."

"Hi, Lexi." His voice softened.

"About Saturday," I said, "I'll be at the church early to help decorate and to take pictures, but if you want to meet me there about five, the ceremony starts at five-thirty. Then there's a dinner and dance reception afterward. Would that work for you?"

"Definitely," he said. "Dress code?"

"Tie and jacket. Suspenders optional," I teased. I hoped he'd wear them. They were different but stylish. "Taking it easy tonight?" I asked. "Relaxin' Man Dan?"

"No, not tonight. Got a lot to get through and no other plans anyway. I'll be here late."

"Well, take it easy," I said.

"I'm looking forward to Saturday," he said.

"Me too." I hung up and went out to the café to thaw.

"Dan?" Sophie asked.

"Yep," I answered. I'd told her all about Saturday night.

"I went to church on Sunday," she said.

"How was it?"

"Nice. I liked being in a calm, peaceful place."

What I'd found boring, she'd found peaceful. Cool.

"Once I move into the apartment, though, it'll have to stop. I can't take the bus there. I can't afford the apartment, my living expenses, and a car payment quite yet. Maybe in six months. I have some debt I have to pay off that I accumulated when I lived with Roger," she said sadly.

"Did Michelle drive you on Sunday?" I asked.

"Yeah, but she's leaving for the summer to do a team project with Microsoft in Indonesia."

"Microsoft!" I said. "I had no idea she worked there."

The rest of the day flew by, and we closed the café together.

"Got plans tonight?" I asked Sophie.

"No."

"Want to learn how to make the vegan cookies? If you're going to manage a bakery, you should know how to bake."

"Yes!" she said. "Would you teach me?"

"*Mais oui,*" I said. "You taught me everything else in the café. It's the least I can do."

I turned on the ovens and set out ingredients. Auguste rolled his eyes as Sophie blasted European techno pop on the music system, but hey—she was the boss now.

I showed her how to make the dough, and she

baked them up on her own, though I took them out of the oven. We didn't have any jelly, so they were just peanut butter cookies. Sophie kept a supply of almond milk in the walk-in to drink during the day, and we had milk and cookies together.

She packed the rest of the cookies to go, and I made a small, round mille-feuille. I was careful not to use too sweet of a crème pâtissèrie this time. I slicked a lemon glaze across the top, then zigzagged dark chocolate across that. I packed it into a mini catering box and taped it shut.

On the way home, I stopped at the Davis, Marks office and took the elevator up. The receptionist wasn't there that late, but the security guard recognized me from the time I'd delivered the catering and buzzed me in.

This time, I confidently strode down the hallway. I stopped short when I saw the same woman was in Dan's office. *Should I go in?*

Dan saw me this time, though, and he came toward the door. He put his palm on the small of my back and ushered me into the office.

"Lexi!" he said. "I'm so glad to see you." He gestured toward the woman. "This is Nancy."

Nancy looked at me. She was brunette, with a sprinkle of tiny freckles across her nose that softened her professional demeanor. "Nice to meet you," she said, betraying no emotion, positive or negative.

"If you'll excuse us, please," Dan said to Nancy. "I'll get back with you later."

He showed Nancy out, as a gentleman would, and then returned to me. I opened up my little brown bag and drew out two plastic forks and two napkins.

"Sugar high to get you through the work," I pronounced. We shared the mille-feuille.

"Delicious! I could get used to this," Dan said, looking at me meaningfully.

I sighed into my pastry. *So could I.*

Sandra Byrd

Nineteen

Tel maître, tel valet.
Like master, like servant.

Wednesday night I drove down to The Ballroom to meet Tanya for a game of pool. When I got in, Tanya was waiting. Sometimes I hated that she was never late. I mean *never*.

"Sorry I'm late," I said. "I had to stalk someone for a parking spot."

"No problem; I think our table is just now ready."

We walked over to the pool table and grabbed a couple of cue sticks. I rubbed the tip of mine in blue chalk and broke the balls.

"Any decision yet?" she asked.

"No," I said. "Not yet. I had a good talk with Dan last night, though. I took him a mille-feuille at work and stayed long enough to share a bite."

She raised her eyebrows mischievously. "Sounds serious."

"Hmm," I said, looking away before she could

321

read my expression. "You, of anyone, sound serious."

She banked her shot and pocketed the ball. "I don't know. I went back to my counselor for one more visit. I think I'm learning how to risk. I have to give up control of what I know in order to find out what's there. With Steve."

We continued to play, and my mind continued to run wild with thoughts.

"What if I go to France and I like it so much that I never come home?" I said.

"Then I'll visit you," she answered. "Don't worry about that." She pocketed the last ball. "I won. What's up with your game tonight?"

"What if it's not safe?"

"Pool or France?" she asked, racking up another round. "Seriously, now you sound like me. Or your dad."

I pretended to be shocked, but she was right. Fear for personal safety had never been a big issue for me. "Well, there's still the money."

"Now that's serious," she said. "You don't get paid?"

"I'll get a stipend—not much, but they'll pay for my training and certification. They pay for my uniforms and my room and board. I have to provide my own spending money and savings, and, of course, pay for flying there and home. I'll probably get some service money—tips. In the French system, you don't make much working your way up, but the training is invaluable."

"How much would the flight be?"

"About a grand one way. Two and a half times that for an open round-trip ticket. I have it in savings, and even a little more, but I don't want to touch too much of that if possible. I'll have to live off something when I get back. The Allrecipes job is unlikely to be open again just then."

"What do you have that's worth twenty-five hundred dollars?" Tanya asked.

I sighed. "My vase might go for that on eBay. I don't know. But I don't really want to sell that."

Tanya shot and missed. "I'll pray for you."

"That's what Dan said," I said.

"Cool. Though I bet he and I pray in different directions," she said, smiling.

I banked a shot, made a combination, and got two balls in at once. "I won," I said.

"You did," Tanya agreed. "In more ways than one."

When I got home that night, my parents were already snoring. I got on the computer to, I'm sorry to admit, look up my reviews at Allrecipes.com. Hey, a little affirmation isn't all bad.

"Someone only gave me three stars!" I snorted in disgust and scrolled down to read the review.

Well, maybe she was right. *I should dry sauté the saffron next time.*

I listened to the increasing traffic outside on the

street. Someone was drag racing. Again. I hope they didn't hit my car.

Suddenly, I had an idea of how I could earn my twenty-five hundred dollars. I searched for the site I needed.

S.H.D.B. CAR VALUE ONLINE

2000 Volkswagen Jetta GL Sedan 4D

Condition
Excellent: $3,805
Good: $3,380
Fair: $2,850

An hour before the wedding, I sat in the church, feet propped on the freshly waxed pew, while the photographer went through the roll call. Nate and Leah were up now. They'd decided to forgo tradition in favor of getting the pictures done before the reception. Peonies blushed throughout the church, and the pew ends were decorated with ecru and pale pink ribbons.

Nate couldn't take his eyes off Leah. She did look gorgeous. *I bet Nate doesn't have one of his headaches tonight!*

I checked my watch. We still had half an hour before anyone else arrived, including Dan. I felt a little dizzy. If I were Nate, I'd have been worrying about an attack of cardiac virus or perhaps an unreported medication side effect. But I wasn't Nate. I knew why my heart kept skipping beats.

I plucked a Bible out of the pew in front of me and started to read aimlessly, waiting for the bridesmaids' turn with the photographer. I turned to Matthew 28, the last chapter. I was proud of myself for getting through a whole book without stopping.

What do you want me to hear from you, Lord? I asked, grateful for the relative silence in the church due to the lack of Sesame Street Squawkers. Leah's flower girl and ring bearer, her cousin's children, were napping in the church nursery.

With light bulbs flashing in the front and the low murmur of the photographer cooing encouraging direction to Leah's high-strung mother, I read quietly.

"Do not be afraid," the angel had said to the woman, and she ran to tell the disciples what she had seen. What they had most feared had happened, and yet what lay ahead was a wonderful plan they could not have imagined on their own. God had things well under control.

I kept reading, moved, but nothing pricked my spirit as being specifically for me. Until I got to the end.

"Therefore go and make disciples of all nations, baptizing them in the name of the Father and of the Son and of the Holy Spirit, and teaching them to obey everything I have commanded you. And surely I am with you always, to the very end of the

age."

I closed the Bible and held on to it while I watched the groomsmen move forward for their photo session. Nate beamed. His buddies were all there. He had a new haircut, and I could see his ears glowing pink. When we were kids and he got excited—looking forward to a vacation or showing Mom and Dad a good grade—his ears always turned pink. I wiped a tear from my eye.

I opened the Bible again and read the sentence that caught my eye. "*Go and make disciples of all nations.*"

Is there work for me to do in France? I asked God. I felt a peace I couldn't understand, at the same time, I felt a wrenching heartache.

I closed the book just as someone slipped into the pew alongside me.

"You look beautiful," Dan said.

I couldn't take my eyes off him either. "Well, you clean up good too," I managed.

He reached into his jacket and lightly snapped a pair of suspenders. "I know you like them," he said.

I blushed, and he laughed.

"I'm glad I can make you blush," he said.

"I still have pictures to take," I said, nodding toward the front.

"It's okay; I know I'm early. I'll watch."

The bridesmaids' turn for photos came, and I went forward, conscious of Dan's eyes on me, although everyone else's were on Leah.

Leah's mother smoothed the textured silk of the

bridesmaids' dresses. Leah had chosen antique rose as the dress color. I was glad she'd picked that one. The color her mother had originally chosen was more ashy, and I'd privately dubbed it Old Lady Lipstick or Dusty Pink, heavy on the dust.

Each of us held a small bouquet of antique roses with little green euphorbia leaves tucked in here and there and a lovely spray of white bacopa instead of baby's breath. I liked that Leah did her own thing. The wedding was sweet and chic and very Leah.

When the photos were done, I rejoined Dan for just a minute. I had to disappear into the bridal room soon.

Tanya and Steve had arrived and were sitting a few rows behind Dan. I'd asked her to come early and sit with Dan so he didn't feel alone.

As I walked down the aisle toward them, I motioned for her to follow me. I slid into the pew first, with Tanya and Steve behind me.

"Dan, I'd like you to meet my best friend, Tanya, and her boyfriend, Steve," I said.

"Steve Dunn," Steve said, sticking his hand out toward Dan.

"Dan Larson."

Tanya beamed at me behind his back and winked.

We chatted for a few minutes, and then I excused myself to help Leah for the final minutes before the ceremony.

The bridal room was a frenzy of makeup touch-ups, but as soon as we heard the music start in the church, the mood became more subdued. I saw Leah's mom tuck a blue-edged hankie into the hidden pocket sewn inside one of the folds of Leah's beautiful petticoats.

I kissed Leah's cheek. "Welcome to our family, *belle-soeur,*" I said. *Belle-soeur* means "sister-in-law," but if you translate it literally, it means "beautiful sister." Leah was about to be both!

We filed into the hallway to wait for the long walk down the aisle. I went last, just before Leah and her dad. As I walked down the aisle, I noticed neighbors who had bandaged Nate's eternally scraped knees. Molly, my mom's church buddy, sat in the same pew where they sat together week after week. Nate's friends from high school, college, and law school. My aunt. Nonna and Stanley, who looked very happy. Tanya and Steve.

And Dan.

I took my place near the altar and waited with everyone else for Leah. When she came down the aisle, it was her perfect moment.

After the ceremony, we had to drive to the country club for the reception. "Can I take you over?" Dan asked.

Of course he could!

I told my parents that I'd be riding with Dan. My dad nodded, pleased and distracted, I knew, for Nate. Not too distracted, though. He bent over to shine a nearly invisible smudge off his patent black shoes.

Dan held the truck door open for me, and I

gathered my full skirt in order to climb in. I liked the way the dress made me feel.

We drove over to the reception, talking about nothing and everything, avoiding the one topic that was on both our minds: France. When we got to the country club, I ignored the long table in front for the bridal party and escorts, instead grabbing two seats next to Nonna and Stanley so I could sit next to Dan.

Dear God, if you'll keep Nonna on a leash tonight, I promise I will make sure the bread gets delivered every Saturday no matter what. For good measure, I'll throw in a pastry whenever I can.

"So," Nonna said, eyeing Dan. "You're Lexi's new boyfriend. You're a lawyer, I hear. That's good. Some lawyers make a good living, and some do too much pro bono work. That's not good. You don't do too much pro bono work, do you?"

Boyfriend? How much money does he make? Oh, Nonna!

Deal's off, God.

"Come on, Nonna," I said. "We need to use the restroom."

"I don't need to use the restroom, dear." Nonna sat in her chair, intransigent as a Yorkie avoiding the vet.

I patted the top of my head, exactly where her balding patch lay, and looked at her pointedly.

"Oh yes, yes," she said, hurriedly standing up.

"Dan is kind of shy," I said to Nonna once we reached the bathroom, knowing he wasn't. It was I who couldn't handle the embarrassment. "And he's

329

not Italian, so he might not be ready for you to, you know, come on too strong."

"So he's weak?" Nonna asked.

"No," I said. "Just behave yourself."

"Oh, all right," she said. We touched up our makeup before returning to the table. On the way back, Nonna stopped a waiter and asked him to deliver two Monster Energy drinks for her and Stanley. Lovely.

I got myself a glass of Cabernet, and one for Dan too. I suspected he'd like Cabernet, and when he sipped and relished it, I knew I'd made the right choice.

After dinner, the lights dimmed and the band began to play.

"Would you like to dance?" Dan asked me.

"I'd love to."

I set my handbag on the table and let him lead me to the floor. After a song or two, "Always On My Mind" came on. How appropriate.

"Want to keep dancing?" Dan asked.

I answered by tightening my hands on his arms, and he pulled me a little closer. He could lead without being obvious. I liked that.

We said nothing during the dance, and I wasn't sure if I was glad or not that those particular lyrics were playing, echoing my own heart. I didn't want to fall in love right now. It made everything too complicated, and we might get our hearts broken.

After the dance, the band took a break.

"Want to take a walk in the garden?" Dan asked.

"Away from my grandmother?"

Dan gave me a guilty look.

"You're a quick study," I said.

"Stanley Jones looks like he's got his hands full with her at the moment, anyway," Dan said, as Nonna fixed Stanley's tie.

"I hope she didn't get on your nerves," I said.

"I think you two are a lot alike."

"I don't know if I've just been insulted or complimented," I replied, and Dan laughed.

We sat on a bench. Handfuls of roses tumbled down the arbor on either side of us, perfuming the night air, already fresh and warm, like sheets hung out to dry in the summer sun.

I sat on the bench with my hands on either side of my legs. Dan did the same thing, so our hands barely touched, side of palm to side of palm. I didn't move my hand, and neither did he. Holding hands while dancing was a lot less serious than holding hands just because.

"So, have you made any decisions?" he asked quietly.

I took a deep breath. "I have," I said. "I'm going."

He didn't meet my eyes. "I figured."

I looked at him and willed him to look me in the face, and he did. "I want to try to make the career I've always wanted work. I want to live in France—I've always wanted to visit. I want to hear what God has to say to me in a place where I have to depend on him alone."

"I'm going to miss you more than I thought

possible." He blushed. "I guess that sounds cheesy."

"I'm glad I can make Strong Man Dan blush," I teased. I lowered my voice but looked into his eyes. "It's a little known fact that I prefer American cheese to French cheese anyway."

He moved his hand so that it covered mine. "I'm not worried about French cheese," he said. "I'm worried about a French Dip. The one that you might fall in love with and stay in France for."

"I'm not going to France to find a guy," I said. "Before, I might have." I held his gaze. "But not now."

He inhaled deeply and then sighed. "But you can't predict what will happen."

I shook my head. "No. I can't. But you may fall in love with a sharp lawyer in your firm."

"Unlikely," he said.

"Unlikely, but still a possibility."

He reluctantly shrugged. "Possible, I suppose," he said. "When do you leave?"

"I'm not certain. A few weeks, I think. Maybe a month."

"Can I see you a few times before then?" he asked.

"I'd love that."

"I could always schedule a trip to visit my sister in Belgium. It's right next to France."

"I'm sure she'd be pleased to know how much her brother cares." I poked him playfully, and he managed a smile.

"The music's back on," Dan said.

He led me back to the dance floor, where we danced until Nonna cut in. I went back to my seat, and Uncle Bennie slid in next to me.

"Got a couple of job offerings, but I hear you might have a big option overseas," he said.

"Yeah," I said. "Top level."

"Really?" His eyes widened in surprise.

"I'll be working at a café. Baking. And doing laundry. But it's *French* laundry." I gave him a triumphant look, daring him to make me feel like the family underachiever for washing tablecloths.

"Ah," he said. "That makes all the difference, then, doesn't it?" He kissed my cheek. "You've grown up, Lexi."

"I have," I agreed. "Thanks for all your help...everywhere."

He patted my hand. "It's nothing at all. Now, my dear, may I have this dance?"

Toward the end of the evening, as Nate and Leah were getting ready to leave, my dad called everyone together for the toasts. And then Leah threw her bouquet.

It flew out over the dance floor. I saw Nonna trying to elbow her way in to catch it, but she and Leah's mother collided in their attempts to catch it while acting like they weren't trying. It threw them both off balance, and the bouquet soared directly into Tanya's hands. She caught it out of reflex, looking more surprised than anyone else.

Dan whispered to me when I got back to the table, "No bouquet? I thought you used to be a catcher on a softball team."

"I haven't found a team I want to play on yet."

He laughed and took my hand. "Maybe mine."

Maybe...

The next morning I got up early to go to church.

My mom appeared in the kitchen. I thought she'd have left for her church by now. "Not feeling good?" I asked.

"I'd like to visit your church," she said. "Is that all right?"

"I would love that," I told her.

Dan had told me he would be at the second service, since he taught Sunday school during the early service. I looked for him in the hallway but didn't see him.

We sat down and settled in to listen. The sermon sank in, and then came my favorite time: praise. The songs seemed to come in through my pores and then back out through me again.

I prayed for Sophie, that she would find her way to God whether it was here or somewhere else. I prayed for Nate and Leah. I prayed for Luc and Marianne, that God would draw them to himself as they began their marriage in a country where God often resided in lovely cathedrals but wasn't as welcome in the day-to-day business of humble homes.

I prayed for Dan, but there I was on emotionally

shaky ground. I pushed away the tender thought of him teaching his Sunday school right at that moment.

And then I felt the Spirit move, felt the urge to stand as the worship leader sang out, "I exalt Thee, oh Lord." I stood and raised my hands into the air along with many others in the congregation, praising God publicly as I felt led to do, not worrying at all about what those around me would think.

I had to live for the audience of One.

My eyes were closed, but I felt the space between my mom and me. Then something completely unexpected happened. My mother stood up next to me. She didn't wobble up; she *stood* up firmly beside me. She didn't raise her hands, but she didn't need to. I knew she wasn't standing because she was led to. She was standing with me, like I had sat with her.

The tears came down my face, and I took one arm and wrapped it about her waist, and she wrapped her arm around my waist too. I knew what this said, in our unspoken language. My mother stood with me in every possible way.

After church, I went home and changed. I had only a few sets of clothes left to choose from. I'd packed the rest and put them into a storage unit, except for the boxes I was sending ahead to France.

Leah and Nate were there, saying good-bye

before leaving for their honeymoon.

"So, Leah, are you guys happy with the condo you're planning to rent?" I asked.

She shrugged. "I guess so. We're moving in next week, right after we get back from our honeymoon. It's not perfect, but we'll definitely make it a home."

I took a deep breath. "I've been thinking. Would you guys like my apartment?"

She nearly dropped the box she was carrying. "What do you mean, would we like your apartment?"

"I mean, do you want it? I'm going to France. I don't need it. And I talked to the manager, and since he felt so bad about giving up my studio, he's arranged for me to be able to transfer the lease to you guys, even though it wasn't in my contract. If you want to, that is."

She did drop the box this time, then leaped over it to hug me.

"Is that out of joy for me or because you get the cool apartment?" I teased.

"Both!" she said. "If you're sure..."

"I'm sure," I said, handing over the keys. "I think it was meant to be yours all along. You can go by there and sign the transfer papers anytime. I already signed my half."

She ran off to make sure it was okay with Nate, but I was sure it would be.

I went back to packing. Deep in a nest inside one of the boxes, I'd packed my bud vase. The tiny stone cottage in France would be my first home on my own, and I'd be proud to take a piece of high-quality American art to a nation that honors and appreciates all forms of art. I'd studied French art in college and couldn't wait to devour the Musée d'Orsay for myself.

I left my room and headed into the living room, where my dad was watching something on ESPN. He stood when I entered the room. He looked at odds with himself, which was unusual.

"Everything okay?" I asked. "I wasn't going to turn the channel or anything."

He relaxed. "I know." He turned off the TV. "Getting packed to go?"

"Yes. I know you're not happy that I'm leaving."

He shrugged. "I'd feel better about it if you were in the States."

"You can visit me and go to the beaches of Normandy."

"That would be nice, Alexandra." He cleared his throat.

"It's a good opportunity for me, Dad."

"I know," he said. "Here." He handed me a black leather travel wallet.

"What—?"

"For safety. Don't carry cash in your purse. Make sure you use the travel wallet wherever you go. And buy a small safe once you're there, or open a safe deposit box."

I looked at the leather wallet. It was nice. Masculine, but nice. And my dad had picked it out for me, special. I figured it was his way of saying I

337

had his blessing to go.

"Open it," he said. I did and saw a piece of paper and some bills.

I was shocked. "Dad! Is this for my ticket to France?"

He nodded. "And back again. I didn't want you to be without some cash when you first get there."

"Thank you, *thank* you, Dad," I said. "I can't believe this. How...?"

My parents had made it clear that they didn't have much money to spare, and I knew they'd already helped Nate and Leah a little with the honeymoon, and plus with building their new house...

"Oh, I'm going to do my own landscaping at the new house," he said. "Only sissies hire people to do their lawn work."

If it had been someone else's dad, I'd have thought he had a tear in his eye.

"I'll miss you, Lexi," he said. "But I want you to enjoy yourself. Bake lots of good things."

"I will, Dad," I said. "But I won't make white cupcakes with sprinkles for anyone but you."

I got to work early on Tuesday, but Sophie was already there.

"Only a couple more weeks until you're gone," she said wistfully. "I hope Luc's sister is as easy to work with as you are. Though she won't be as good a friend."

She told me all about moving into her apartment. "What did you do with the one you'd reserved?" she asked.

"Gave it to my brother and Leah," I said. "They'll repay me for the deposit. I'd known for a long time they were supposed to have it; I just didn't know why. And now I do—I'm going to live in France!"

We poured ourselves cups of hot, nutty coffee. I drank mine with an almond croissant, Sophie with a piece of baguette with strawberry confiture.

"She might be easy to work with *and* a friend," I said. "You never know. Hey, I thought about you at church yesterday."

"Really?" Sophie perked up.

"Really," I said. "I think it'd be a shame if you couldn't keep going just because Michelle and I won't be here."

"Yeah, well, another time," she said wistfully.

"Here." I handed her an envelope.

"What is it?"

"Open it," I said.

She pulled out a key and a piece of paper—the title to my Jetta.

"I'll need it until I go, but then it's yours."

"Are you...are you sure?" Her eyes filled with tears.

"I'm sure," I said. And thanks to my dad, I could make the offer. "I took my blood type card out. I think I'll need the reminder to be positive in France," I said, "but the rest is yours. Insurance on this baby is cheap. Trust me."

"Why are you doing this?" she asked.

I not only wanted to pass on my car, I wanted to pass on my faith. "I think it's time you drove yourself to church if you're going to go."

I could tell she understood. "Yeah, it is."

"You have to make me one promise, though."

"What?"

"Take the bread to Pete on Saturday nights."

She stuck out her hand. "Deal." She gave me a big hug.

Luc came into the café, wiping flour dust from his hands onto his apron. "What is this? A sorority party?"

We all laughed.

"In my office, I have some paperwork for you, Alexandra, in order to prepare for your trip for France," Luc continued. "Are you ready?"

"*Mais oui!*" I said. And I was.

Air France Boarding Pass

Flight and Date: 0625 June 25
Gate/Porte: D25
Seat/Place: H34
From: Seattle, WA (SEA)
To/Destination: Paris, France (CDG)

Name: Alexandra Stuart

The End

I hope you enjoyed the read, and I'd love to tell you about new releases and contests. Please visit my website, www.sandrabyrd.com, and sign up for my newsletter! And for stunning photos of the French Twist series' delicious recipes, click on the link to my Pinterest boards.

After enjoying the delicious series intro, tuck into the second book in the French Twist series, *Bon Appétit*.

Lexi Stuart is risking it all. Saying *au revoir* to the security of home, her job, and could-be boyfriend Dan, Lexi embarks on a culinary adventure in France to fulfill her life dream of becoming a pastry chef.

As she settles into her new home in the village of *Presque le Chateau* to study and work in a local bakery, her twenty-something optimism meets resistance in the seemingly crusty nature of the people and culture around her. Determined to gain her footing, she finds a church, meets a new friend, and makes the acquaintance of a child named Céline—as well as Céline's attractive, widowed father, Philippe. Even Patricia, the gruff pastry cook, shows a softer side as she mentors Lexi in the art of baking.

As Lexi lives her dream, the only thing she has to do is choose from the array in life's patisserie display window: her familiar home, friends, and family in Seattle or her new life in France. Lexi discovers that as she leans more on God the choices become a little clearer—and making them, well, *c'est la vie!*

This book is written from a lightly Christian point of view.

After savoring *Bon Appétit*, indulge in the sweet and final book in the series, *Pièce de Résistance*.

www.sandrabyrd.com

60737751R00191

Made in the USA
Lexington, KY
17 February 2017